JAMES TYNION IV * RIAN SYGH * WALTER BAIAMONTE

THE BACKSTAGERS ™

VOLUME TWO: THE SHOW MUST GO ON

BOOM! BOX™

BOOM! BOX™

ross richie...ceo & founder
joy huffman...cfo
matt gagnon...editor-in-chief
filip sablik....................president , publishing & marketing
stephen christy........................president, development
lance kreiter......vice president, licensing & merchandising
phil barbaro......vice president, finance & human resources
arune singh.................................vice president, marketing
bryce carlson..vice president, editorial & creative strategy
scott newman............................manager, production design
kate henning...................................manager, operations
spencer simpson.......................................manager, sales
sierra hahn...executive editor
jeanine schaefer....................................executive editor
dafna pleban...senior editor
shannon watters...senior editor
eric harburn...senior editor
whitney leopard...editor
cameron chittock...editor
chris rosa...editor
matthew levine..editor
sophie philips-roberts.........................assistant editor
gavin gronenthal..................................assistant editor
michael moccio.......................................assistant editor
amanda lafranco...................................executive assistant
jillian crab...design coordinator
michelle ankley..................................design coordinator
kara leopard...production designer
marie krupina...production designer
grace park...........................production design assistant
chelsea roberts..................production design assistant
samantha knapp.................production design assistant
elizabeth loughridge.......................accounting coordinator
stephanie hocutt.....................social media coordinator
josé meza...event coordinator
holly aitchison............................operations coordinator
megan christopher..........................operations assistant
rodrigo hernandez..........................mailroom assistant
morgan perry.......................direct market representative
cat o'grady.................................marketing assistant
breanna sarpy..................................executive assistant

THE BACKSTAGERS Volume Two, February 2019. Published by BOOM! Box, a division of Boom Entertainment, Inc. The Backstagers is ™ & © 2019 Rian Sygh & James Tynion. Originally published in single magazine form as THE BACKSTAGERS No. 5-8. ™ & © 2016, 2017 Rian Sygh & James Tynion. All rights reserved. BOOM! Box™ and the BOOM! Box logo are trademarks of Boom Entertainment, Inc., registered in various countries and categories. All characters, events, and institutions depicted herein are fictional. Any similarity between any of the names, characters, persons, events, and/or institutions in this publication to actual names, characters, and persons, whether living or dead, events, and/or institutions is unintended and purely coincidental. BOOM! Box does not read or accept unsolicited submissions of ideas, stories, or artwork.

BOOM! Studios, 5670 Wilshire Boulevard, Suite 400, Los Angeles, CA 90036-5679. Printed in China. Second Printing.

ISBN: 978-1-68415-057-1, eISBN: 978-1-61398-787-2

THE BACKSTAGERS™

CREATED BY JAMES TYNION IV AND RIAN SYGH

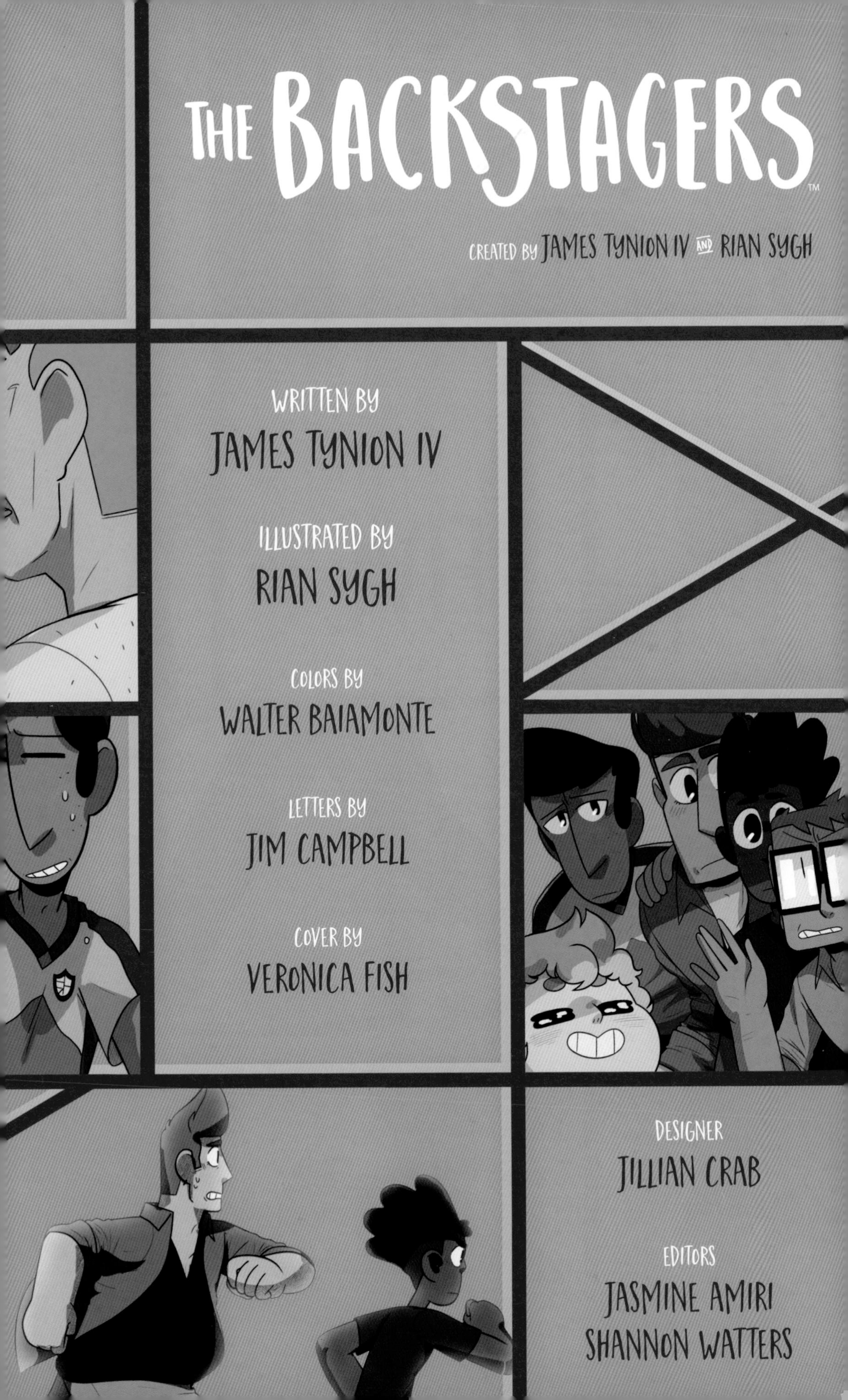

WRITTEN BY
JAMES TYNION IV

ILLUSTRATED BY
RIAN SYGH

COLORS BY
WALTER BAIAMONTE

LETTERS BY
JIM CAMPBELL

COVER BY
VERONICA FISH

DESIGNER
JILLIAN CRAB

EDITORS
JASMINE AMIRI
SHANNON WATTERS

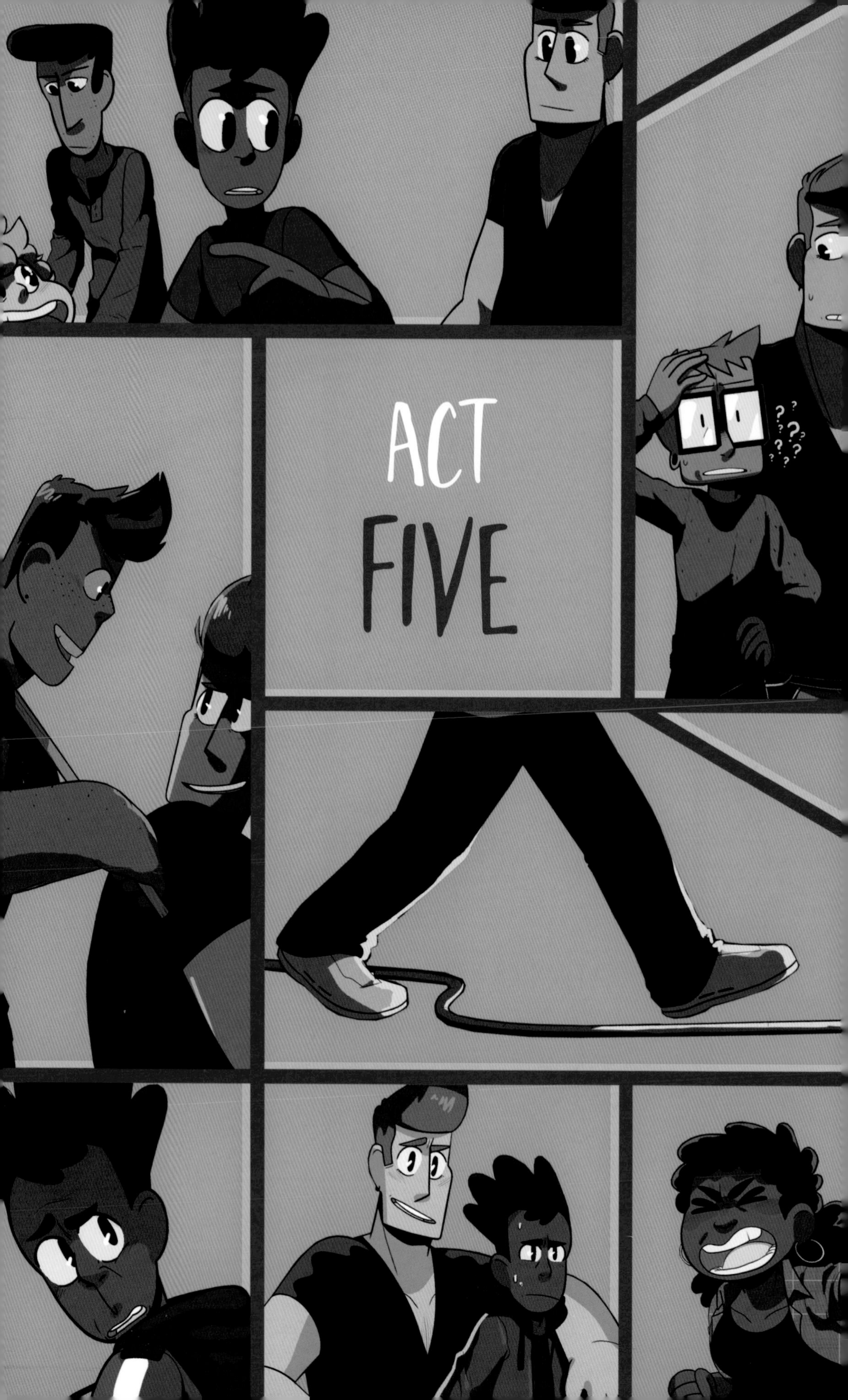
ACT
FIVE

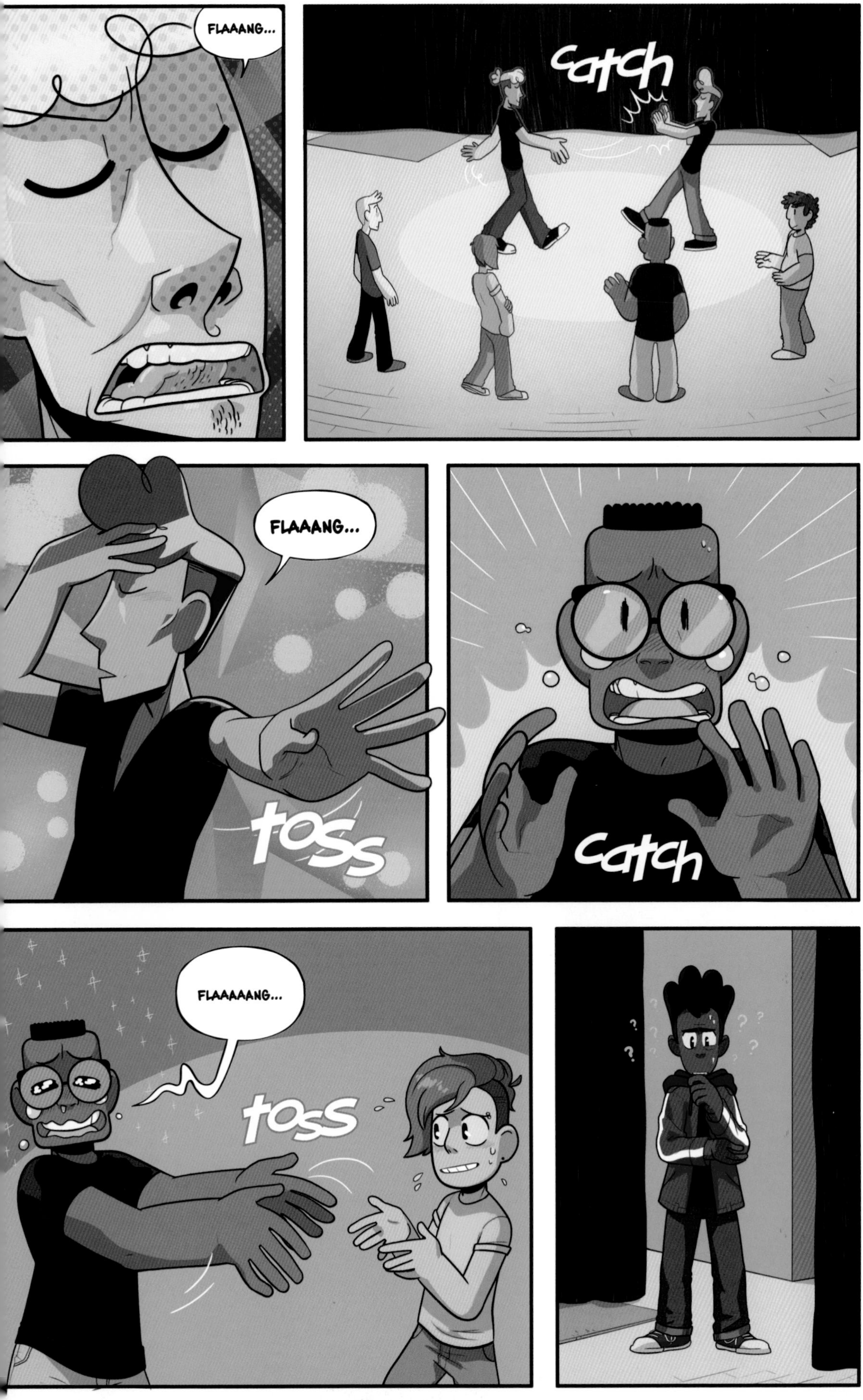
FLAAANG...
catch
FLAAANG...
toss
catch
FLAAAAANG...
toss

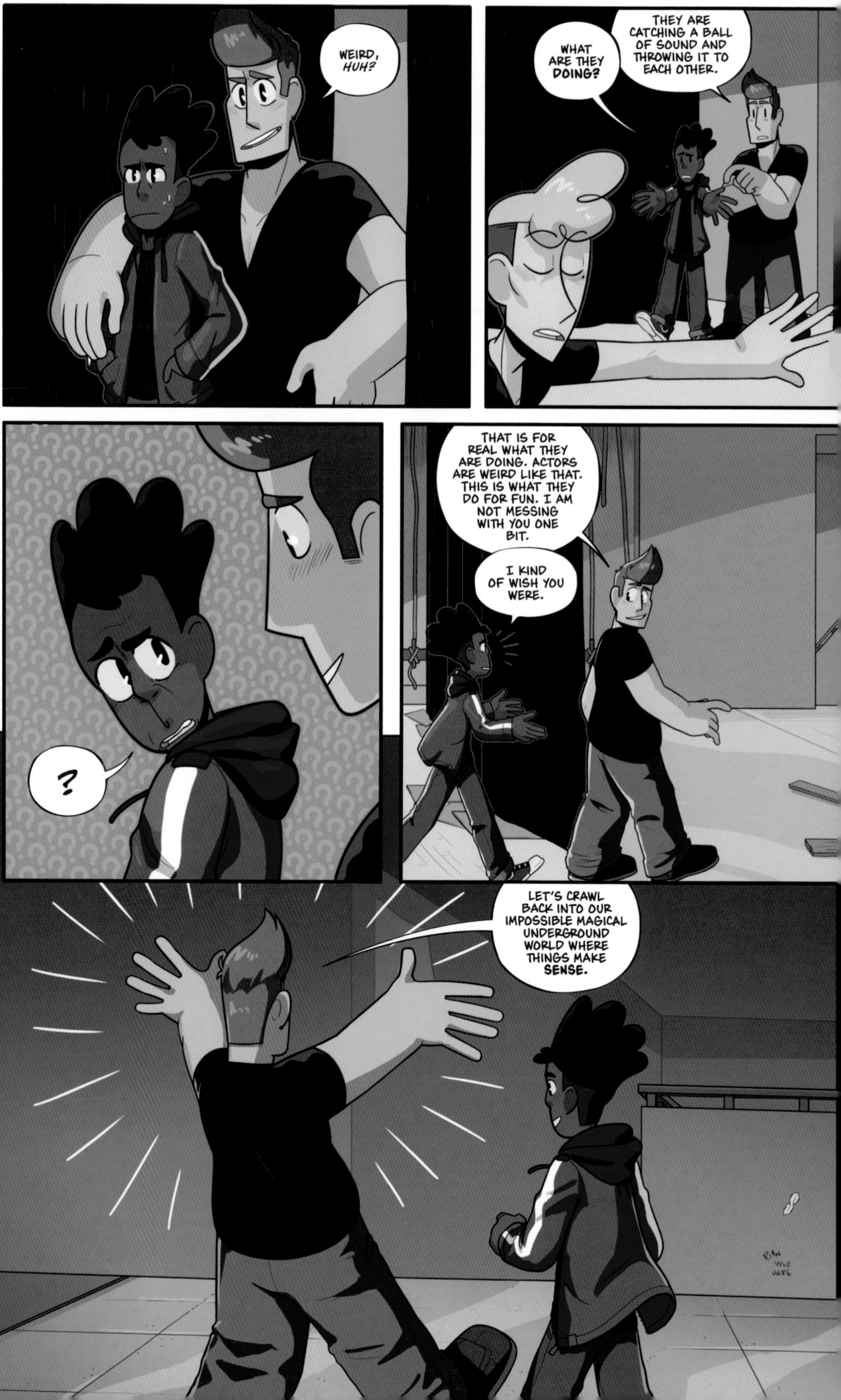
WEIRD, *HUH?*
WHAT ARE THEY **DOING?**
THEY ARE CATCHING A BALL OF SOUND AND THROWING IT TO EACH OTHER.
?
THAT IS FOR REAL WHAT THEY ARE DOING. ACTORS ARE WEIRD LIKE THAT. THIS IS WHAT THEY DO FOR FUN. I AM NOT MESSING WITH YOU ONE BIT.
I KIND OF WISH YOU WERE.
LET'S CRAWL BACK INTO OUR IMPOSSIBLE MAGICAL UNDERGROUND WORLD WHERE THINGS MAKE **SENSE.**

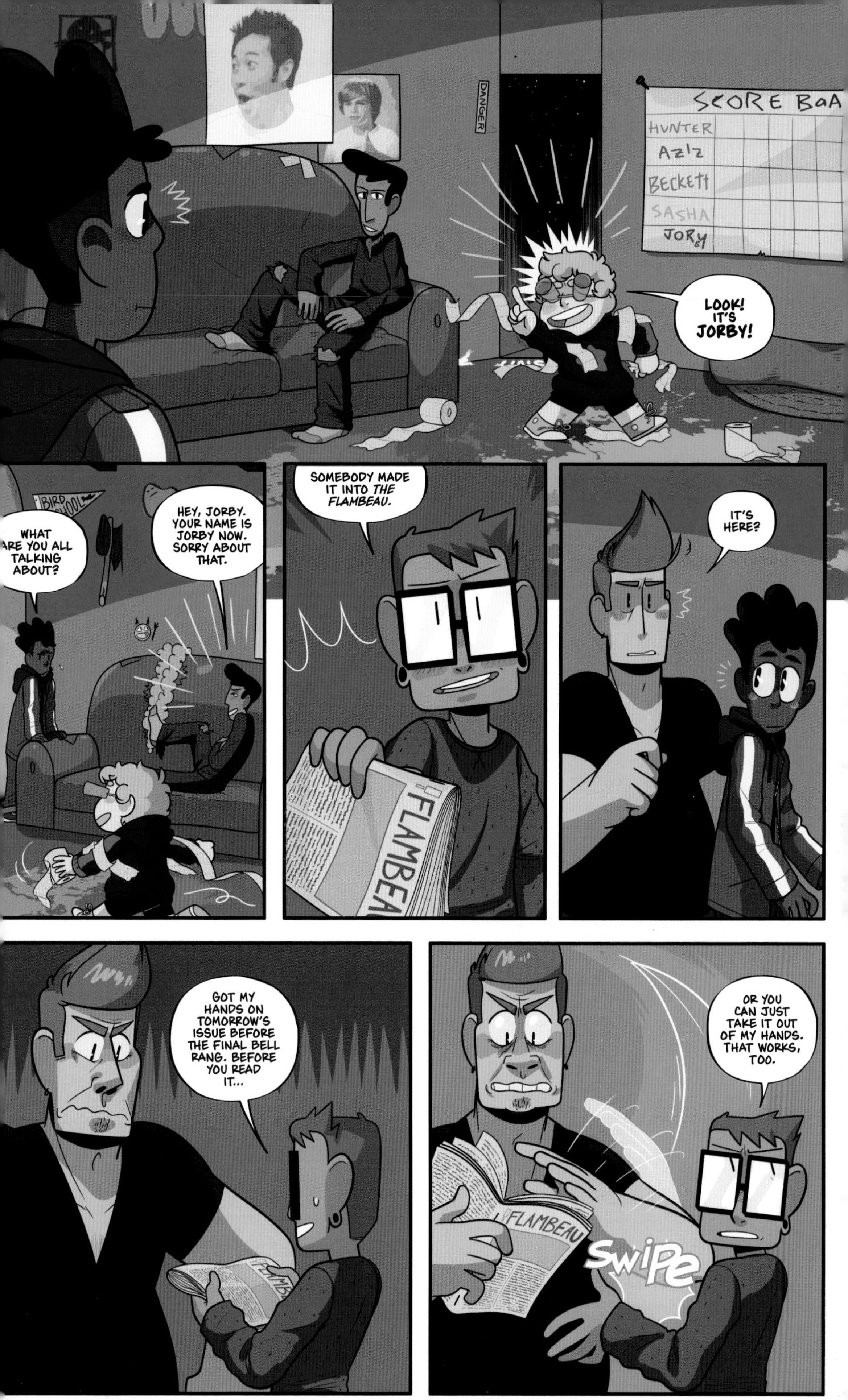
DANGER
SCORE BOA
HUNTER
BECKETT
SASHA
JORY
LOOK! IT'S JORBY!
WHAT ARE YOU ALL TALKING ABOUT?
HEY, JORBY. YOUR NAME IS JORBY NOW. SORRY ABOUT THAT.
SOMEBODY MADE IT INTO *THE FLAMBEAU.*
FLAMBEAU
IT'S HERE?
GOT MY HANDS ON TOMORROW'S ISSUE BEFORE THE FINAL BELL RANG. BEFORE YOU READ IT...
OR YOU CAN JUST TAKE IT OUT OF MY HANDS. THAT WORKS, TOO.
FLAMBEAU
SWIPE

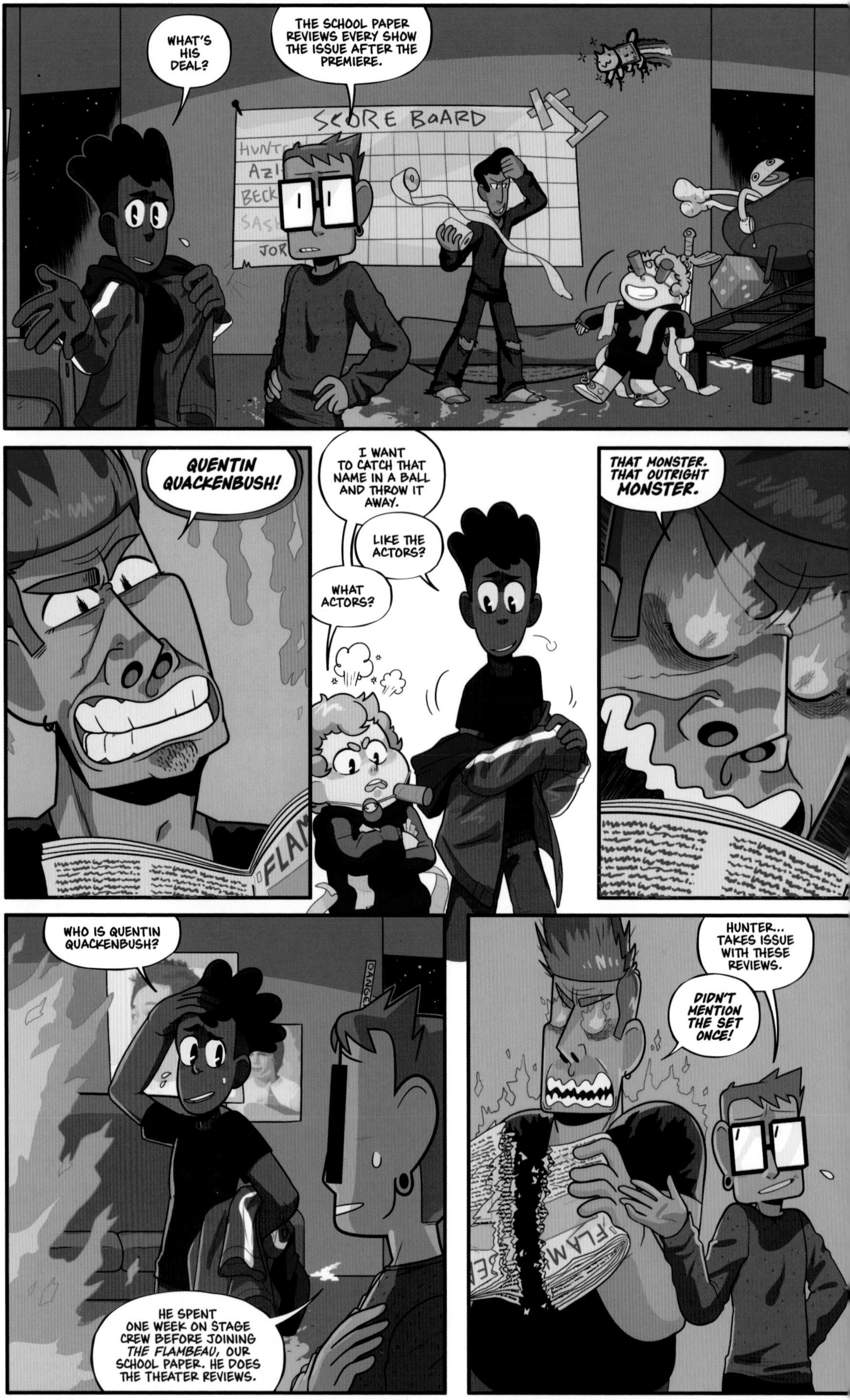
WHAT'S HIS DEAL?
THE SCHOOL PAPER REVIEWS EVERY SHOW THE ISSUE AFTER THE PREMIERE.
SCORE BOARD
QUENTIN QUACKENBUSH!
I WANT TO CATCH THAT NAME IN A BALL AND THROW IT AWAY.
LIKE THE ACTORS?
WHAT ACTORS?
THAT MONSTER. THAT OUTRIGHT MONSTER.
WHO IS QUENTIN QUACKENBUSH?
HE SPENT ONE WEEK ON STAGE CREW BEFORE JOINING THE FLAMBEAU, OUR SCHOOL PAPER. HE DOES THE THEATER REVIEWS.
HUNTER... TAKES ISSUE WITH THESE REVIEWS.
DIDN'T MENTION THE SET ONCE!

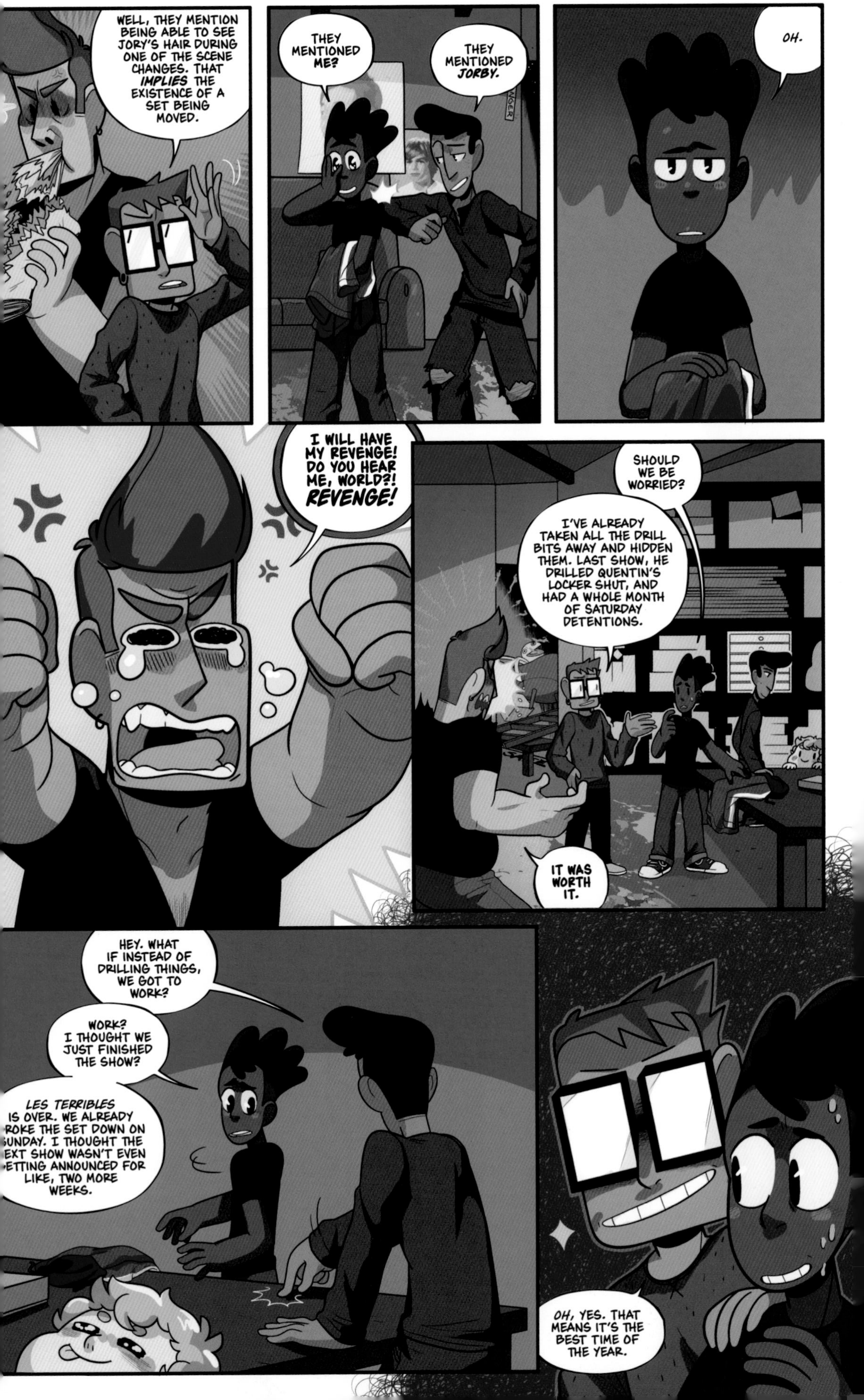

WELL, THEY MENTION BEING ABLE TO SEE JORY'S HAIR DURING ONE OF THE SCENE CHANGES. THAT *IMPLIES* THE EXISTENCE OF A SET BEING MOVED.
THEY MENTIONED ME?
THEY MENTIONED *JORBY.*
OH.
I WILL HAVE MY REVENGE! DO YOU HEAR ME, WORLD?! **REVENGE!**
SHOULD WE BE WORRIED?
I'VE ALREADY TAKEN ALL THE DRILL BITS AWAY AND HIDDEN THEM. LAST SHOW, HE DRILLED QUENTIN'S LOCKER SHUT, AND HAD A WHOLE MONTH OF SATURDAY DETENTIONS.
IT WAS WORTH IT.
HEY. WHAT IF INSTEAD OF DRILLING THINGS, WE GOT TO WORK?
WORK? I THOUGHT WE JUST FINISHED THE SHOW?
LES TERRIBLES IS OVER. WE ALREADY BROKE THE SET DOWN ON SUNDAY. I THOUGHT THE NEXT SHOW WASN'T EVEN GETTING ANNOUNCED FOR LIKE, TWO MORE WEEKS.
OH, YES. THAT MEANS IT'S THE BEST TIME OF THE YEAR.

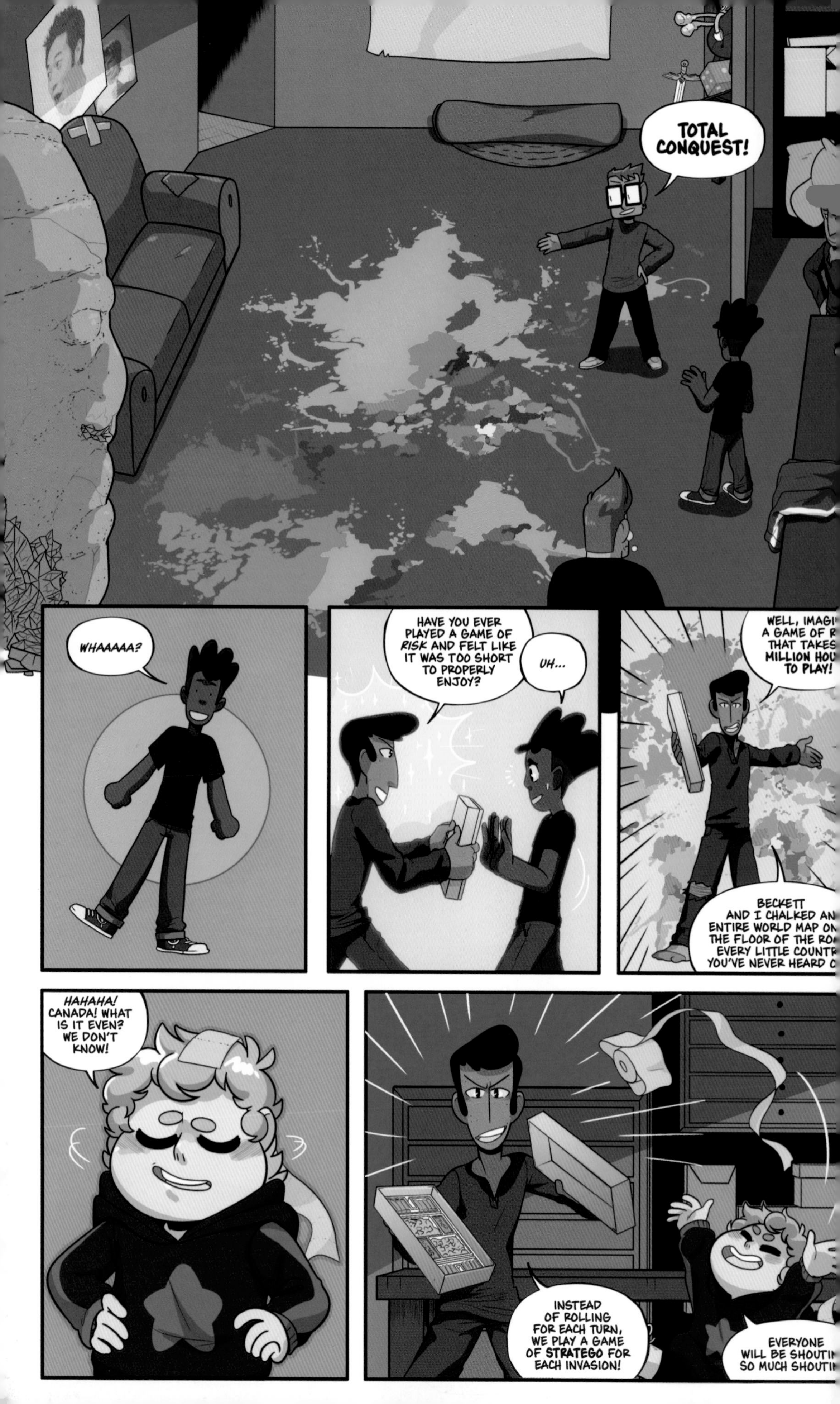

TOTAL CONQUEST!
WHAAAAA?
HAVE YOU EVER PLAYED A GAME OF *RISK* AND FELT LIKE IT WAS TOO SHORT TO PROPERLY ENJOY?
UH...
WELL, IMAGI
A GAME OF R
THAT TAKES
MILLION HOU
TO PLAY!
BECKETT AND I CHALKED AN ENTIRE WORLD MAP ON THE FLOOR OF THE RO EVERY LITTLE COUNTR YOU'VE NEVER HEARD O
HAHAHA! CANADA! WHAT IS IT EVEN? WE DON'T KNOW!
INSTEAD OF ROLLING FOR EACH TURN, WE PLAY A GAME OF **STRATEGO** FOR EACH INVASION!
EVERYONE WILL BE SHOUTIN SO MUCH SHOUTIN

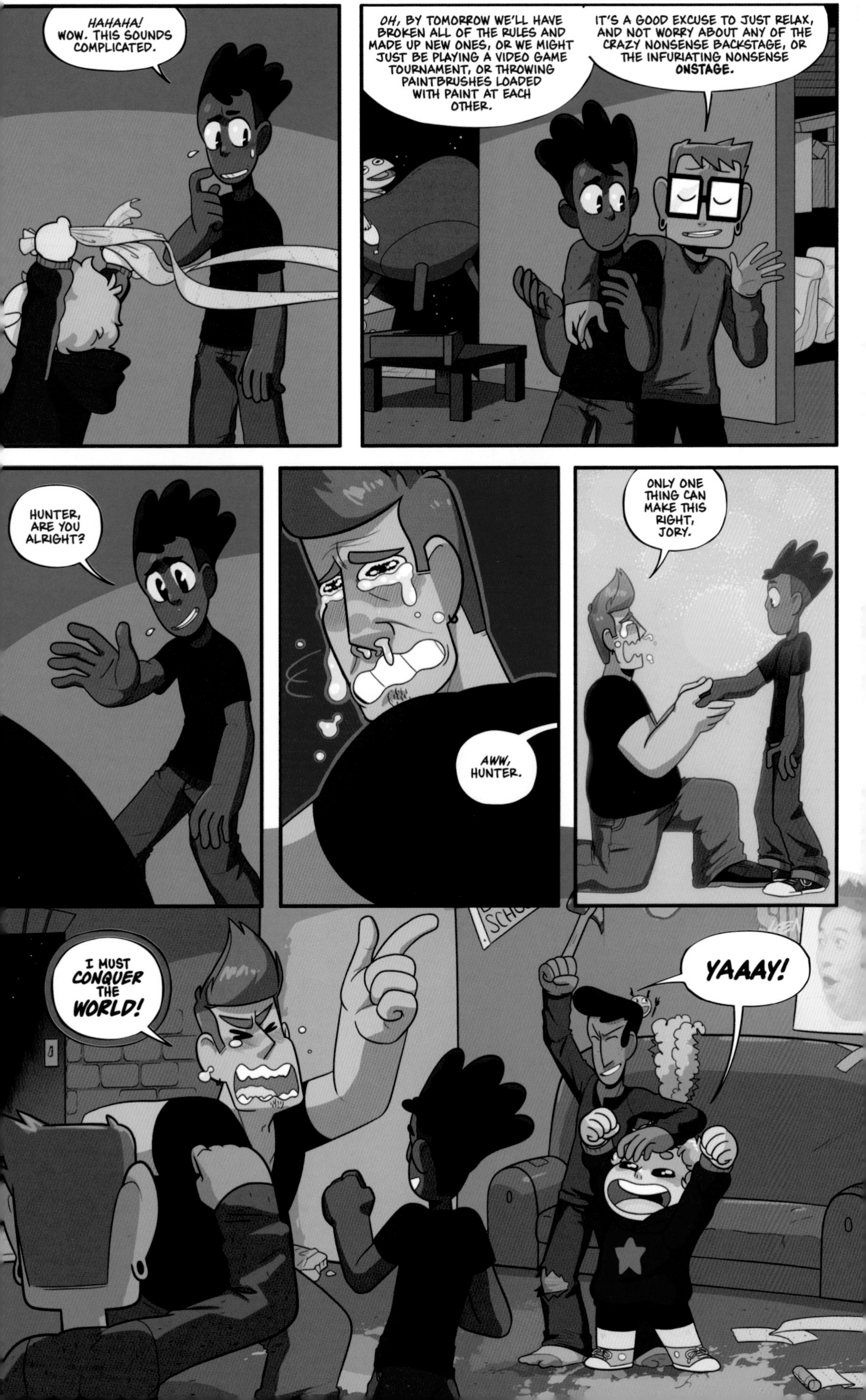

HAHAHA! WOW. THIS SOUNDS COMPLICATED.
OH, BY TOMORROW WE'LL HAVE BROKEN ALL OF THE RULES AND MADE UP NEW ONES, OR WE MIGHT JUST BE PLAYING A VIDEO GAME TOURNAMENT, OR THROWING PAINTBRUSHES LOADED WITH PAINT AT EACH OTHER.
IT'S A GOOD EXCUSE TO JUST RELAX, AND NOT WORRY ABOUT ANY OF THE CRAZY NONSENSE BACKSTAGE, OR THE INFURIATING NONSENSE ONSTAGE.
HUNTER, ARE YOU ALRIGHT?
AWW, HUNTER.
ONLY ONE THING CAN MAKE THIS RIGHT, JORY.
I MUST CONQUER THE WORLD!
YAAAY!

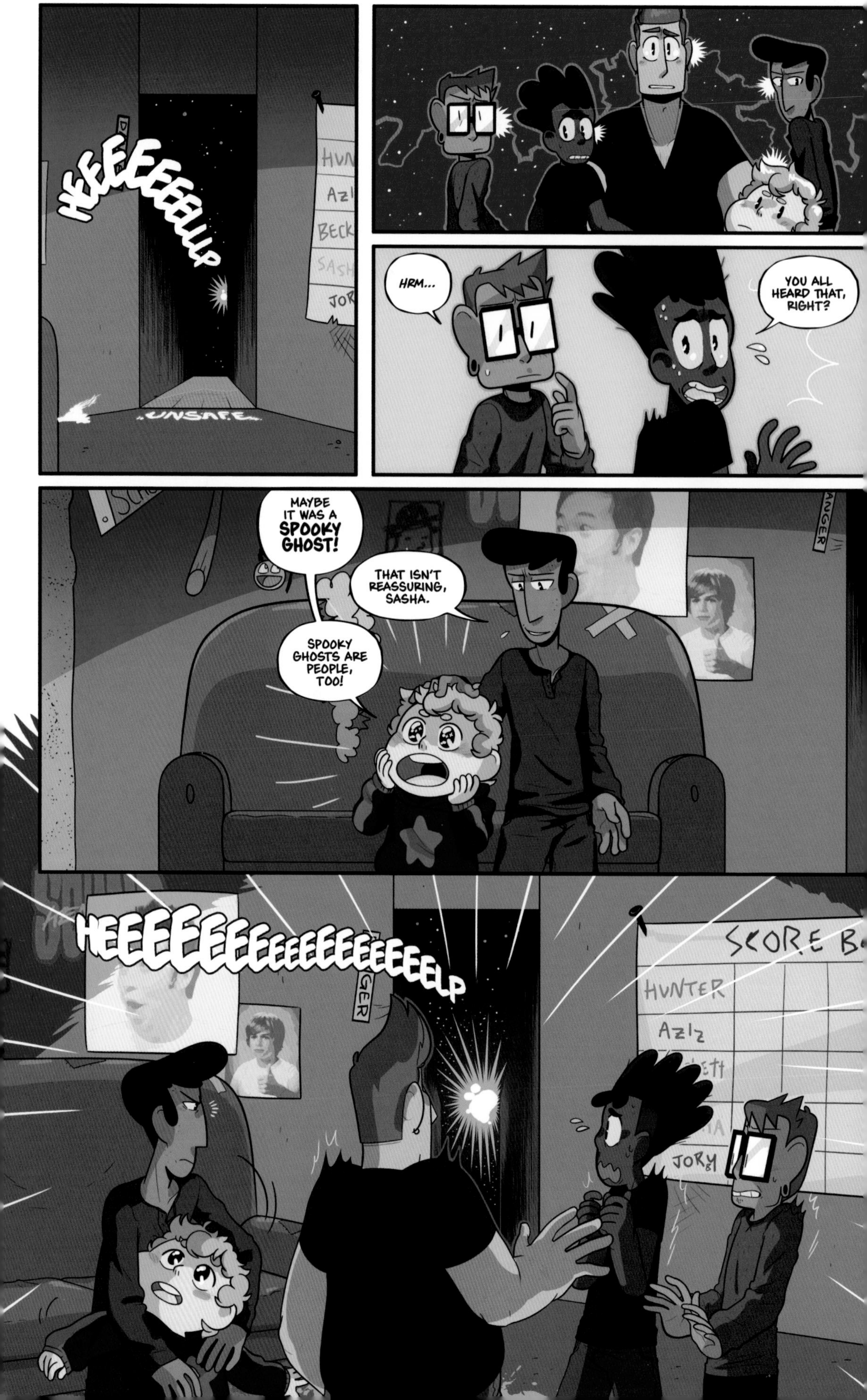

HEEEEEEELLLP
HUN
AZI
BECK
SASH
JOR
UNSAFE
HRM...
YOU ALL HEARD THAT, RIGHT?
MAYBE IT WAS A SPOOKY GHOST!
THAT ISN'T REASSURING, SASHA.
SPOOKY GHOSTS ARE PEOPLE, TOO!
HEEEEEEEEEEEEEEEEEEEELP
SCORE B
HUNTER
AZIZ
JORY

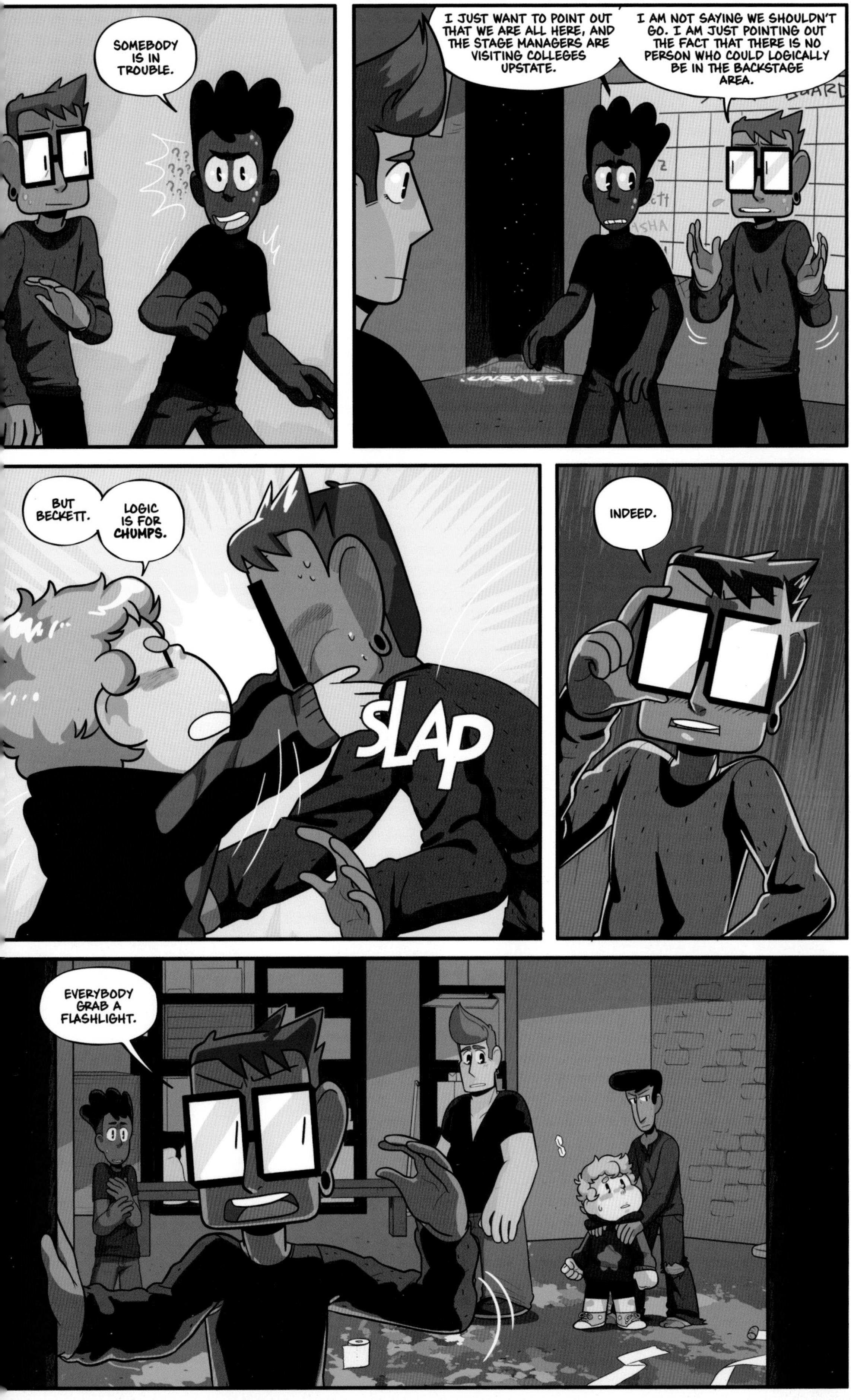
SOMEBODY IS IN TROUBLE.
I JUST WANT TO POINT OUT THAT WE ARE ALL HERE, AND THE STAGE MANAGERS ARE VISITING COLLEGES UPSTATE.
I AM NOT SAYING WE SHOULDN'T GO. I AM JUST POINTING OUT THE FACT THAT THERE IS NO PERSON WHO COULD LOGICALLY BE IN THE BACKSTAGE AREA.
UNSAFE
BUT BECKETT.
LOGIC IS FOR CHUMPS.
SLAP
INDEED.
EVERYBODY GRAB A FLASHLIGHT.

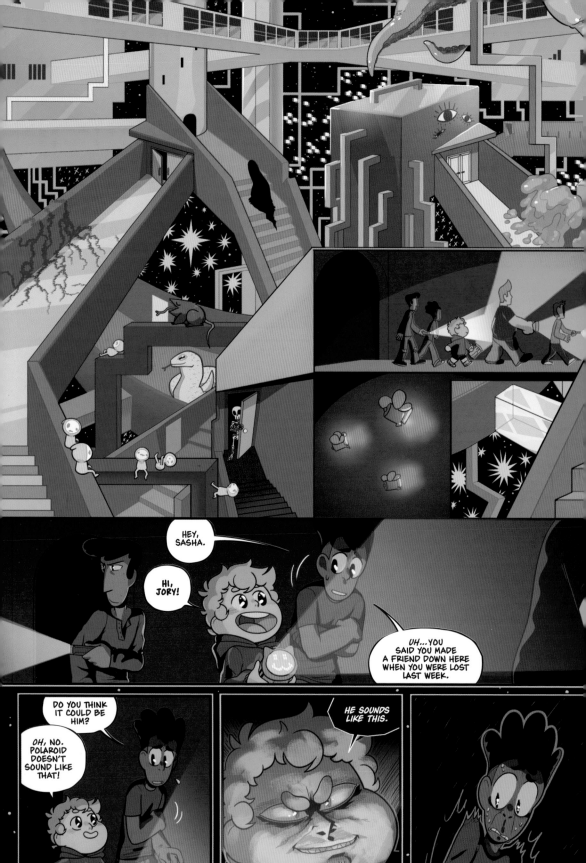

HEY, SASHA.

HI, JORY!

UH...YOU SAID YOU MADE A FRIEND DOWN HERE WHEN YOU WERE LOST LAST WEEK.

DO YOU THINK IT COULD BE HIM?

OH, NO. POLAROID DOESN'T SOUND LIKE THAT!

HE SOUNDS LIKE THIS.

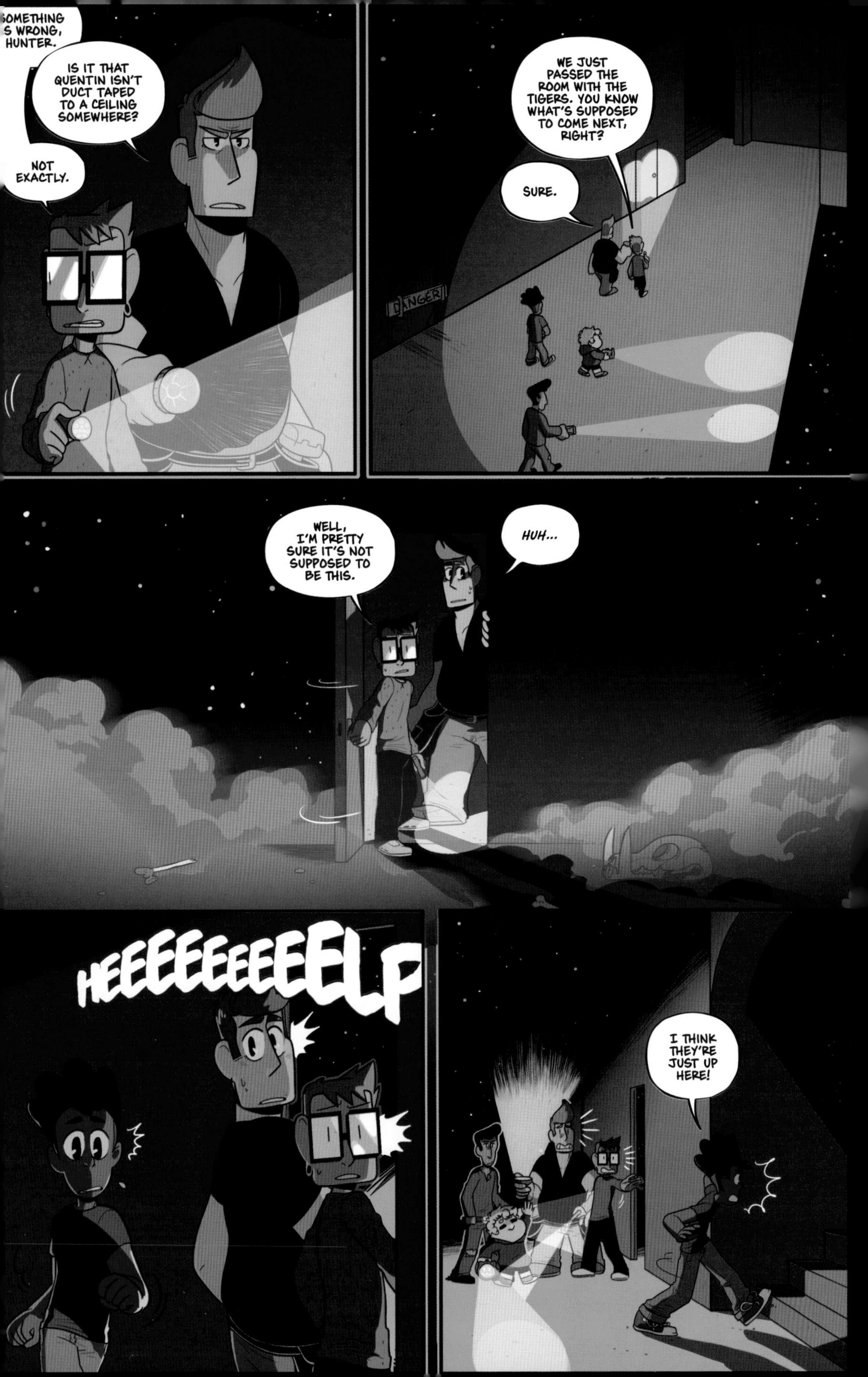
SOMETHING 'S WRONG, HUNTER.
IS IT THAT QUENTIN ISN'T DUCT TAPED TO A CEILING SOMEWHERE?
NOT EXACTLY.
WE JUST PASSED THE ROOM WITH THE TIGERS. YOU KNOW WHAT'S SUPPOSED TO COME NEXT, RIGHT?
SURE.
DANGER
WELL, I'M PRETTY SURE IT'S NOT SUPPOSED TO BE THIS.
HUH...
HEEEEEEEEEELP
I THINK THEY'RE JUST UP HERE!

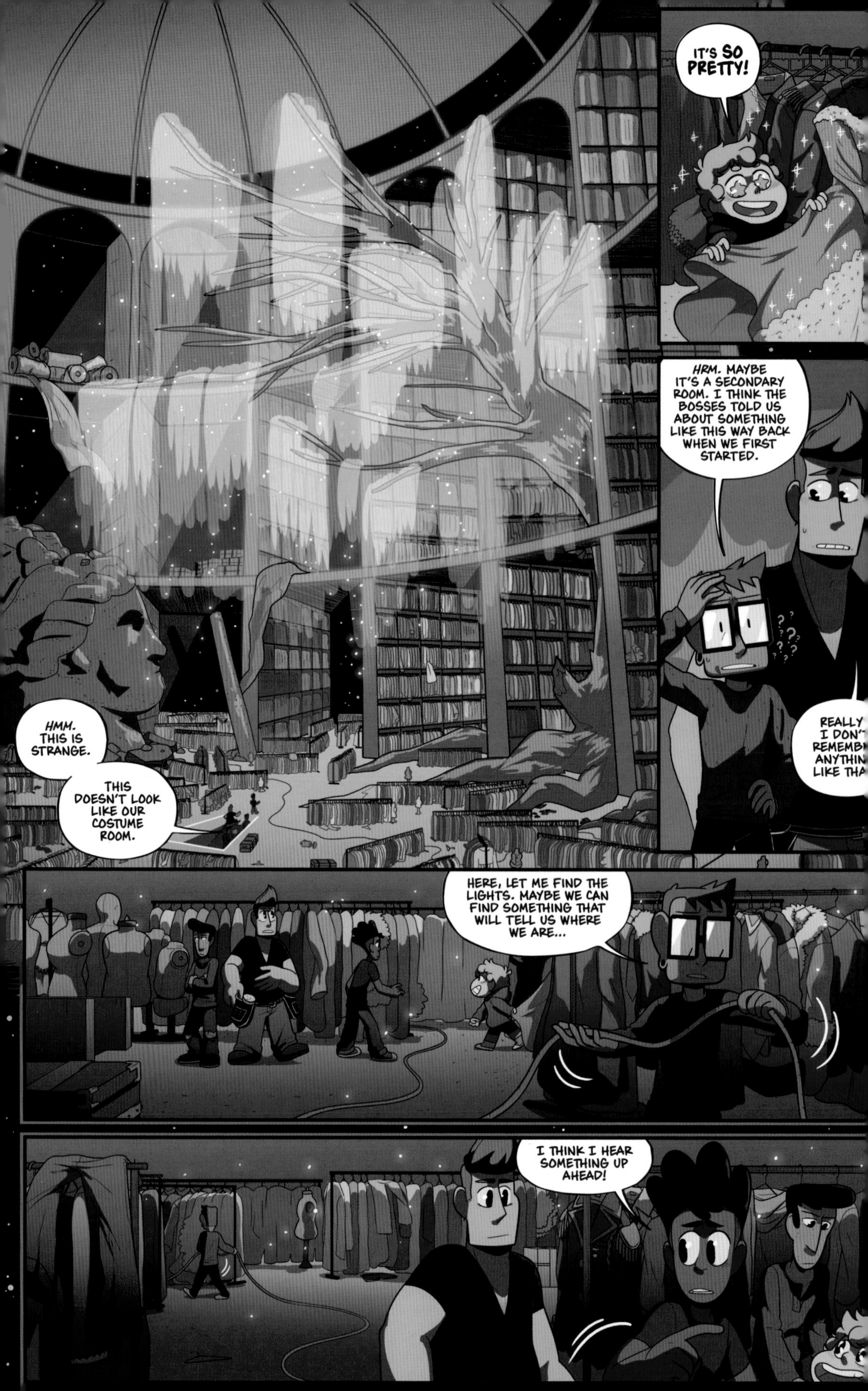
HMM. THIS IS STRANGE.
THIS DOESN'T LOOK LIKE OUR COSTUME ROOM.
IT'S SO PRETTY!
HRM. MAYBE IT'S A SECONDARY ROOM. I THINK THE BOSSES TOLD US ABOUT SOMETHING LIKE THIS WAY BACK WHEN WE FIRST STARTED.
HERE, LET ME FIND THE LIGHTS. MAYBE WE CAN FIND SOMETHING THAT WILL TELL US WHERE WE ARE...
I THINK I HEAR SOMETHING UP AHEAD!

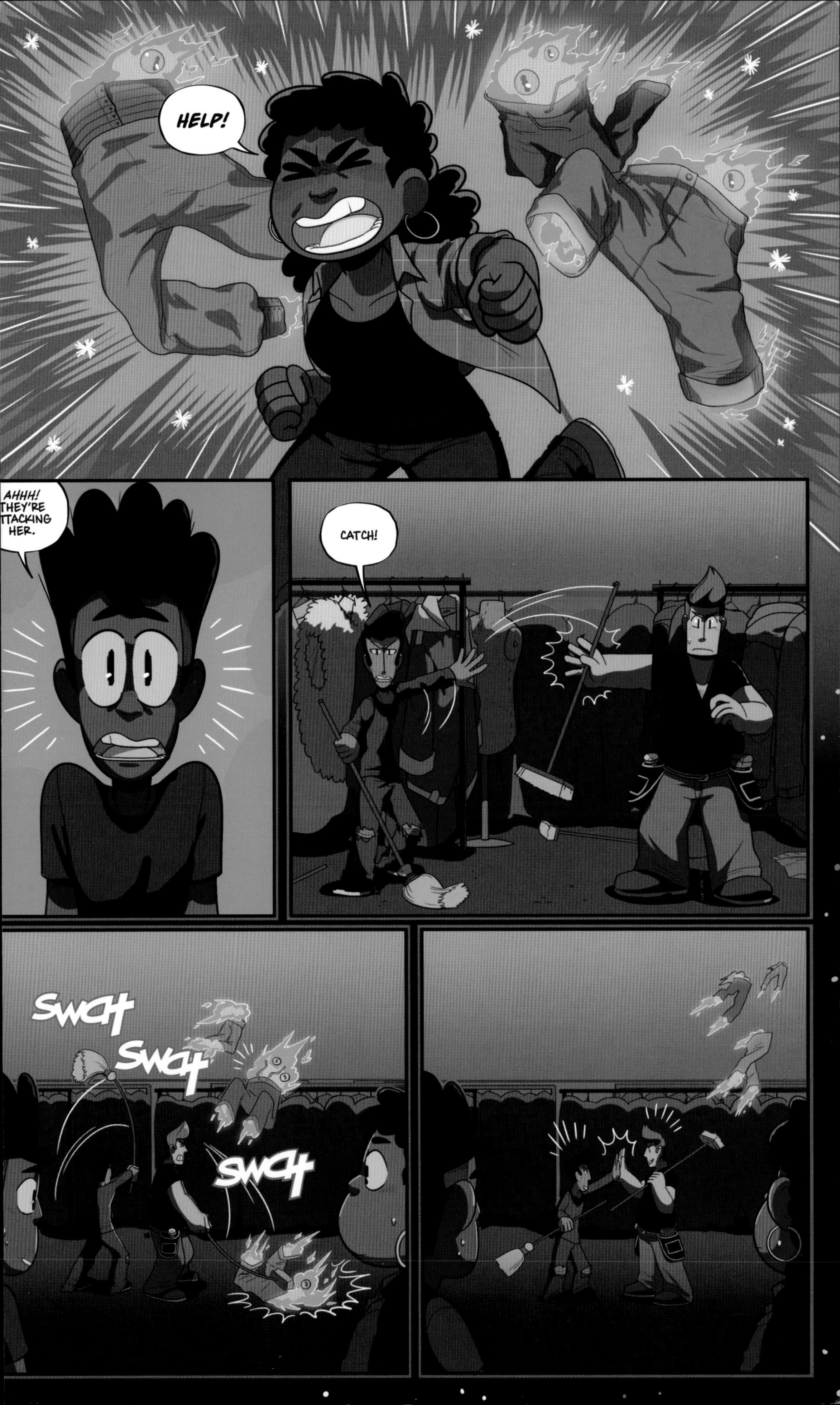

HELP!
AHHH! THEY'RE ATTACKING HER.
CATCH!
SWCH
SWCH
SWCH

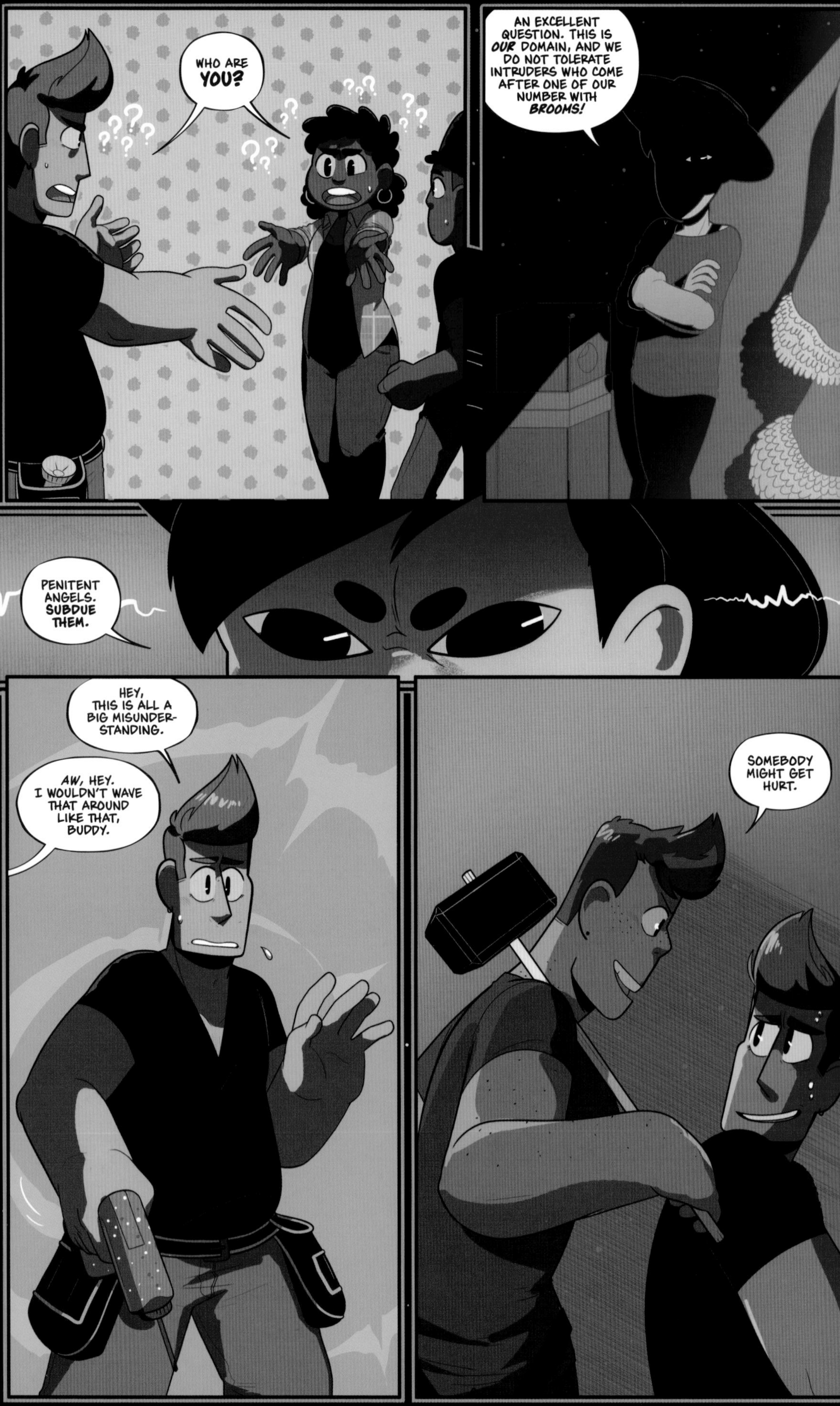
WHO ARE YOU?
AN EXCELLENT QUESTION. THIS IS OUR DOMAIN, AND WE DO NOT TOLERATE INTRUDERS WHO COME AFTER ONE OF OUR NUMBER WITH BROOMS!
PENITENT ANGELS. SUBDUE THEM.
HEY, THIS IS ALL A BIG MISUNDER-STANDING.
AW, HEY. I WOULDN'T WAVE THAT AROUND LIKE THAT, BUDDY.
SOMEBODY MIGHT GET HURT.

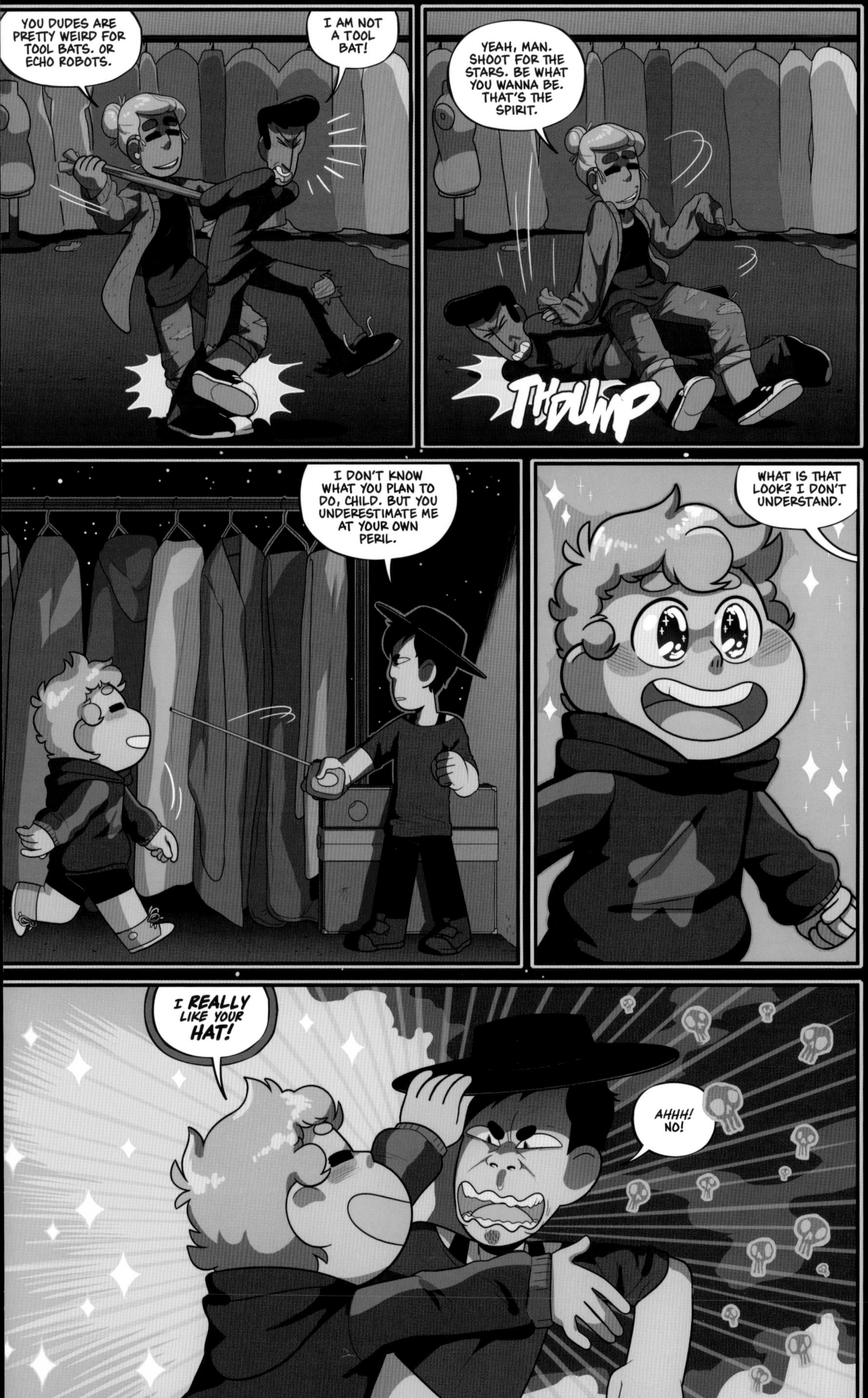
YOU DUDES ARE PRETTY WEIRD FOR TOOL BATS. OR ECHO ROBOTS.
I AM NOT A TOOL BAT!
YEAH, MAN. SHOOT FOR THE STARS. BE WHAT YOU WANNA BE. THAT'S THE SPIRIT.
THDUMP
I DON'T KNOW WHAT YOU PLAN TO DO, CHILD. BUT YOU UNDERESTIMATE ME AT YOUR OWN PERIL.
WHAT IS THAT LOOK? I DON'T UNDERSTAND.
I REALLY LIKE YOUR HAT!
AHHH! NO!

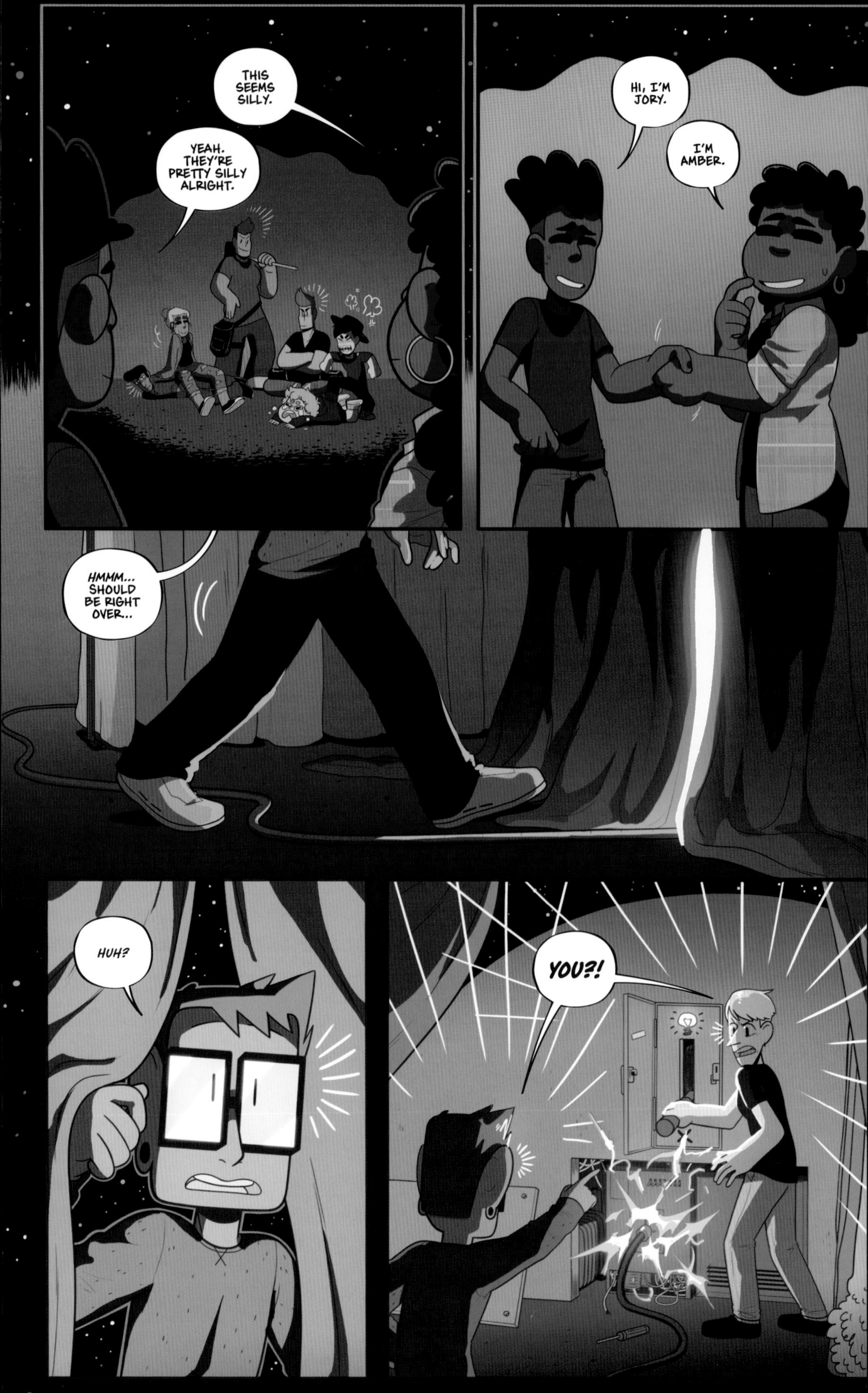
THIS SEEMS SILLY.
YEAH. THEY'RE PRETTY SILLY ALRIGHT.
HI, I'M JORY.
I'M AMBER.
HMMM... SHOULD BE RIGHT OVER...
HUH?
YOU?!

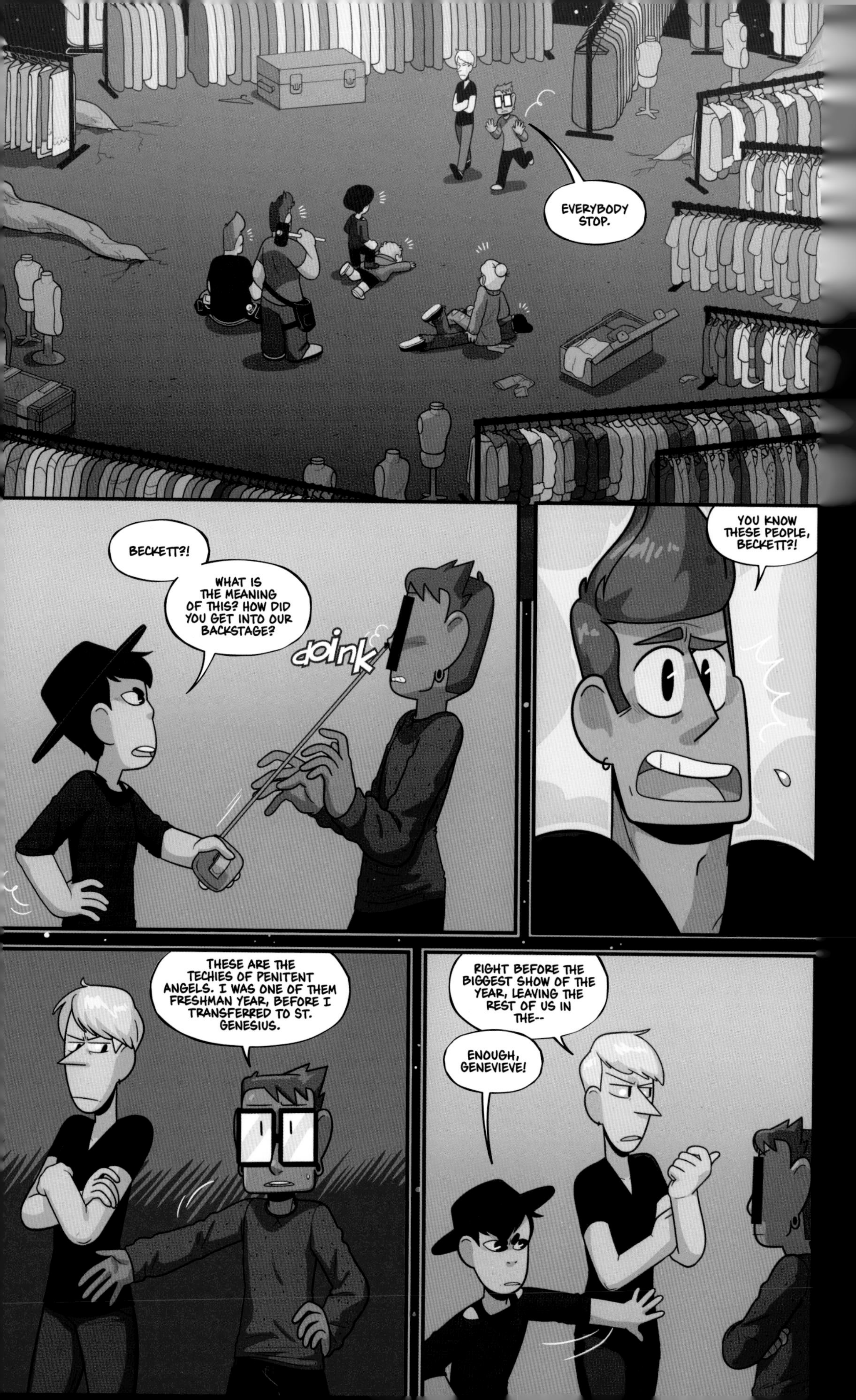
EVERYBODY STOP.
BECKETT?!
WHAT IS THE MEANING OF THIS? HOW DID YOU GET INTO OUR BACKSTAGE?
doink
YOU KNOW THESE PEOPLE, BECKETT?!
THESE ARE THE TECHIES OF PENITENT ANGELS. I WAS ONE OF THEM FRESHMAN YEAR, BEFORE I TRANSFERRED TO ST. GENESIUS.
RIGHT BEFORE THE BIGGEST SHOW OF THE YEAR, LEAVING THE REST OF US IN THE--
ENOUGH, GENEVIEVE!

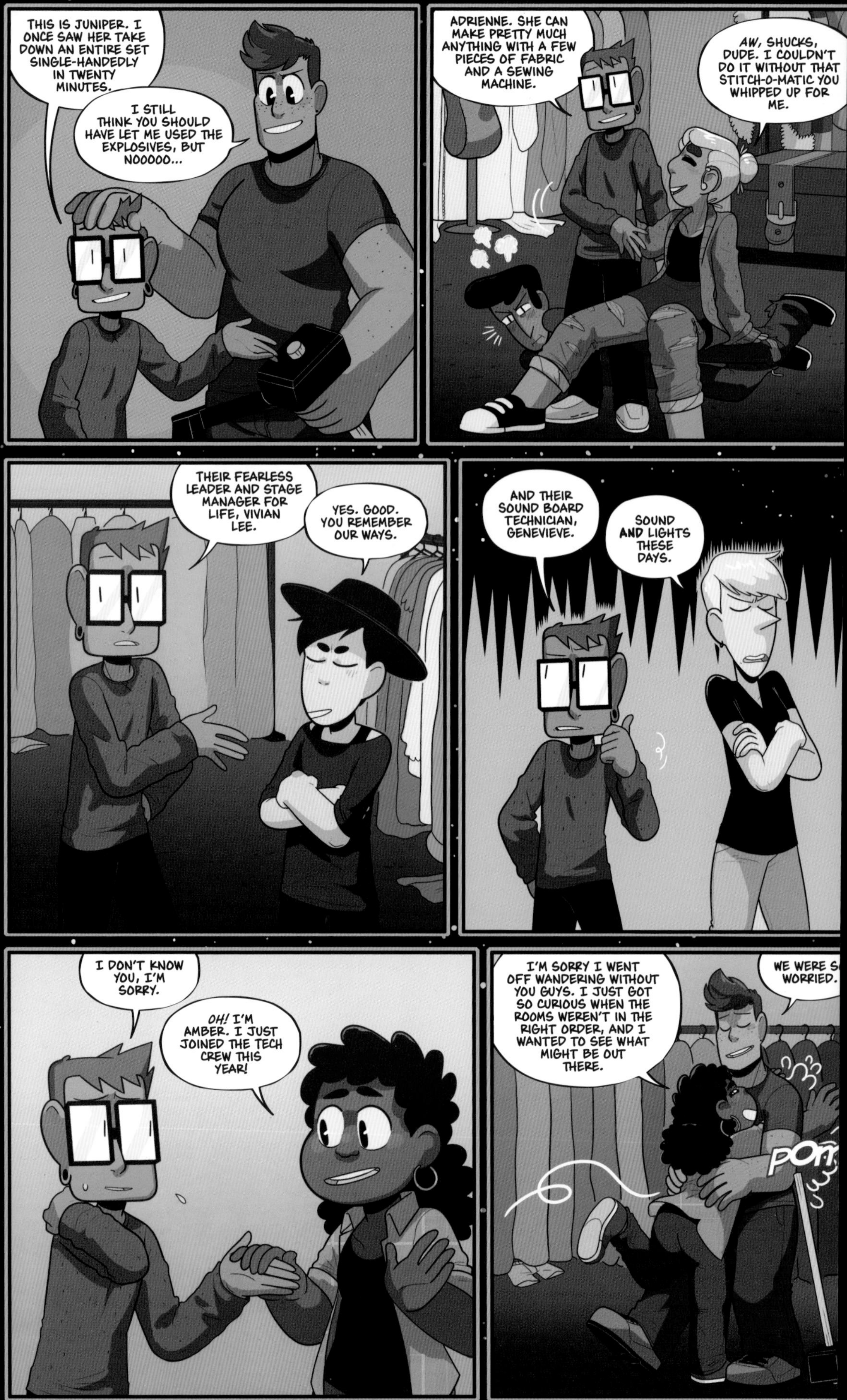
THIS IS JUNIPER. I ONCE SAW HER TAKE DOWN AN ENTIRE SET SINGLE-HANDEDLY IN TWENTY MINUTES.
I STILL THINK YOU SHOULD HAVE LET ME USED THE EXPLOSIVES, BUT NOOOOO...
ADRIENNE. SHE CAN MAKE PRETTY MUCH ANYTHING WITH A FEW PIECES OF FABRIC AND A SEWING MACHINE.
AW, SHUCKS, DUDE. I COULDN'T DO IT WITHOUT THAT STITCH-O-MATIC YOU WHIPPED UP FOR ME.
THEIR FEARLESS LEADER AND STAGE MANAGER FOR LIFE, VIVIAN LEE.
YES. GOOD. YOU REMEMBER OUR WAYS.
AND THEIR SOUND BOARD TECHNICIAN, GENEVIEVE.
SOUND AND LIGHTS THESE DAYS.
I DON'T KNOW YOU, I'M SORRY.
OH! I'M AMBER. I JUST JOINED THE TECH CREW THIS YEAR!
I'M SORRY I WENT OFF WANDERING WITHOUT YOU GUYS. I JUST GOT SO CURIOUS WHEN THE ROOMS WEREN'T IN THE RIGHT ORDER, AND I WANTED TO SEE WHAT MIGHT BE OUT THERE.
WE WERE S WORRIED.

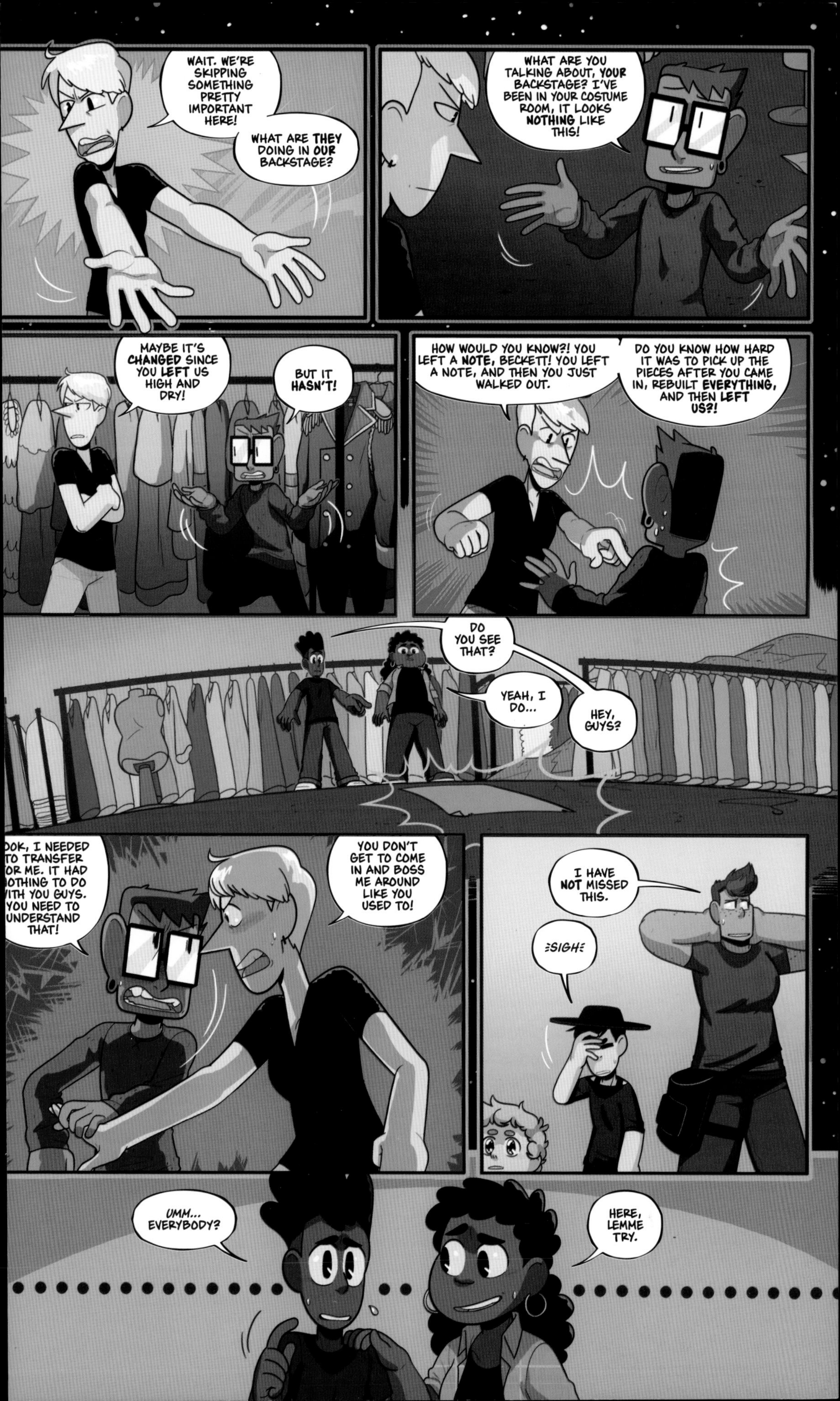
WAIT. WE'RE SKIPPING SOMETHING PRETTY IMPORTANT HERE!
WHAT ARE THEY DOING IN OUR BACKSTAGE?
WHAT ARE YOU TALKING ABOUT, YOUR BACKSTAGE? I'VE BEEN IN YOUR COSTUME ROOM, IT LOOKS NOTHING LIKE THIS!
MAYBE IT'S CHANGED SINCE YOU LEFT US HIGH AND DRY!
BUT IT HASN'T!
HOW WOULD YOU KNOW?! YOU LEFT A NOTE, BECKETT! YOU LEFT A NOTE, AND THEN YOU JUST WALKED OUT.
DO YOU KNOW HOW HARD IT WAS TO PICK UP THE PIECES AFTER YOU CAME IN, REBUILT EVERYTHING, AND THEN LEFT US?!
DO YOU SEE THAT?
YEAH, I DO...
HEY, GUYS?
OOK, I NEEDED TO TRANSFER FOR ME. IT HAD NOTHING TO DO WITH YOU GUYS. YOU NEED TO UNDERSTAND THAT!
YOU DON'T GET TO COME IN AND BOSS ME AROUND LIKE YOU USED TO!
I HAVE NOT MISSED THIS.
SIGH
UMM... EVERYBODY?
HERE, LEMME TRY.

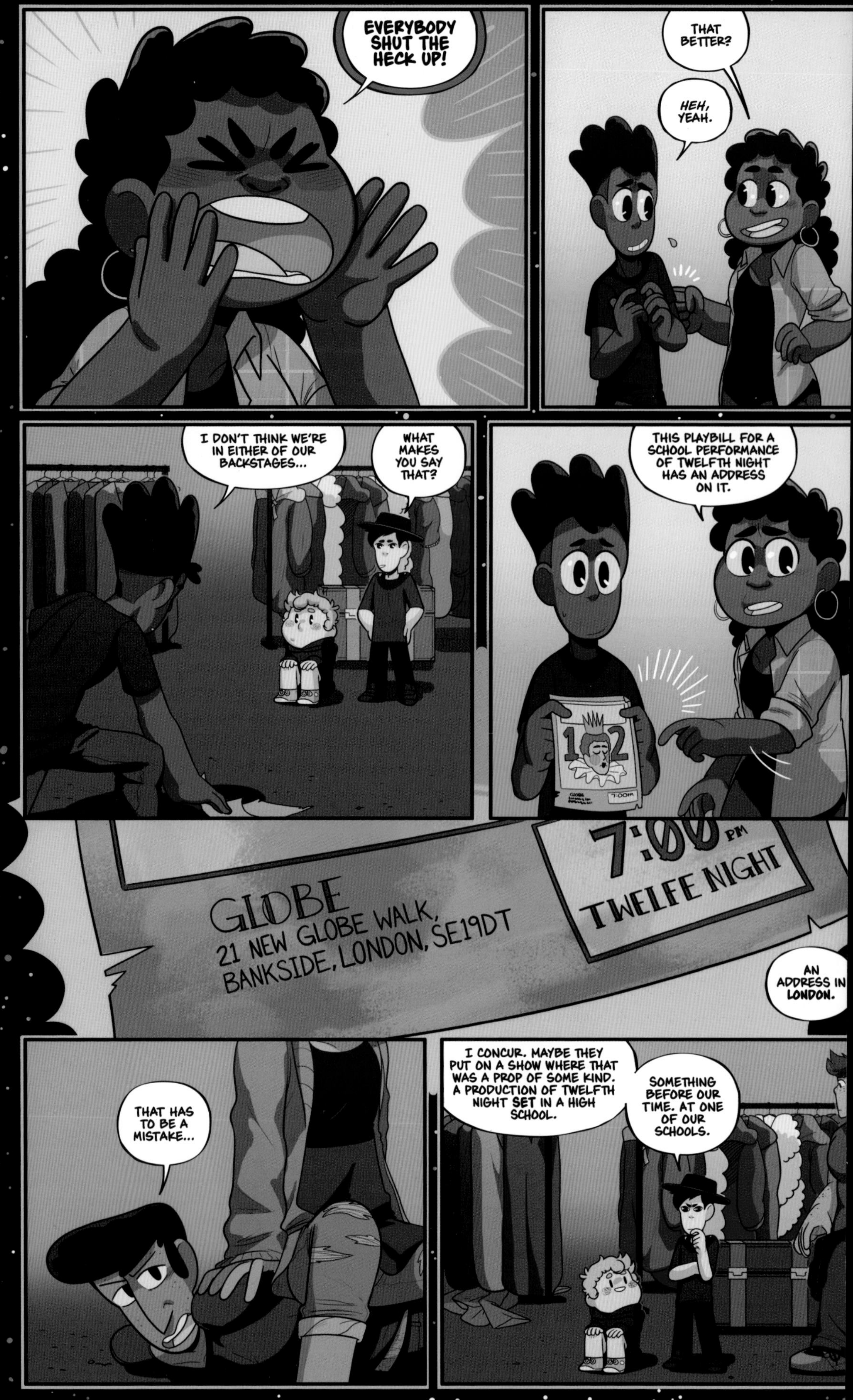
EVERYBODY SHUT THE HECK UP!
THAT BETTER?
HEH, YEAH.
I DON'T THINK WE'RE IN EITHER OF OUR BACKSTAGES...
WHAT MAKES YOU SAY THAT?
THIS PLAYBILL FOR A SCHOOL PERFORMANCE OF TWELFTH NIGHT HAS AN ADDRESS ON IT.
GLOBE
21 NEW GLOBE WALK,
BANKSIDE, LONDON, SE19DT
7:00 PM
TWELFE NIGHT
AN ADDRESS IN LONDON.
THAT HAS TO BE A MISTAKE...
I CONCUR. MAYBE THEY PUT ON A SHOW WHERE THAT WAS A PROP OF SOME KIND. A PRODUCTION OF TWELFTH NIGHT SET IN A HIGH SCHOOL.
SOMETHING BEFORE OUR TIME. AT ONE OF OUR SCHOOLS.

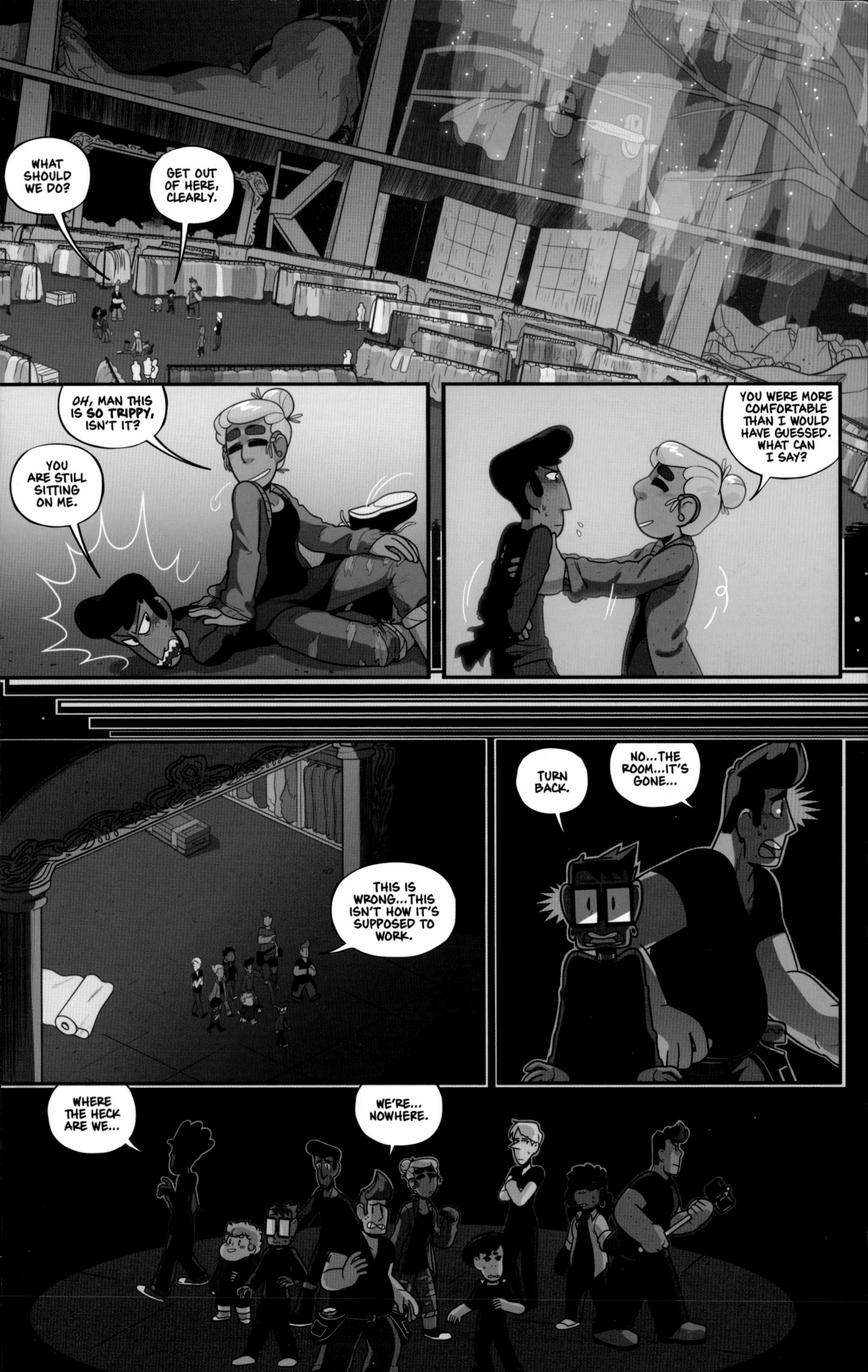
WHAT SHOULD WE DO?
GET OUT OF HERE, CLEARLY.
OH, MAN THIS IS SO TRIPPY, ISN'T IT?
YOU ARE STILL SITTING ON ME.
YOU WERE MORE COMFORTABLE THAN I WOULD HAVE GUESSED. WHAT CAN I SAY?
THIS IS WRONG...THIS ISN'T HOW IT'S SUPPOSED TO WORK.
TURN BACK.
NO...THE ROOM...IT'S GONE...
WHERE THE HECK ARE WE...
WE'RE... NOWHERE.

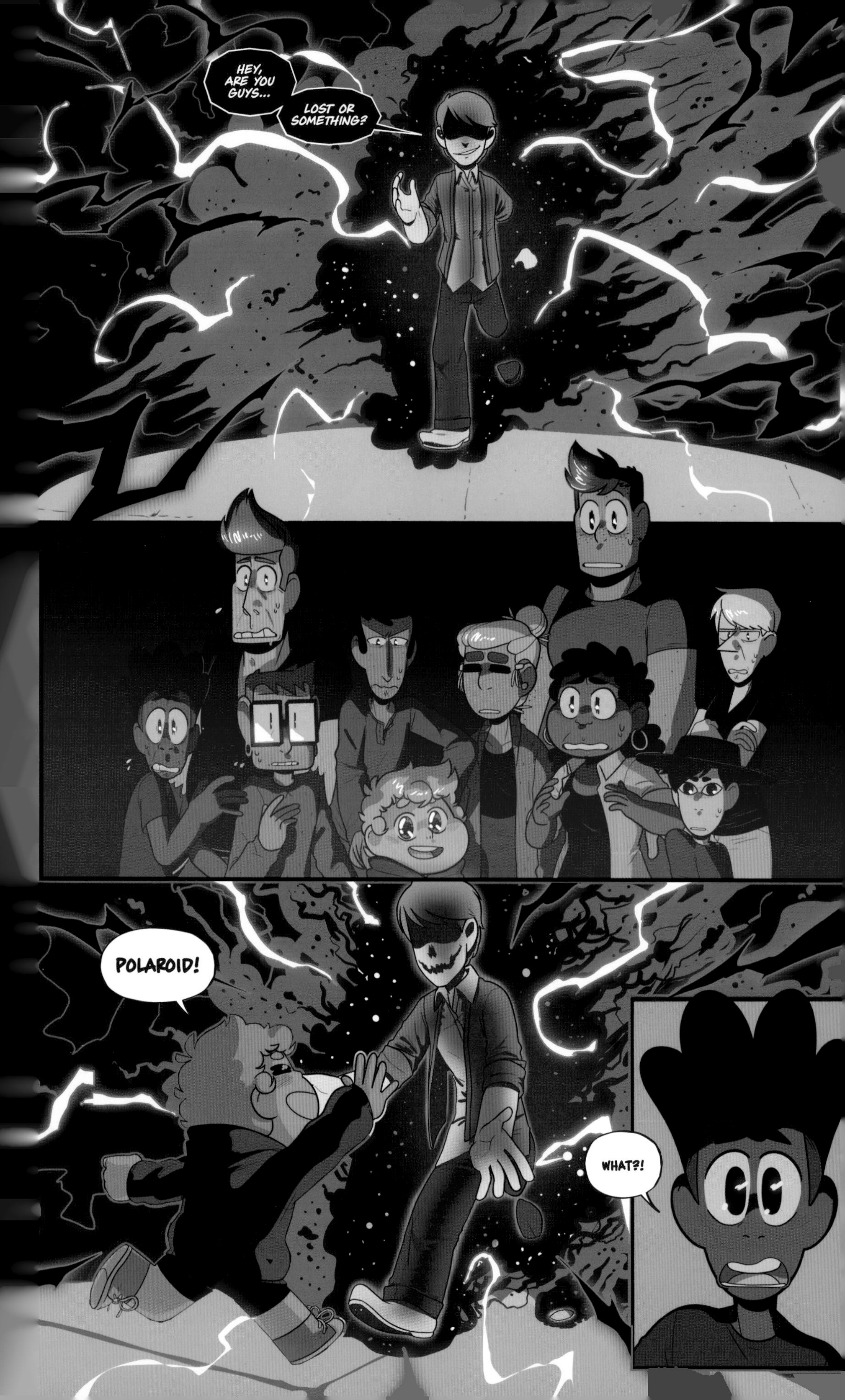
HEY, ARE YOU GUYS...
LOST OR SOMETHING?
POLAROID!
WHAT?!

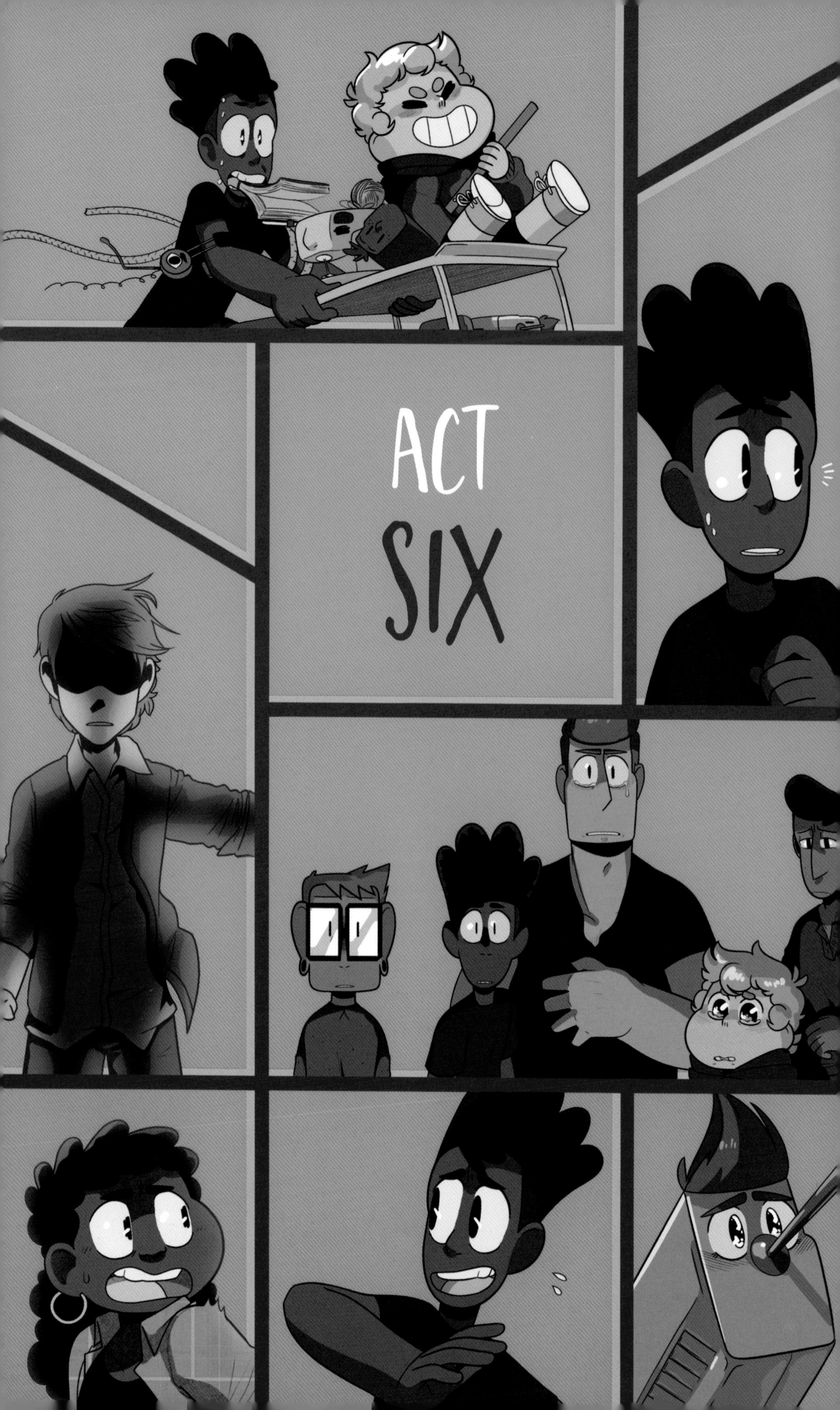
ACT
SIX

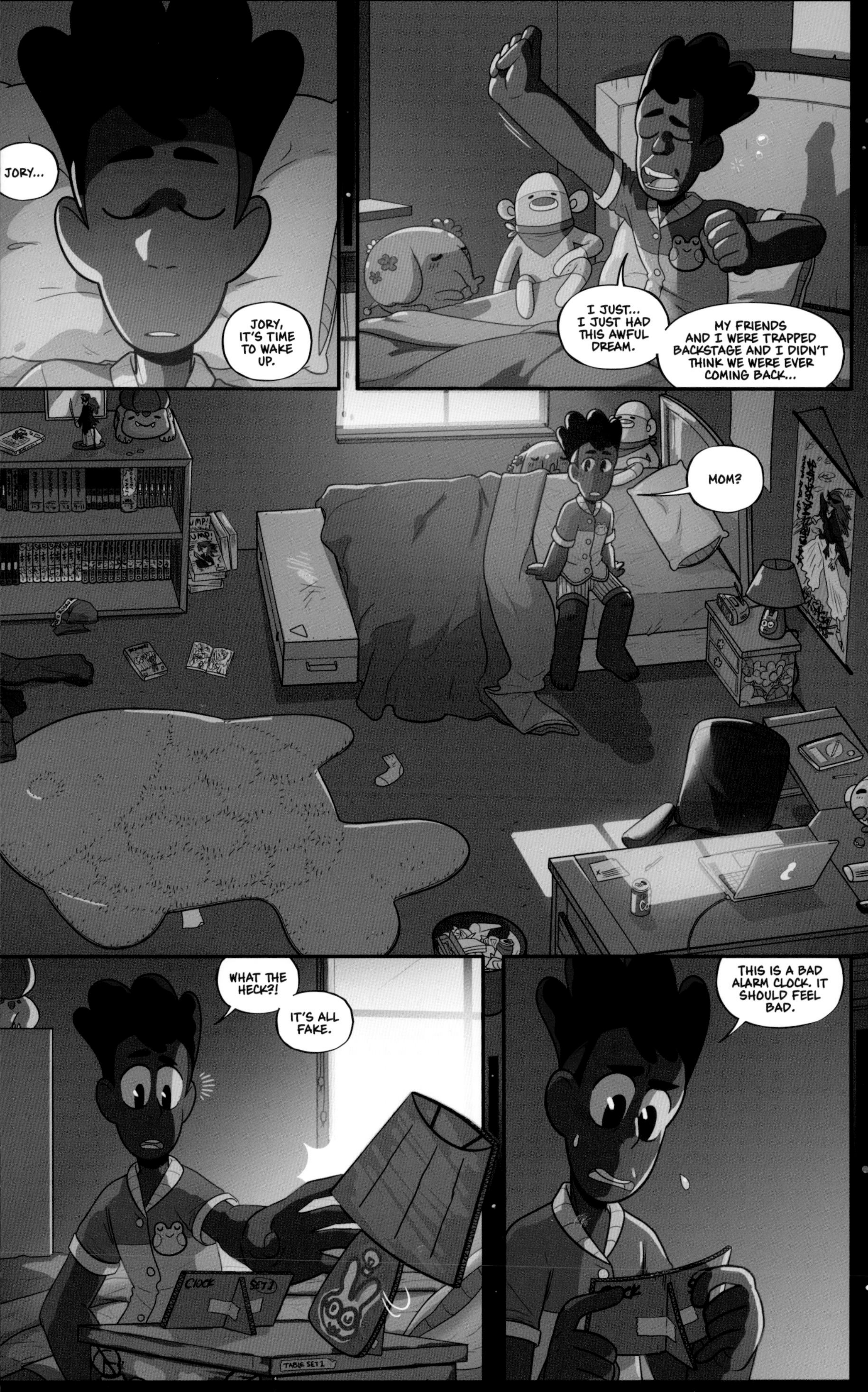

JORY...
JORY, IT'S TIME TO WAKE UP.
I JUST... I JUST HAD THIS AWFUL DREAM.
MY FRIENDS AND I WERE TRAPPED BACKSTAGE AND I DIDN'T THINK WE WERE EVER COMING BACK...
MOM?
WHAT THE HECK?!
IT'S ALL FAKE.
CLOCK
SET 1
TABLE SET 1
THIS IS A BAD ALARM CLOCK. IT SHOULD FEEL BAD.

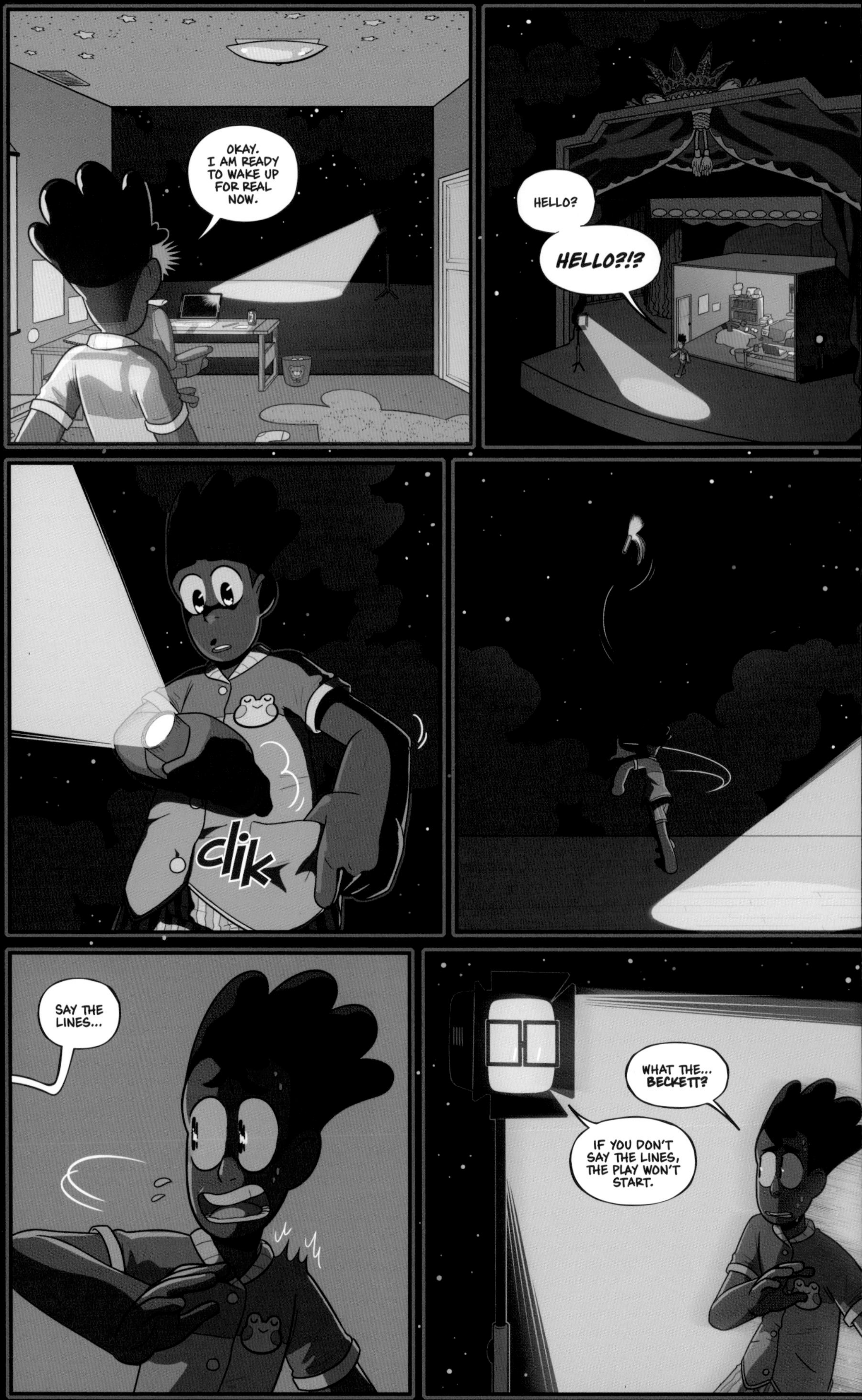
OKAY. I AM READY TO WAKE UP FOR REAL NOW.
HELLO?
HELLO?!?
CLIK
SAY THE LINES...
WHAT THE... BECKETT?
IF YOU DON'T SAY THE LINES, THE PLAY WON'T START.

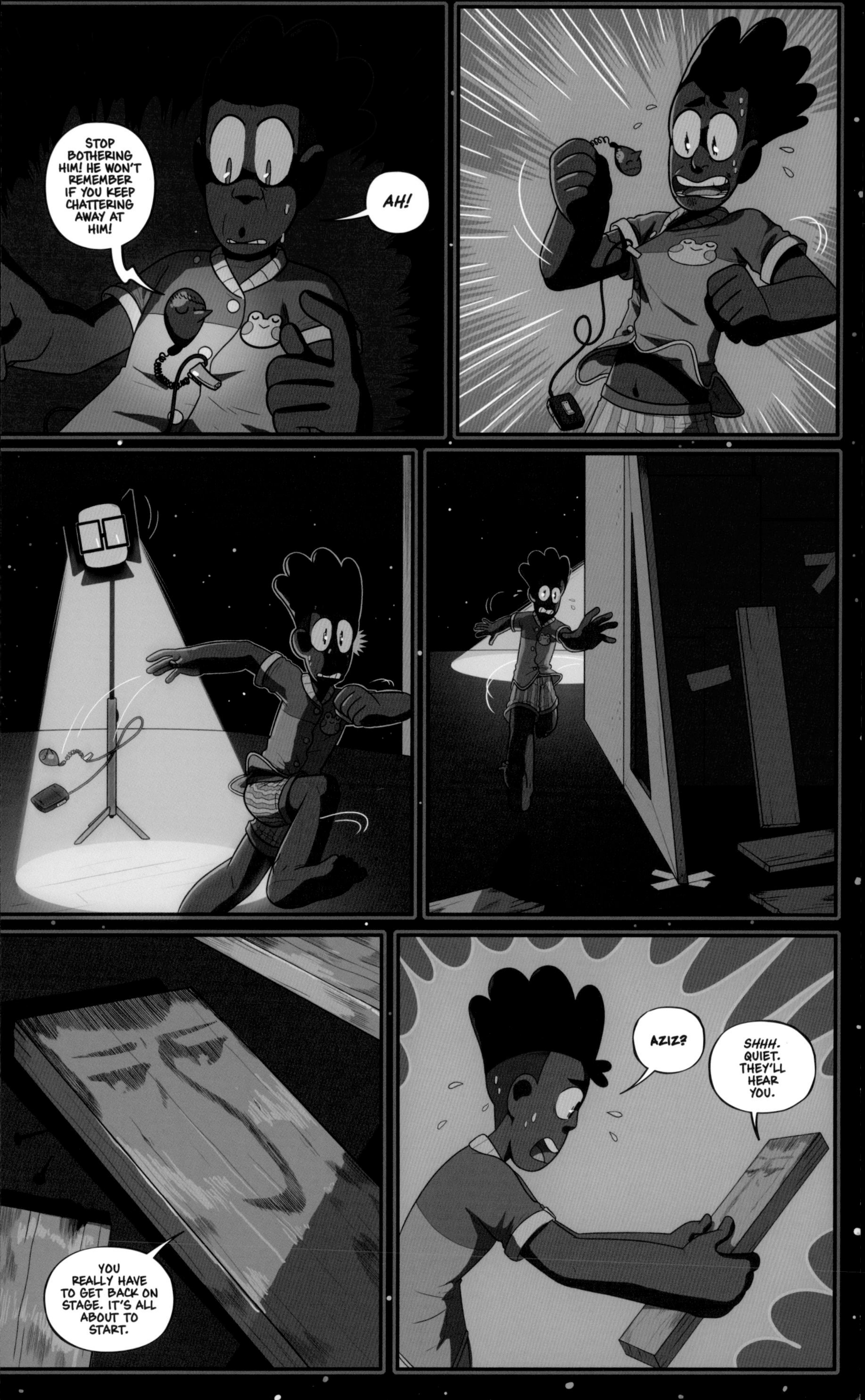
STOP BOTHERING HIM! HE WON'T REMEMBER IF YOU KEEP CHATTERING AWAY AT HIM!
AH!
YOU REALLY HAVE TO GET BACK ON STAGE. IT'S ALL ABOUT TO START.
AZIZ?
SHHH. QUIET. THEY'LL HEAR YOU.

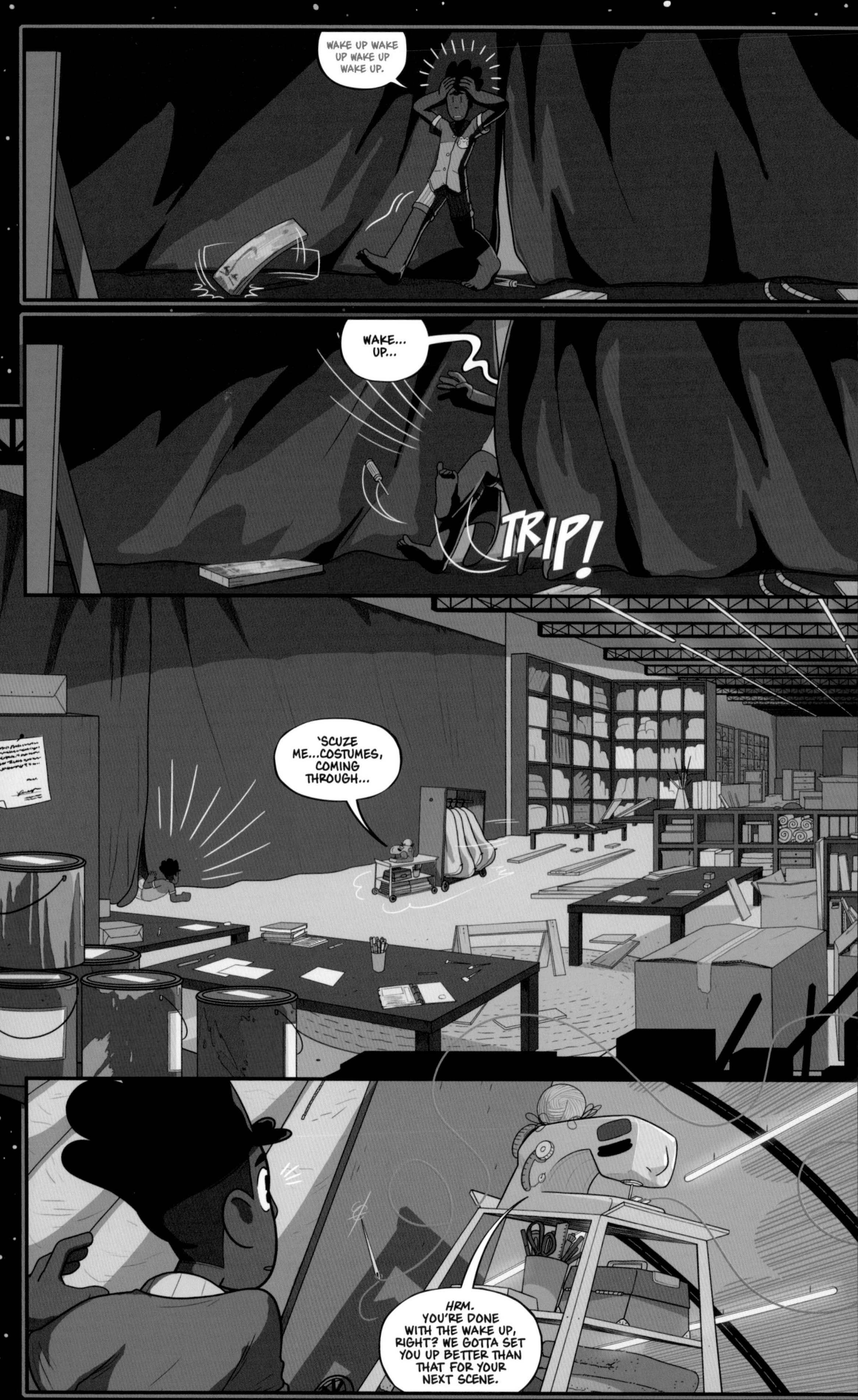
WAKE UP WAKE UP WAKE UP WAKE UP.
WAKE... UP...
TRIP!
'SCUZE ME...COSTUMES, COMING THROUGH...
HRM. YOU'RE DONE WITH THE WAKE UP, RIGHT? WE GOTTA SET YOU UP BETTER THAN THAT FOR YOUR NEXT SCENE.

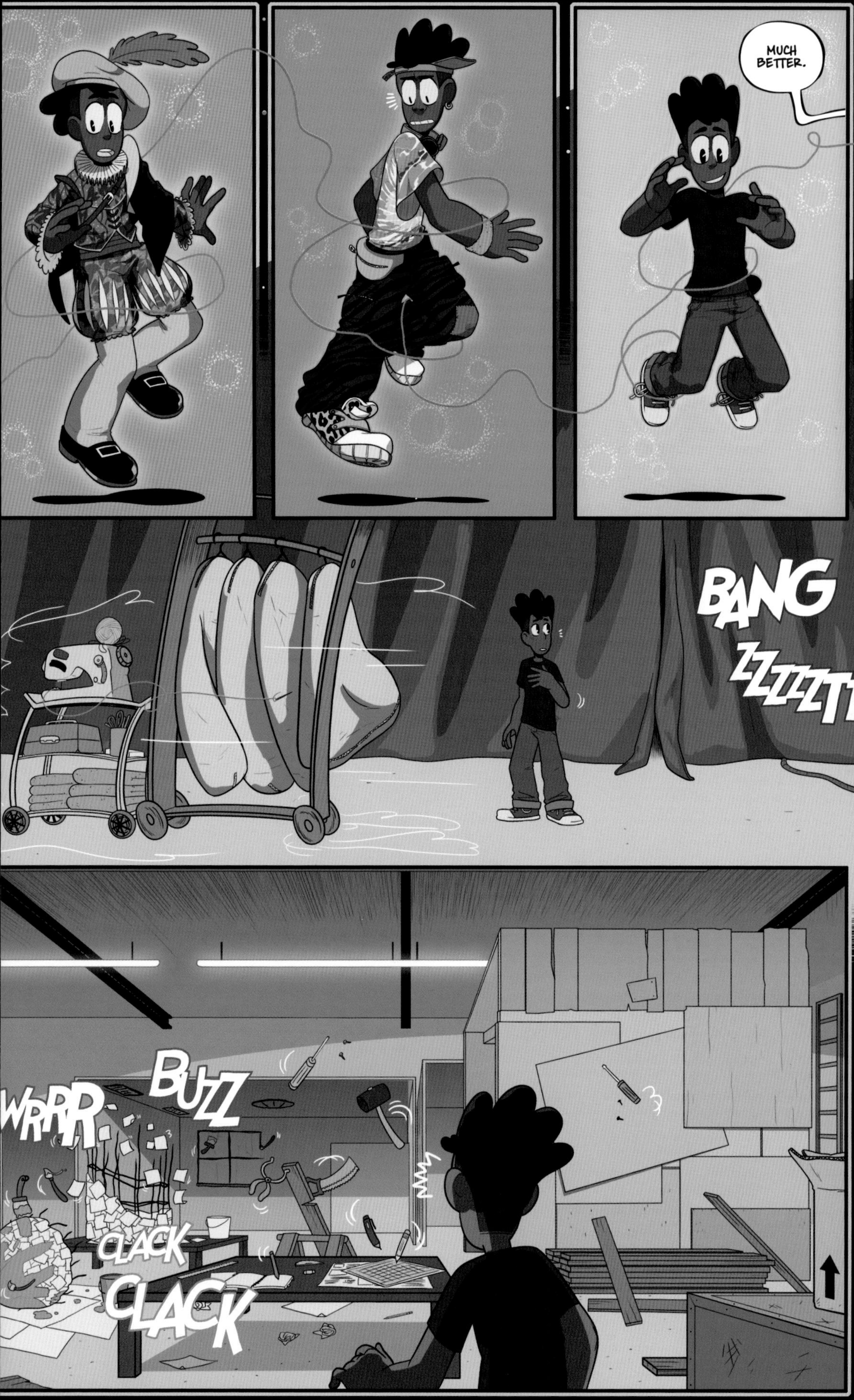
MUCH BETTER.
BANG
ZZZZZTTT
WRRRR
BUZZ
CLACK
CLACK

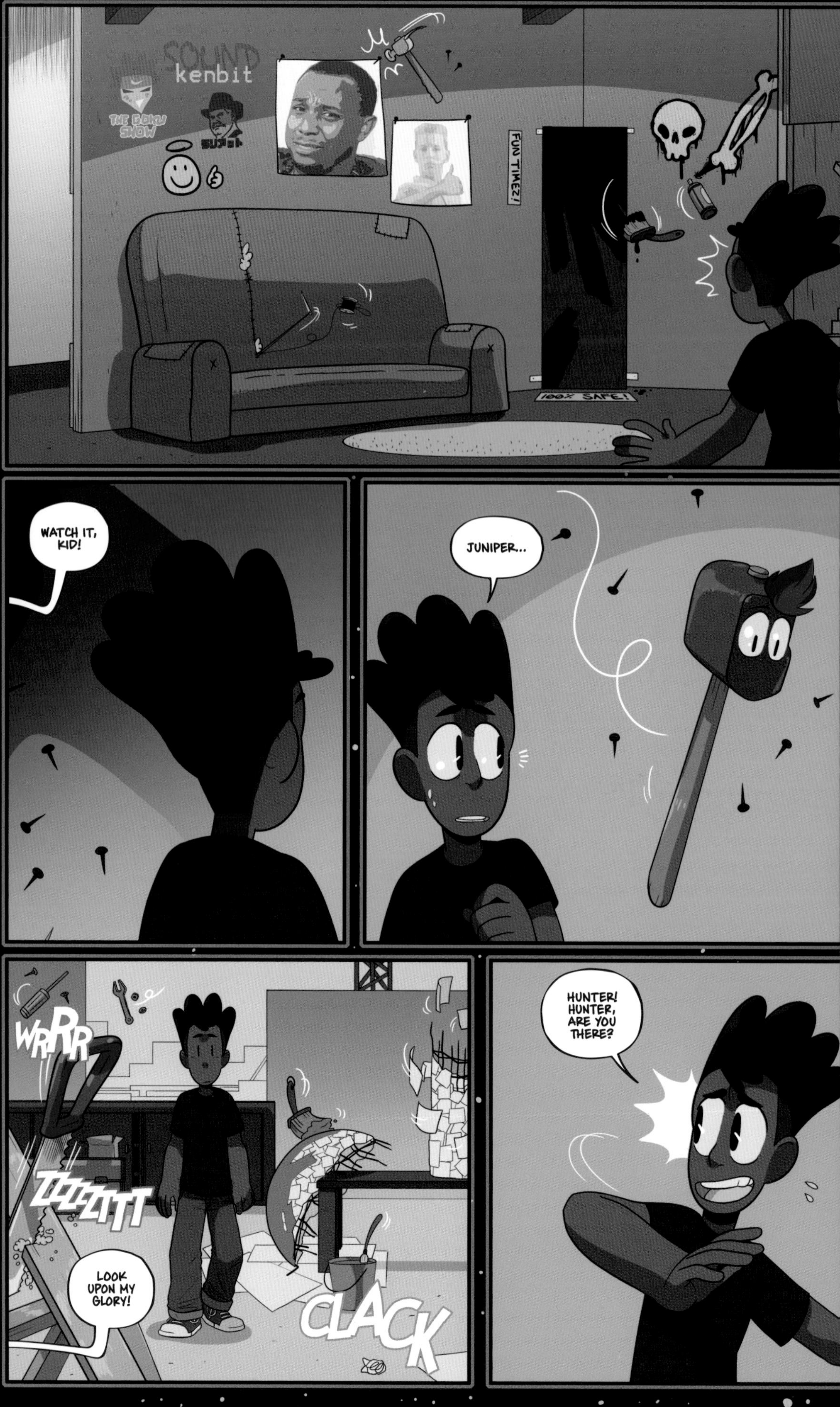
SOUND
kenbit
THE GOKU SHOW
FUN TIMEZ!
100% SAFE!
WATCH IT, KID!
JUNIPER...
WRRR
ZZZZZTTT
LOOK UPON MY GLORY!
CLACK
HUNTER! HUNTER, ARE YOU THERE?

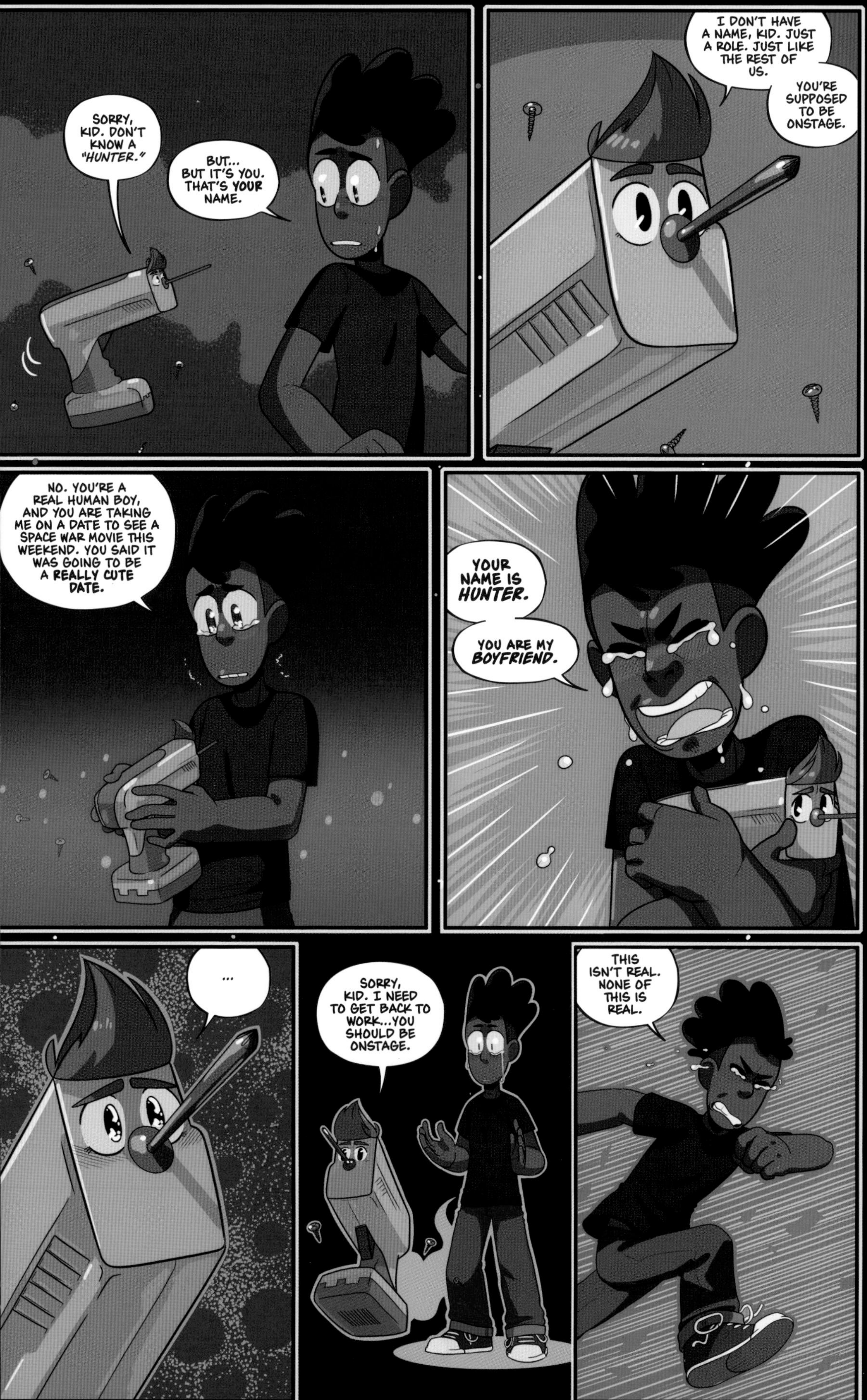
SORRY, KID. DON'T KNOW A "HUNTER."
BUT... BUT IT'S YOU. THAT'S YOUR NAME.
I DON'T HAVE A NAME, KID. JUST A ROLE. JUST LIKE THE REST OF US.
YOU'RE SUPPOSED TO BE ONSTAGE.
NO. YOU'RE A REAL HUMAN BOY, AND YOU ARE TAKING ME ON A DATE TO SEE A SPACE WAR MOVIE THIS WEEKEND. YOU SAID IT WAS GOING TO BE A REALLY CUTE DATE.
YOUR NAME IS HUNTER.
YOU ARE MY BOYFRIEND.
...
SORRY, KID. I NEED TO GET BACK TO WORK...YOU SHOULD BE ONSTAGE.
THIS ISN'T REAL. NONE OF THIS IS REAL.

JORY?

AMBER?!

OH THANK GOD!

WHAT THE HECK IS THIS PLACE?

EVERYONE BACK TO THEIR PLACES IMMEDIATELY. THIS WILL NOT STAND!

VIVIAN LEE?! IS THAT YOU?!

THIS ISN'T THE TIME FOR QUESTIONS! WE NEED TO BE READY!

I DON'T UNDERSTAND WHAT'S GOING ON?! WHAT DO YOU WANT FROM ME?

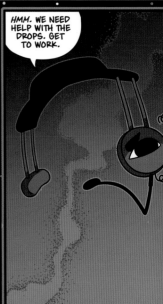

HMM. WE NEED HELP WITH THE DROPS. GET TO WORK.

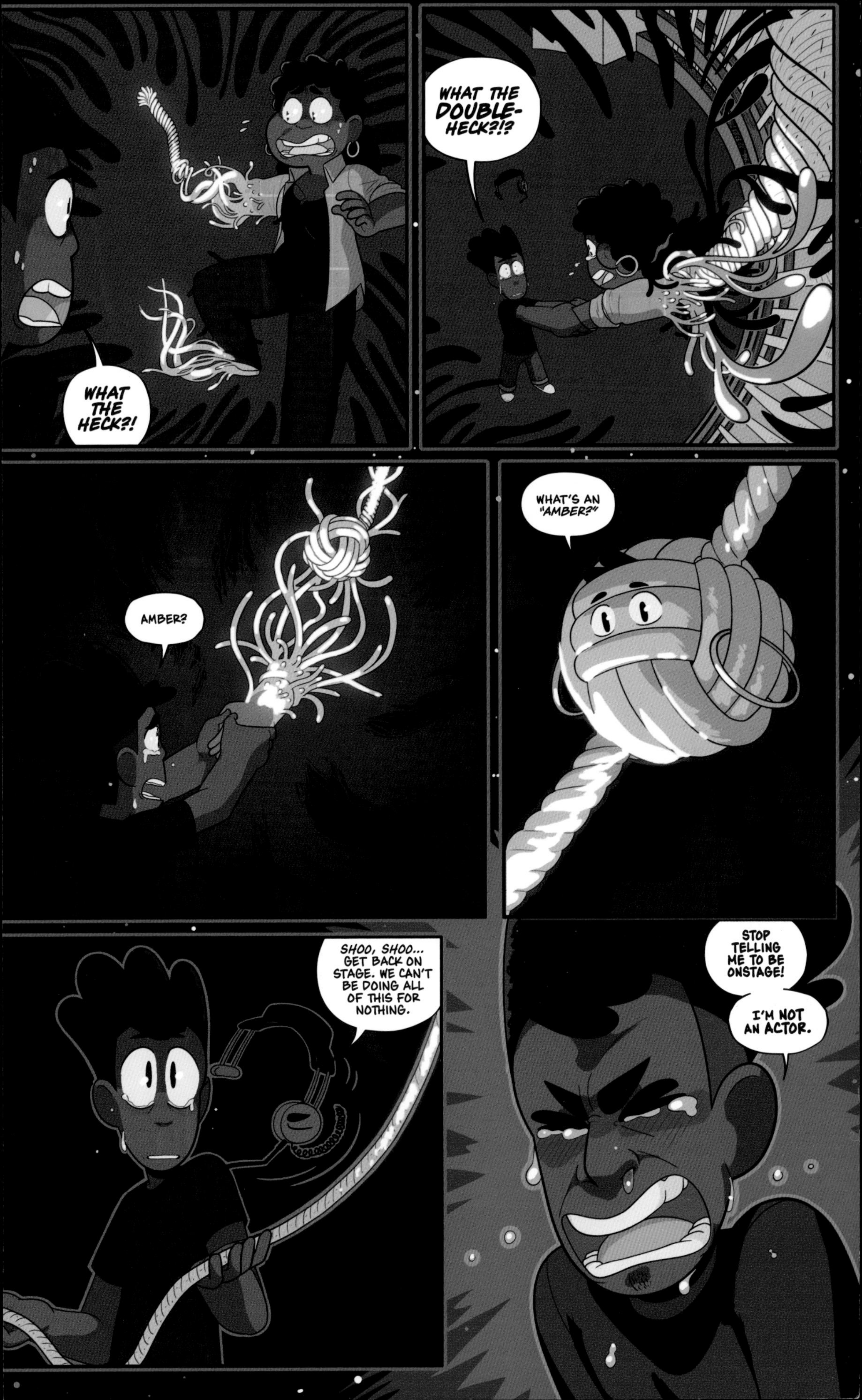
WHAT THE HECK?!
WHAT THE DOUBLE-HECK?!?
AMBER?
WHAT'S AN "AMBER?"
SHOO, SHOO... GET BACK ON STAGE. WE CAN'T BE DOING ALL OF THIS FOR NOTHING.
STOP TELLING ME TO BE ONSTAGE!
I'M NOT AN ACTOR.

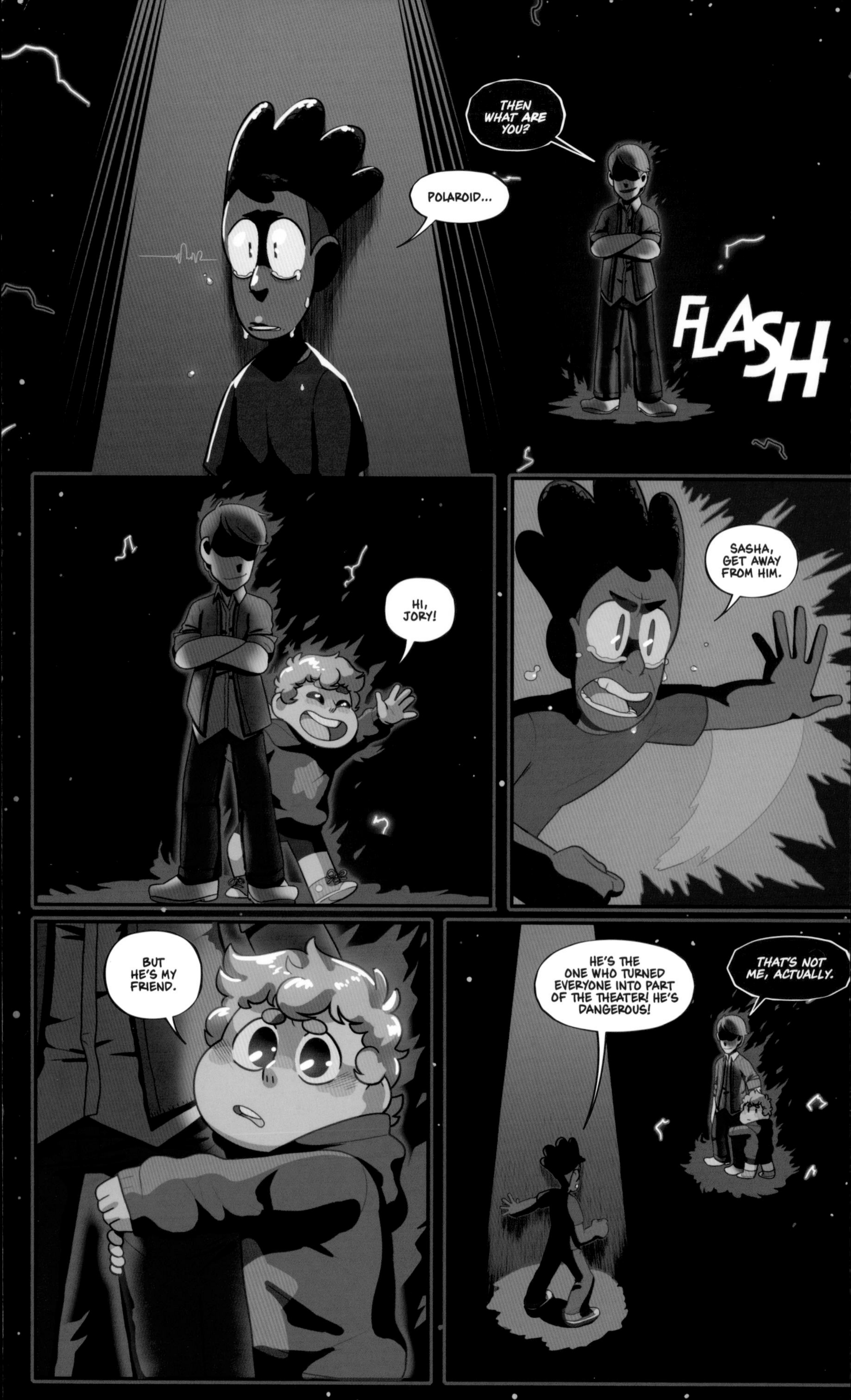
POLAROID...
THEN WHAT ARE YOU?
FLASH
HI, JORY!
SASHA, GET AWAY FROM HIM.
BUT HE'S MY FRIEND.
HE'S THE ONE WHO TURNED EVERYONE INTO PART OF THE THEATER! HE'S DANGEROUS!
THAT'S NOT ME, ACTUALLY.

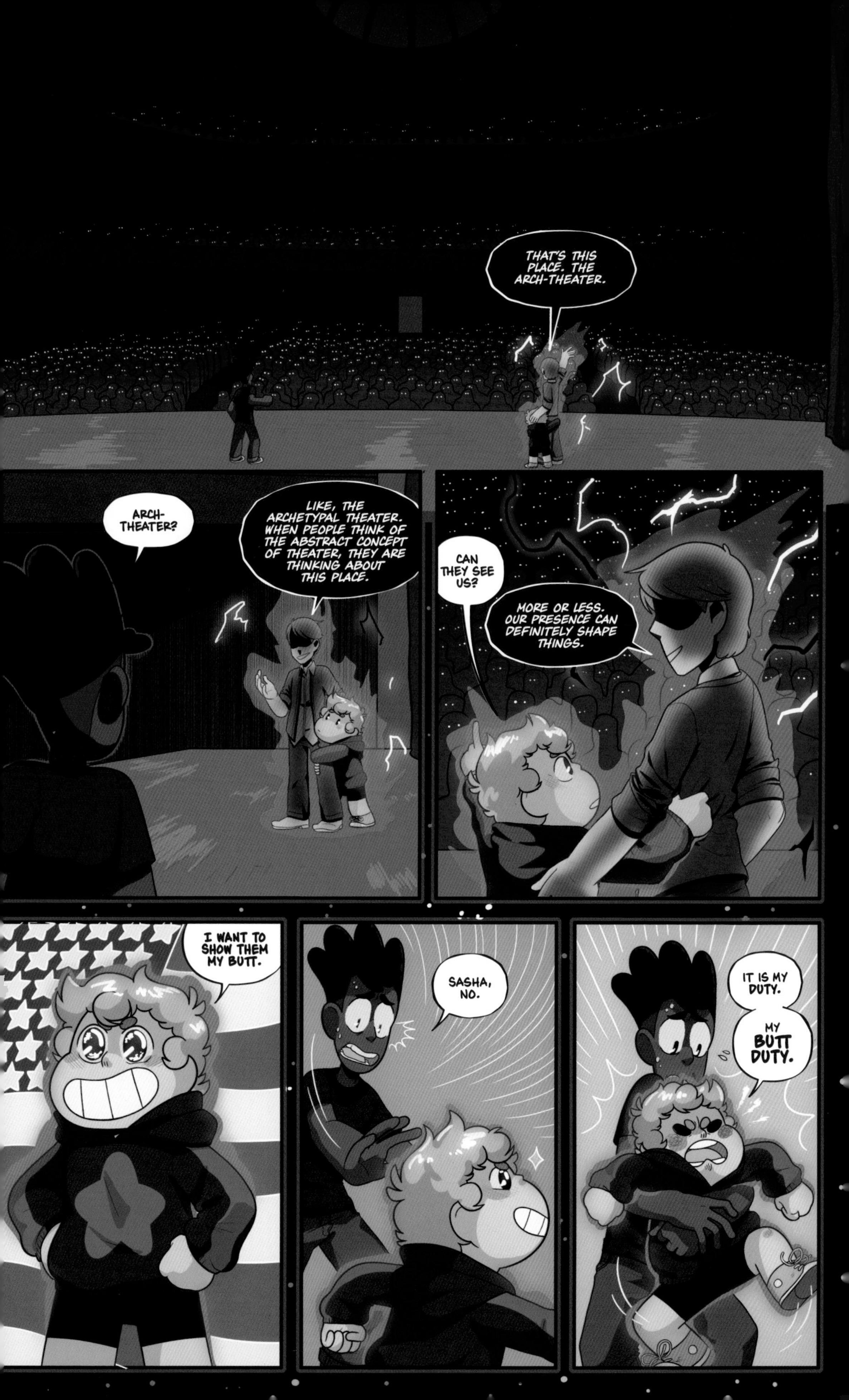
THAT'S THIS PLACE. THE ARCH-THEATER.
ARCH-THEATER?
LIKE, THE ARCHETYPAL THEATER. WHEN PEOPLE THINK OF THE ABSTRACT CONCEPT OF THEATER, THEY ARE THINKING ABOUT THIS PLACE.
CAN THEY SEE US?
MORE OR LESS. OUR PRESENCE CAN DEFINITELY SHAPE THINGS.
I WANT TO SHOW THEM MY BUTT.
SASHA, NO.
IT IS MY DUTY.
MY BUTT DUTY.

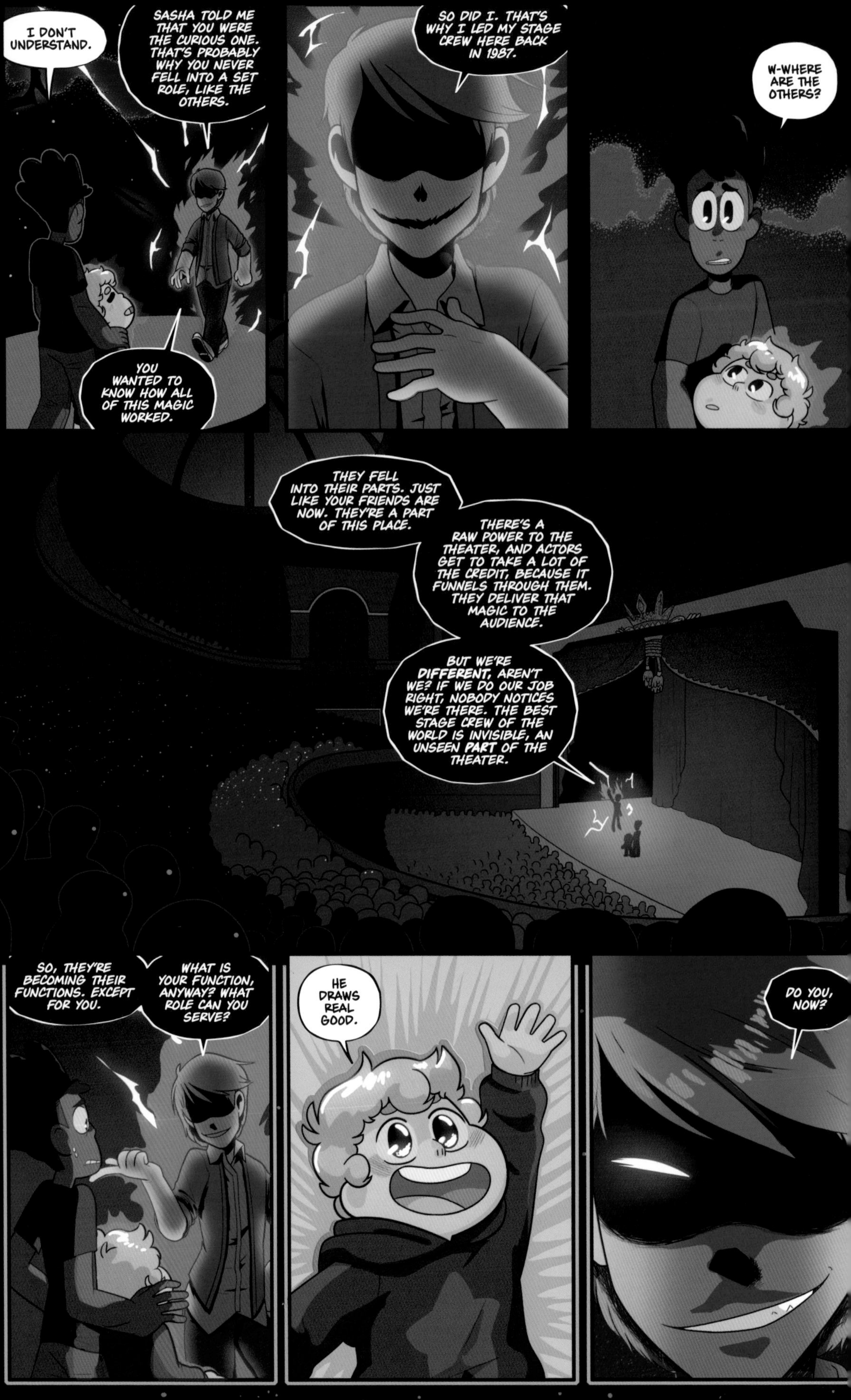
I DON'T UNDERSTAND.
SASHA TOLD ME THAT YOU WERE THE CURIOUS ONE. THAT'S PROBABLY WHY YOU NEVER FELL INTO A SET ROLE, LIKE THE OTHERS.
YOU WANTED TO KNOW HOW ALL OF THIS MAGIC WORKED.
SO DID I. THAT'S WHY I LED MY STAGE CREW HERE BACK IN 1987.
W-WHERE ARE THE OTHERS?
THEY FELL INTO THEIR PARTS. JUST LIKE YOUR FRIENDS ARE NOW. THEY'RE A PART OF THIS PLACE.
THERE'S A RAW POWER TO THE THEATER, AND ACTORS GET TO TAKE A LOT OF THE CREDIT, BECAUSE IT FUNNELS THROUGH THEM. THEY DELIVER THAT MAGIC TO THE AUDIENCE.
BUT WE'RE DIFFERENT, AREN'T WE? IF WE DO OUR JOB RIGHT, NOBODY NOTICES WE'RE THERE. THE BEST STAGE CREW OF THE WORLD IS INVISIBLE, AN UNSEEN PART OF THE THEATER.
SO, THEY'RE BECOMING THEIR FUNCTIONS. EXCEPT FOR YOU.
WHAT IS YOUR FUNCTION, ANYWAY? WHAT ROLE CAN YOU SERVE?
HE DRAWS REAL GOOD.
DO YOU, NOW?

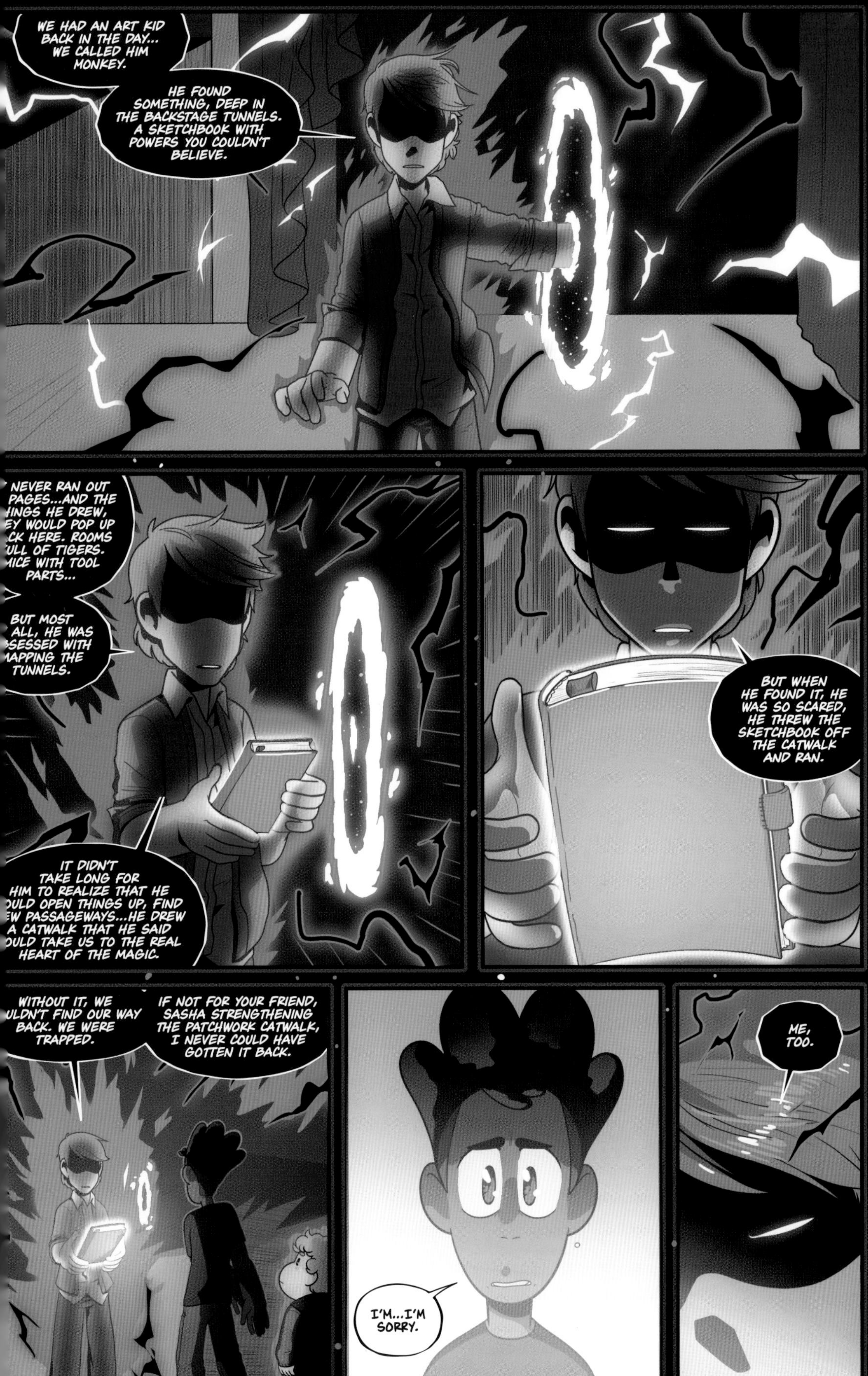

WE HAD AN ART KID BACK IN THE DAY... WE CALLED HIM MONKEY.
HE FOUND SOMETHING, DEEP IN THE BACKSTAGE TUNNELS. A SKETCHBOOK WITH POWERS YOU COULDN'T BELIEVE.
NEVER RAN OUT PAGES...AND THE INGS HE DREW, EY WOULD POP UP CK HERE. ROOMS ULL OF TIGERS. MICE WITH TOOL PARTS...
BUT MOST ALL, HE WAS SESSED WITH APPING THE TUNNELS.
IT DIDN'T TAKE LONG FOR HIM TO REALIZE THAT HE OULD OPEN THINGS UP, FIND EW PASSAGEWAYS...HE DREW A CATWALK THAT HE SAID OULD TAKE US TO THE REAL HEART OF THE MAGIC.
BUT WHEN HE FOUND IT, HE WAS SO SCARED, HE THREW THE SKETCHBOOK OFF THE CATWALK AND RAN.
WITHOUT IT, WE ULDN'T FIND OUR WAY BACK. WE WERE TRAPPED.
IF NOT FOR YOUR FRIEND, SASHA STRENGTHENING THE PATCHWORK CATWALK, I NEVER COULD HAVE GOTTEN IT BACK.
I'M...I'M SORRY.
ME, TOO.

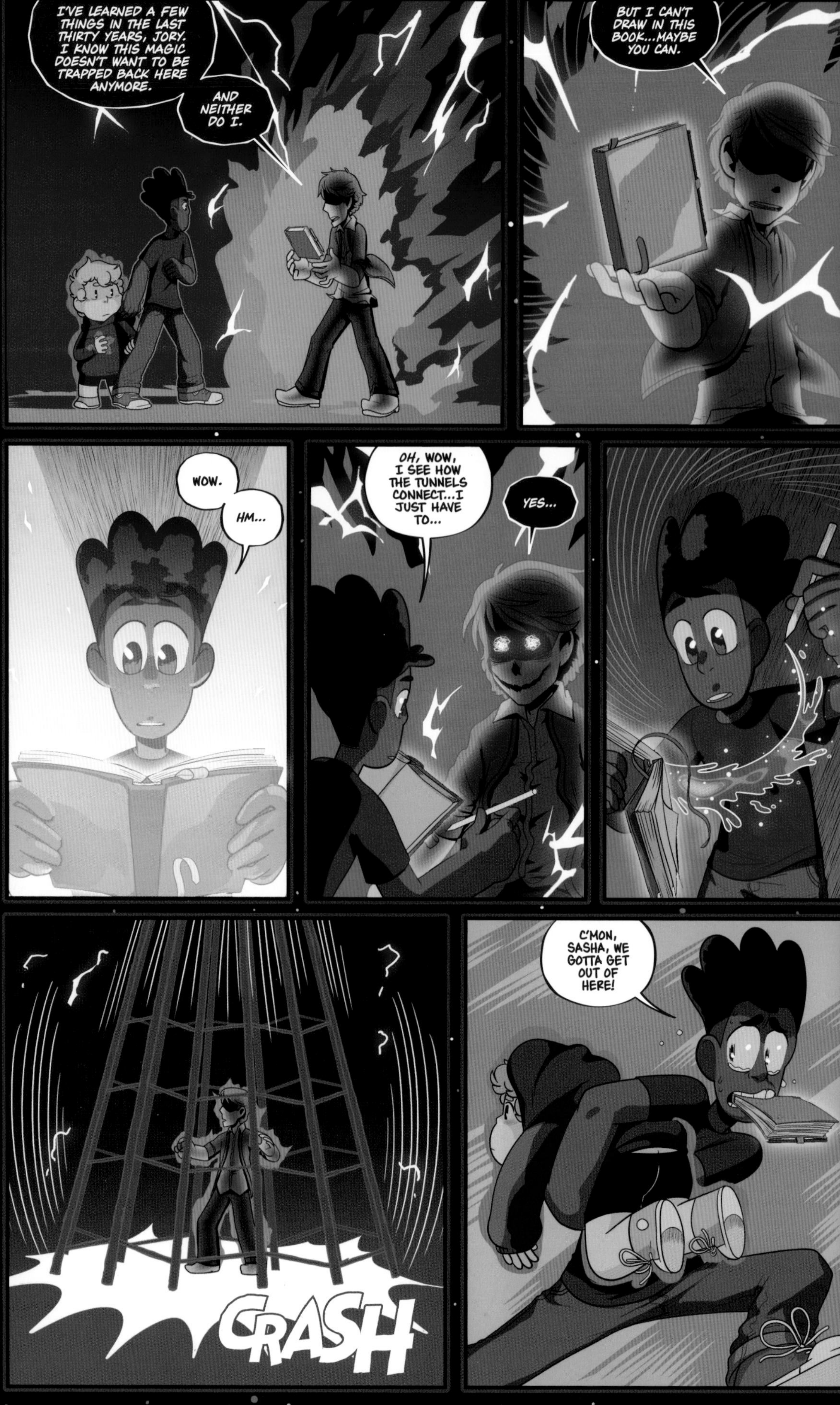
I'VE LEARNED A FEW THINGS IN THE LAST THIRTY YEARS, JORY. I KNOW THIS MAGIC DOESN'T WANT TO BE TRAPPED BACK HERE ANYMORE.
AND NEITHER DO I.
BUT I CAN'T DRAW IN THIS BOOK...MAYBE YOU CAN.
WOW.
HM...
OH, WOW, I SEE HOW THE TUNNELS CONNECT...I JUST HAVE TO...
YES...
CRASH
C'MON, SASHA, WE GOTTA GET OUT OF HERE!

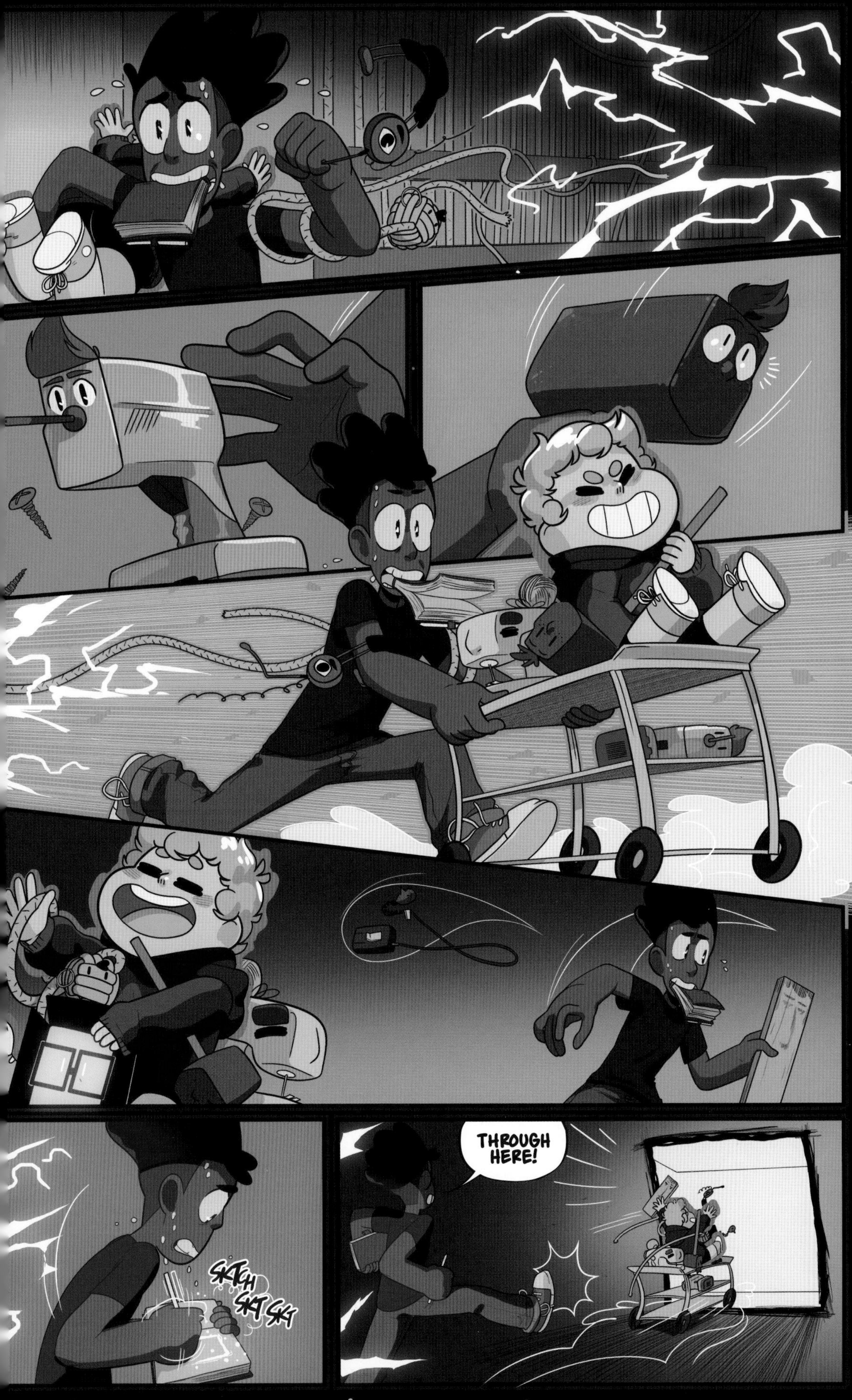
SKTCH
SKT SKT
THROUGH HERE!

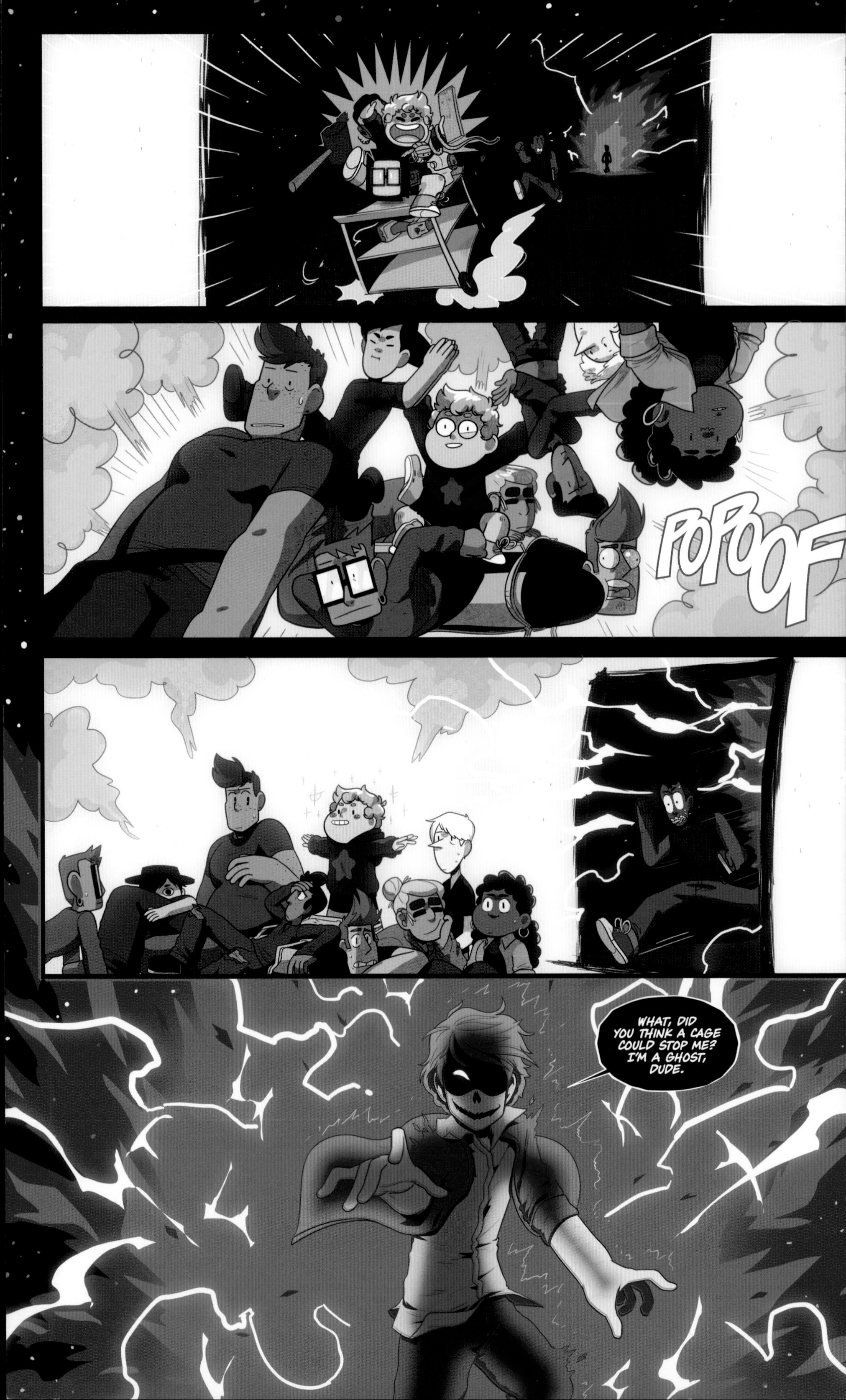
POPOOF
WHAT, DID YOU THINK A CAGE COULD STOP ME? I'M A GHOST, DUDE.

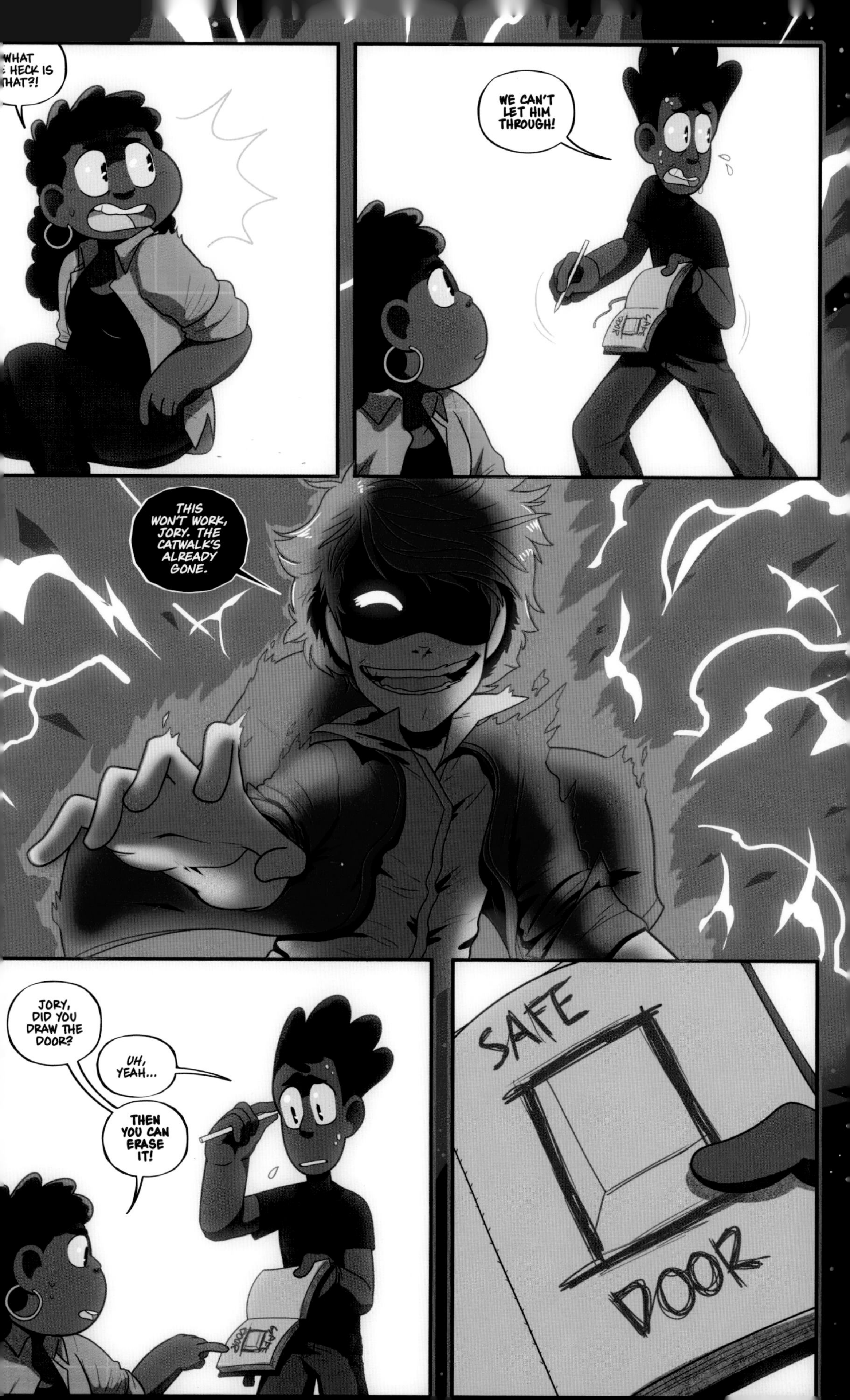
WHAT
THE HECK IS
THAT?!
WE CAN'T
LET HIM
THROUGH!
SAFE
DOOR
THIS
WON'T WORK,
JORY. THE
CATWALK'S
ALREADY
GONE.
JORY,
DID YOU
DRAW THE
DOOR?
UH,
YEAH...
THEN
YOU CAN
ERASE
IT!
SAFE
DOOR
SAFE
DOOR

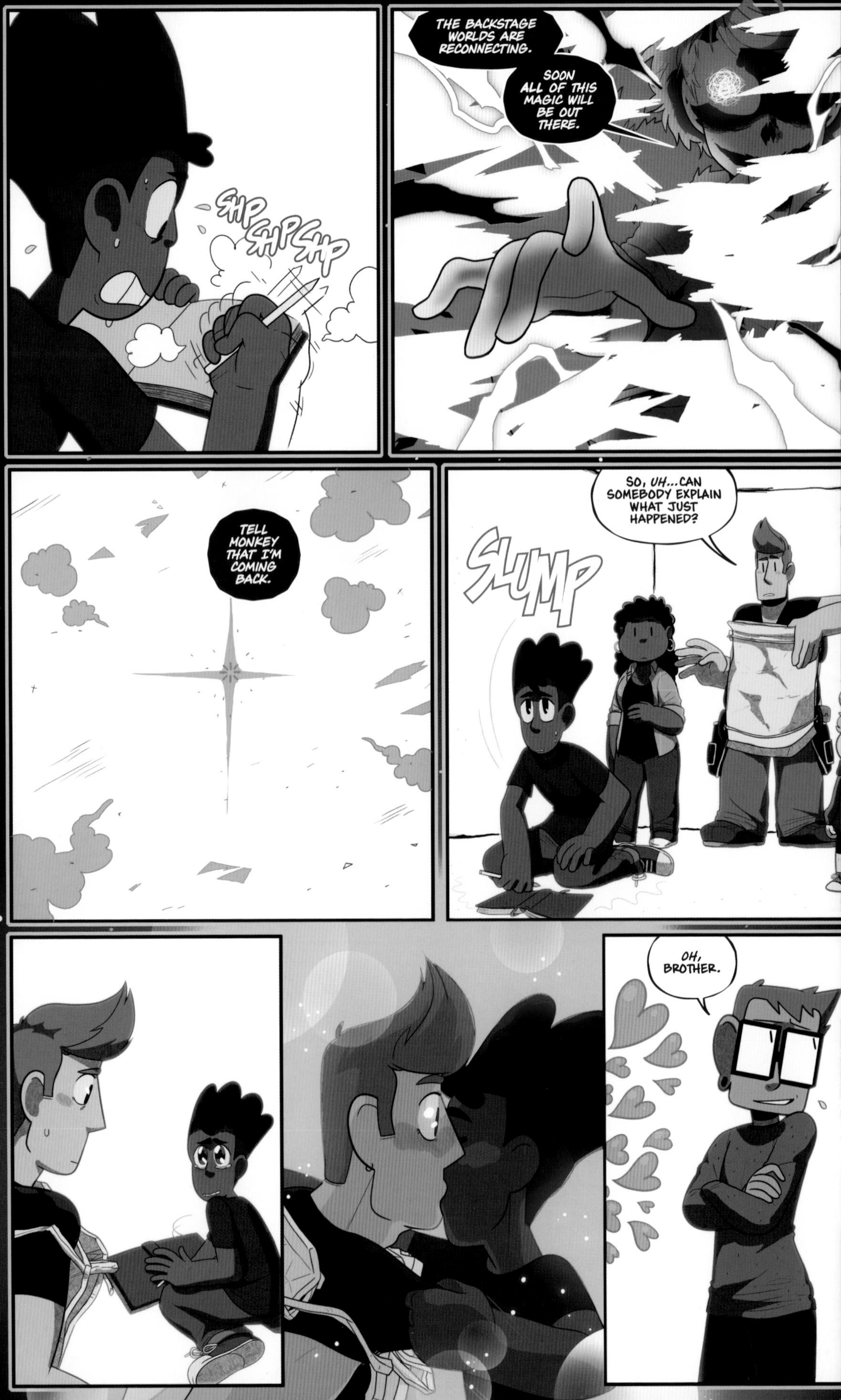
SHP SHP SHP
THE BACKSTAGE WORLDS ARE RECONNECTING.
SOON ALL OF THIS MAGIC WILL BE OUT THERE.
TELL MONKEY THAT I'M COMING BACK.
SLUMP
SO, UH...CAN SOMEBODY EXPLAIN WHAT JUST HAPPENED?
OH, BROTHER.

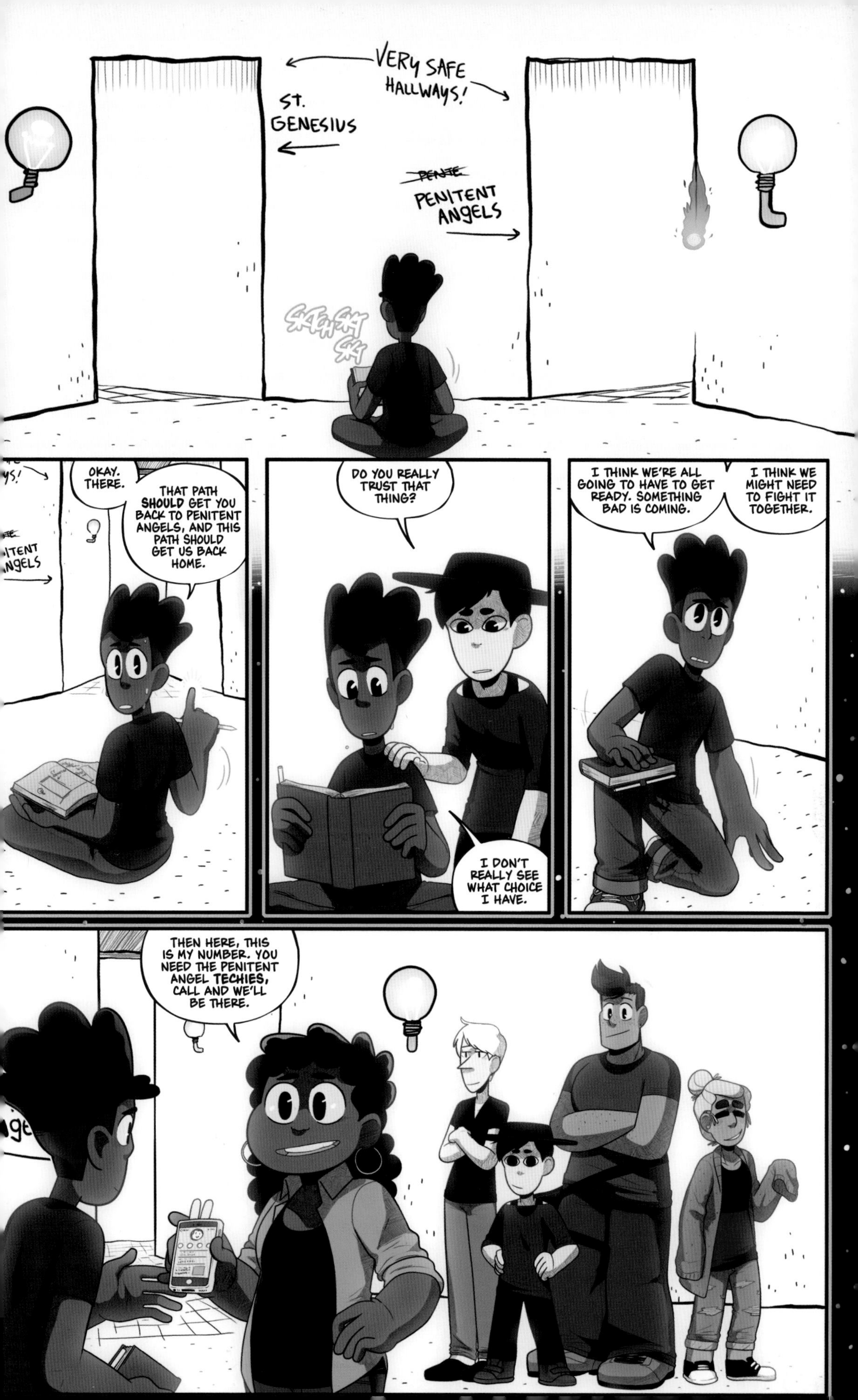
VERY SAFE HALLWAYS!
ST. GENESIUS
PENITENT ANGELS
OKAY. THERE.
THAT PATH **SHOULD** GET YOU BACK TO PENITENT ANGELS, AND THIS PATH SHOULD GET US BACK HOME.
DO YOU REALLY TRUST THAT THING?
I DON'T REALLY SEE WHAT CHOICE I HAVE.
I THINK WE'RE ALL GOING TO HAVE TO GET READY. SOMETHING BAD IS COMING.
I THINK WE MIGHT NEED TO FIGHT IT TOGETHER.
THEN HERE, THIS IS MY NUMBER. YOU NEED THE PENITENT ANGEL **TECHIES**, CALL AND WE'LL BE THERE.

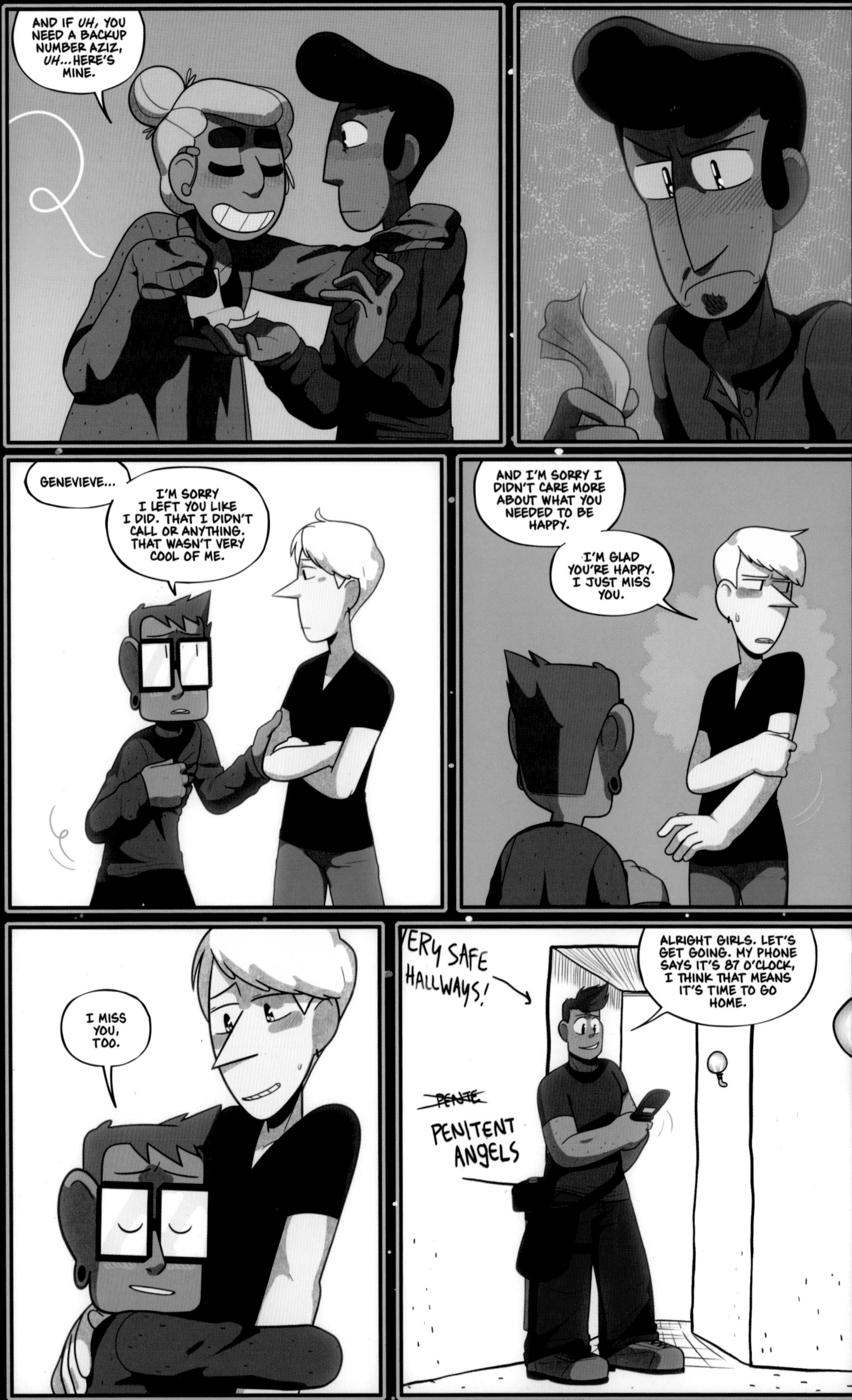
AND IF UH, YOU NEED A BACKUP NUMBER AZIZ, UH... HERE'S MINE.
GENEVIEVE...
I'M SORRY I LEFT YOU LIKE I DID. THAT I DIDN'T CALL OR ANYTHING. THAT WASN'T VERY COOL OF ME.
AND I'M SORRY I DIDN'T CARE MORE ABOUT WHAT YOU NEEDED TO BE HAPPY.
I'M GLAD YOU'RE HAPPY. I JUST MISS YOU.
I MISS YOU, TOO.
ERY SAFE HALLWAYS!
~~PENJE~~
PENITENT ANGELS
ALRIGHT GIRLS. LET'S GET GOING. MY PHONE SAYS IT'S 87 O'CLOCK, I THINK THAT MEANS IT'S TIME TO GO HOME.

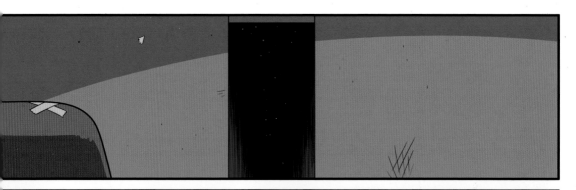

OH, THANK THE STAGE GODS...

WE'RE ACTUALLY HOME.

THAT WAS A FUN ADVENTURE.

NO, SASHA. THAT WAS TERRIFYING.

OH.

PAP

WHAT'S WRONG, JORY?

I JUST GET THE SENSE THAT THIS IS ALL GOING TO GET SO MUCH WORSE BEFORE IT GETS BETTER.

YOU CAN SAY THAT AGAIN.

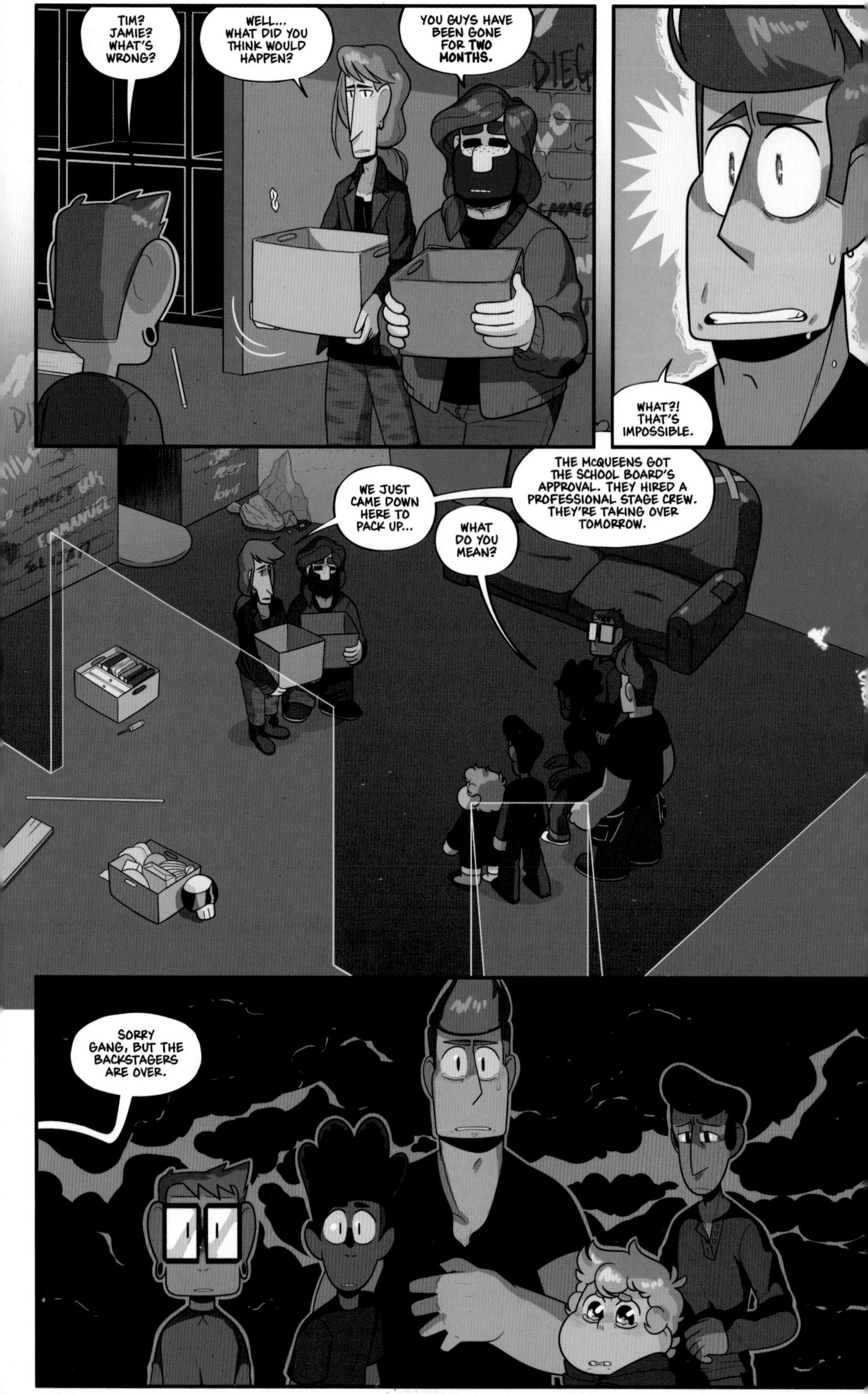
TIM? JAMIE? WHAT'S WRONG?
WELL... WHAT DID YOU THINK WOULD HAPPEN?
YOU GUYS HAVE BEEN GONE FOR TWO MONTHS.
WHAT?! THAT'S IMPOSSIBLE.
WE JUST CAME DOWN HERE TO PACK UP...
WHAT DO YOU MEAN?
THE McQUEENS GOT THE SCHOOL BOARD'S APPROVAL. THEY HIRED A PROFESSIONAL STAGE CREW. THEY'RE TAKING OVER TOMORROW.
SORRY GANG, BUT THE BACKSTAGERS ARE OVER.

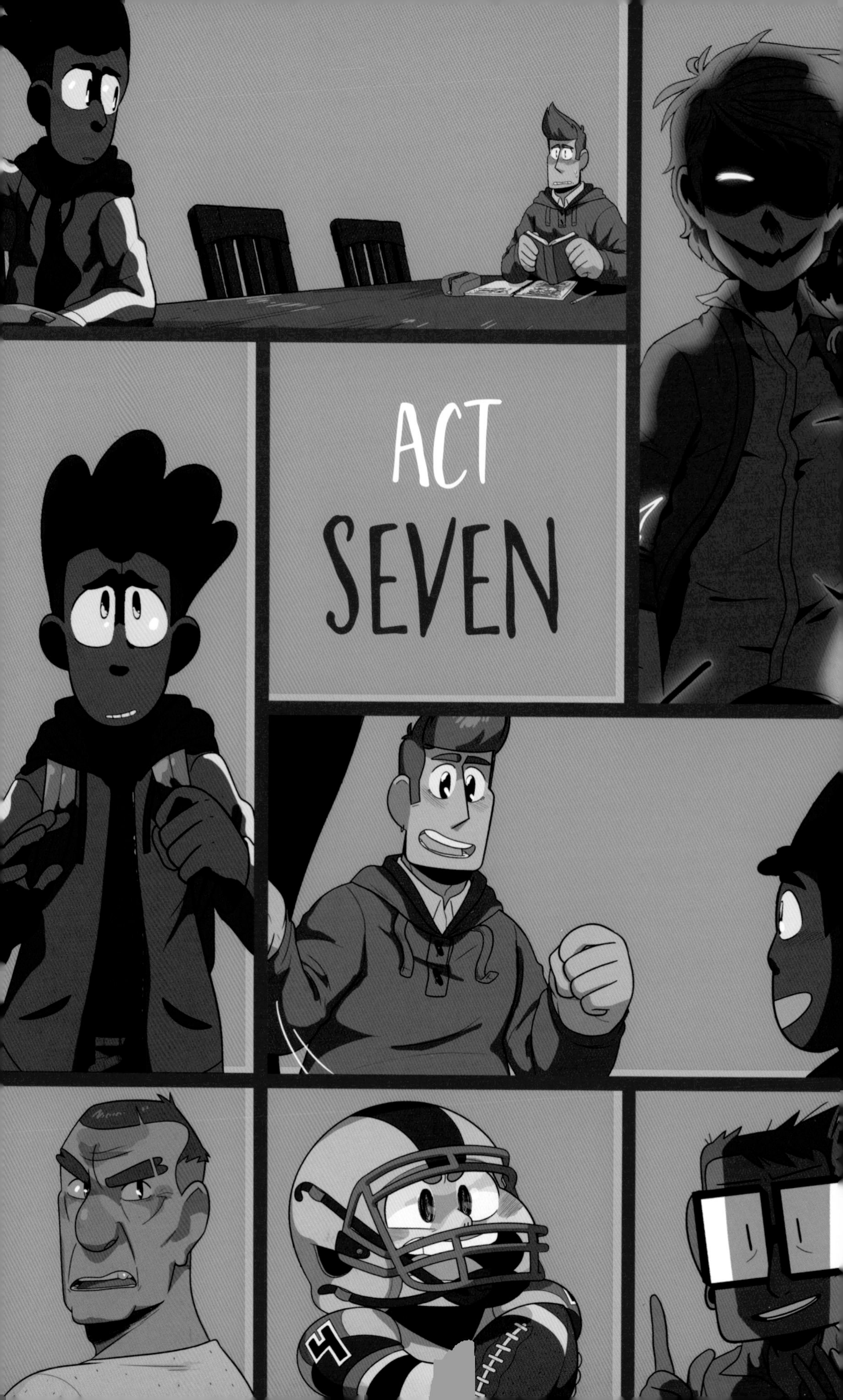
ACT
SEVEN

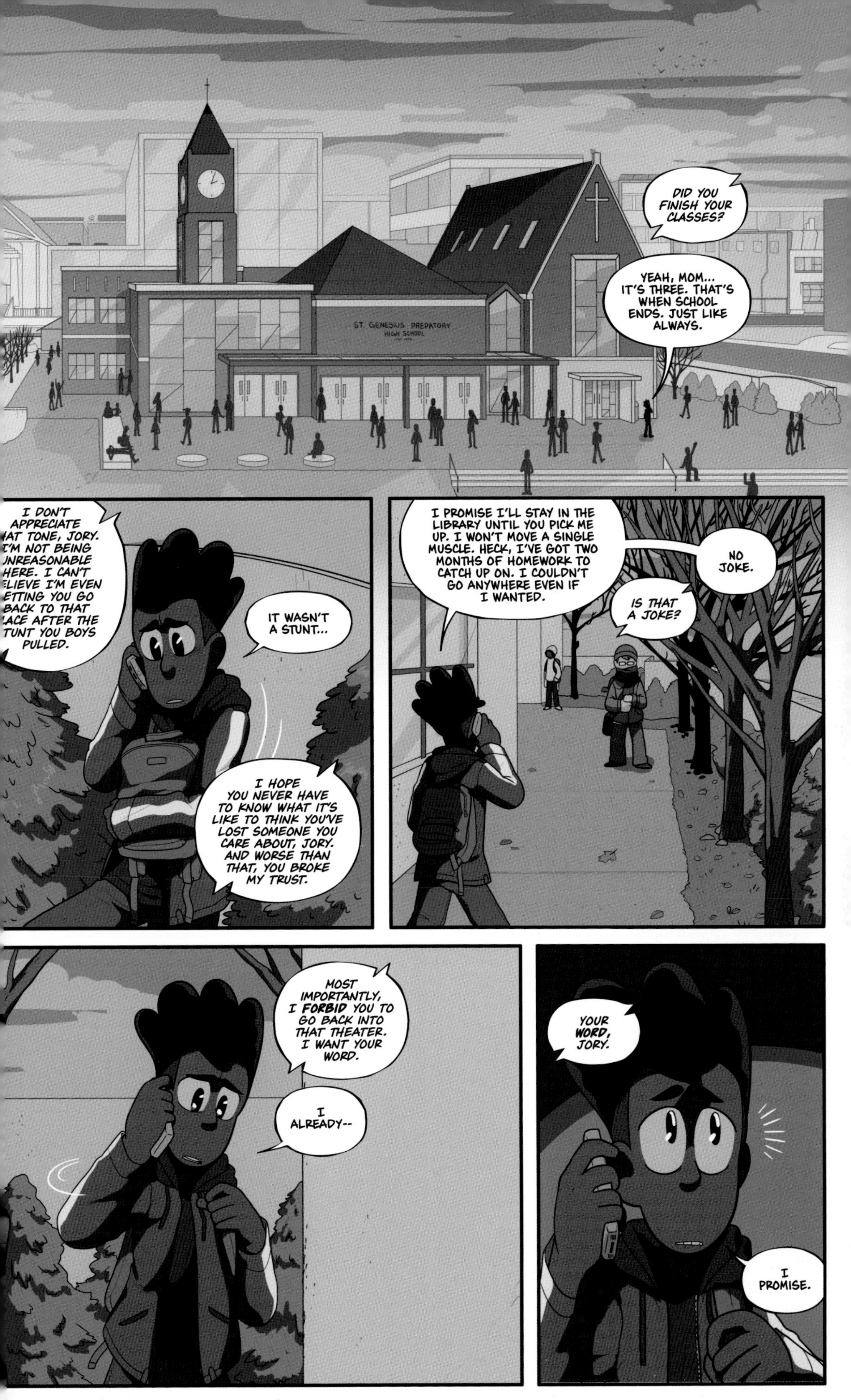
ST. GENESIUS PREPARATORY HIGH SCHOOL
DID YOU FINISH YOUR CLASSES?
YEAH, MOM... IT'S THREE. THAT'S WHEN SCHOOL ENDS. JUST LIKE ALWAYS.
I DON'T APPRECIATE THAT TONE, JORY. I'M NOT BEING UNREASONABLE HERE. I CAN'T BELIEVE I'M EVEN LETTING YOU GO BACK TO THAT PLACE AFTER THE STUNT YOU BOYS PULLED.
IT WASN'T A STUNT...
I HOPE YOU NEVER HAVE TO KNOW WHAT IT'S LIKE TO THINK YOU'VE LOST SOMEONE YOU CARE ABOUT, JORY. AND WORSE THAN THAT, YOU BROKE MY TRUST.
I PROMISE I'LL STAY IN THE LIBRARY UNTIL YOU PICK ME UP. I WON'T MOVE A SINGLE MUSCLE. HECK, I'VE GOT TWO MONTHS OF HOMEWORK TO CATCH UP ON. I COULDN'T GO ANYWHERE EVEN IF I WANTED.
IS THAT A JOKE?
NO JOKE.
MOST IMPORTANTLY, I **FORBID** YOU TO GO BACK INTO THAT THEATER. I WANT YOUR WORD.
I ALREADY--
YOUR **WORD**, JORY.
I PROMISE.

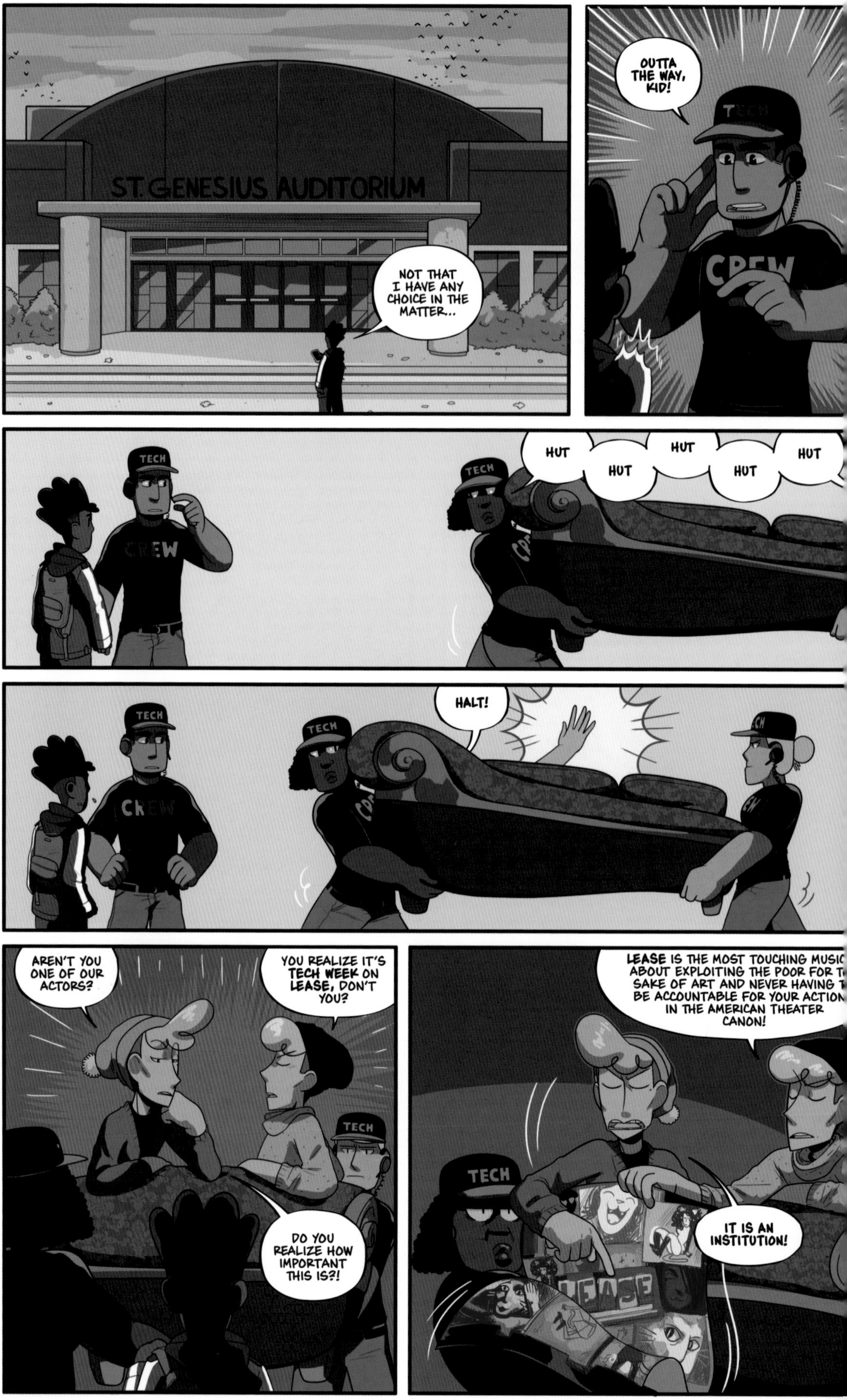
ST. GENESIUS AUDITORIUM
NOT THAT I HAVE ANY CHOICE IN THE MATTER...
OUTTA THE WAY, KID!
TECH
CREW
HUT
HUT
HUT
HUT
HUT
HALT!
AREN'T YOU ONE OF OUR ACTORS?
YOU REALIZE IT'S TECH WEEK ON LEASE, DON'T YOU?
DO YOU REALIZE HOW IMPORTANT THIS IS?!
LEASE IS THE MOST TOUCHING MUSIC ABOUT EXPLOITING THE POOR FOR T SAKE OF ART AND NEVER HAVING T BE ACCOUNTABLE FOR YOUR ACTION IN THE AMERICAN THEATER CANON!
IT IS AN INSTITUTION!
LEASE

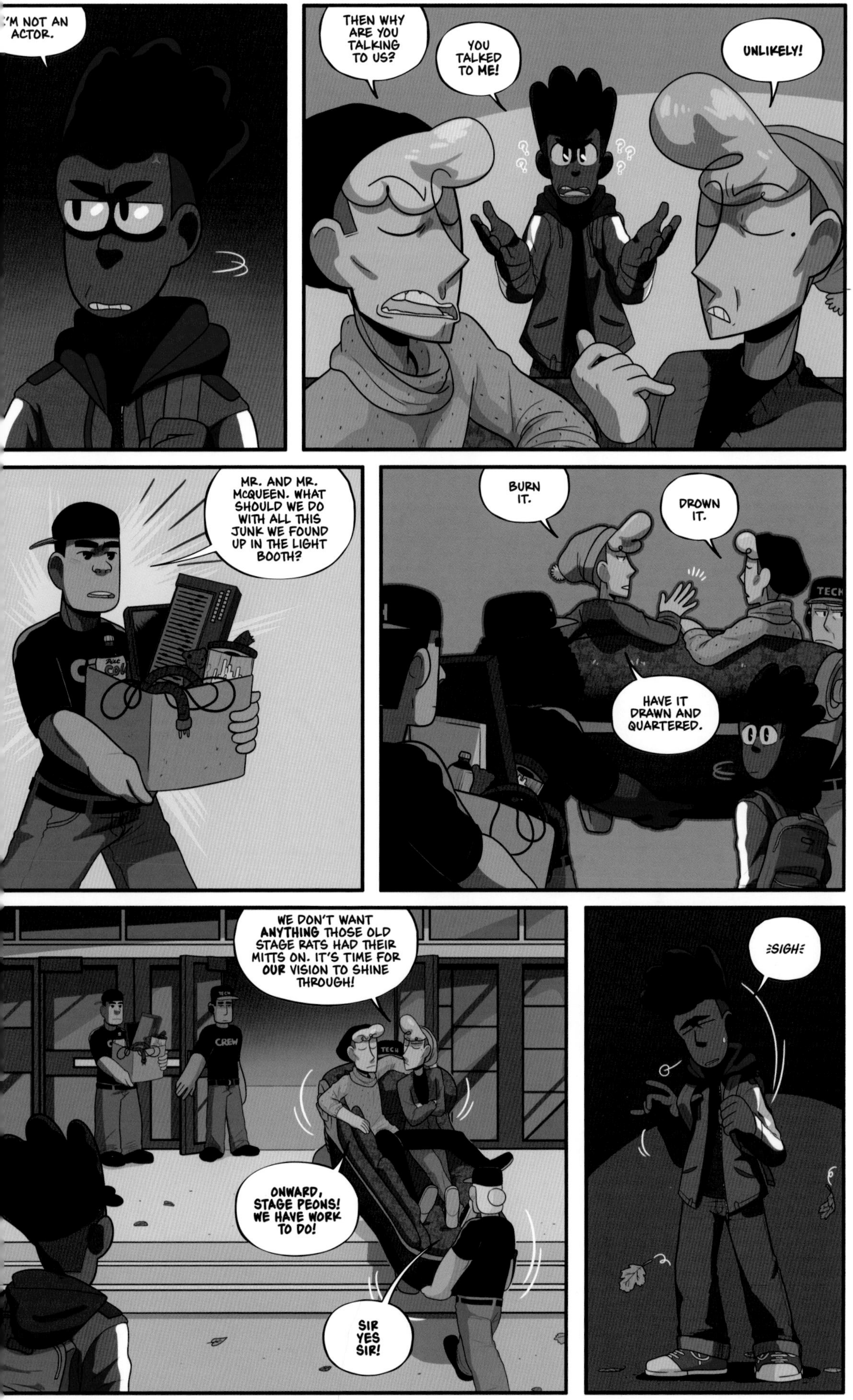
I'M NOT AN ACTOR.
THEN WHY ARE YOU TALKING TO US?
YOU TALKED TO ME!
UNLIKELY!
MR. AND MR. MCQUEEN. WHAT SHOULD WE DO WITH ALL THIS JUNK WE FOUND UP IN THE LIGHT BOOTH?
BURN IT.
DROWN IT.
HAVE IT DRAWN AND QUARTERED.
WE DON'T WANT ANYTHING THOSE OLD STAGE RATS HAD THEIR MITTS ON. IT'S TIME FOR OUR VISION TO SHINE THROUGH!
ONWARD, STAGE PEONS! WE HAVE WORK TO DO!
SIR YES SIR!
SIGH
TECH
CREW

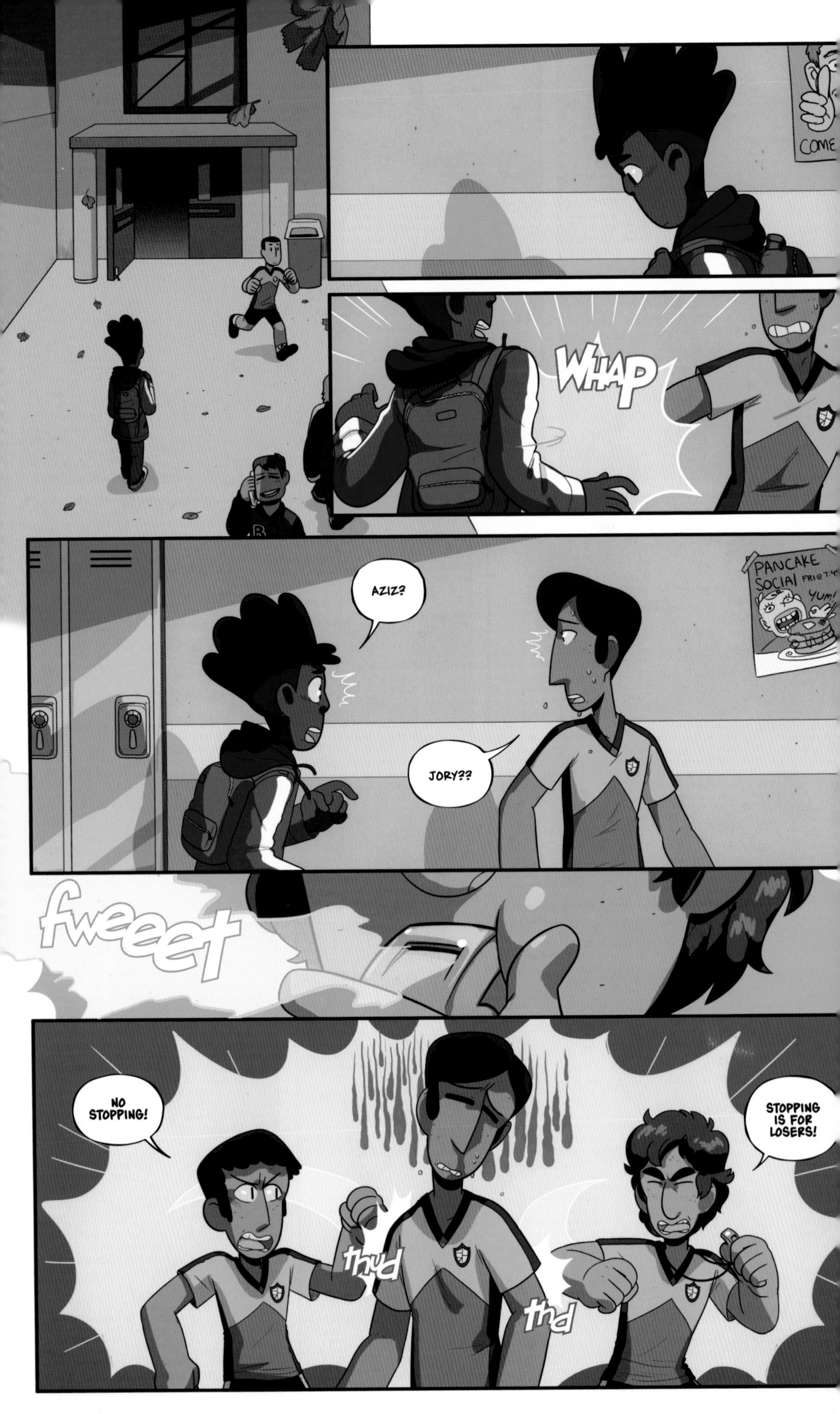
COME
WHAP
PANCAKE SOCIAL FRI @ 7:45
YUM!
AZIZ?
JORY??
fweeet
NO STOPPING!
STOPPING IS FOR LOSERS!
thud
thd

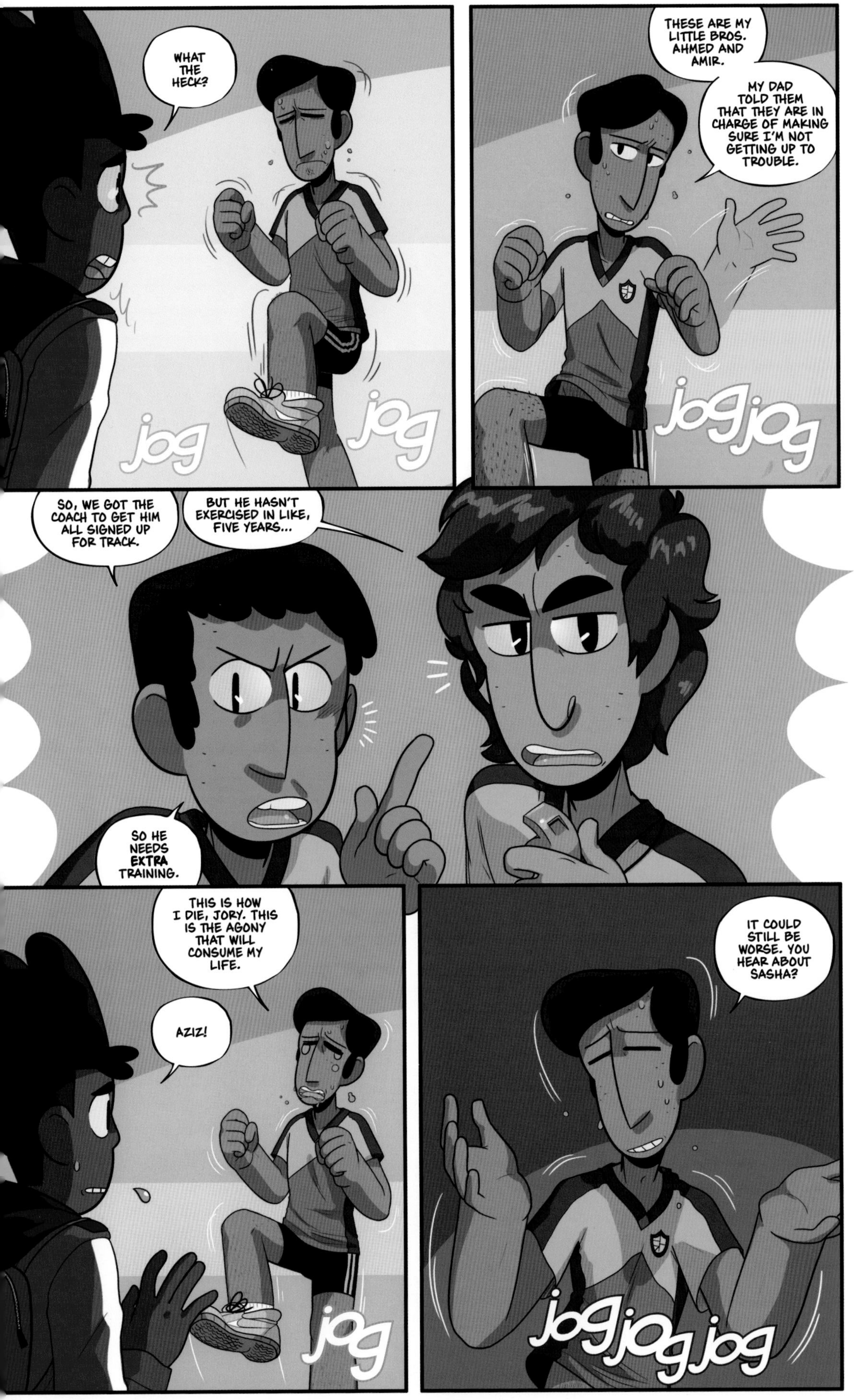

WHAT THE HECK?
jog
jog
THESE ARE MY LITTLE BROS. AHMED AND AMIR.
MY DAD TOLD THEM THAT THEY ARE IN CHARGE OF MAKING SURE I'M NOT GETTING UP TO TROUBLE.
jog jog
SO, WE GOT THE COACH TO GET HIM ALL SIGNED UP FOR TRACK.
BUT HE HASN'T EXERCISED IN LIKE, FIVE YEARS...
SO HE NEEDS **EXTRA** TRAINING.
THIS IS HOW I DIE, JORY. THIS IS THE AGONY THAT WILL CONSUME MY LIFE.
AZIZ!
jog
IT COULD STILL BE WORSE. YOU HEAR ABOUT SASHA?
jog jog jog

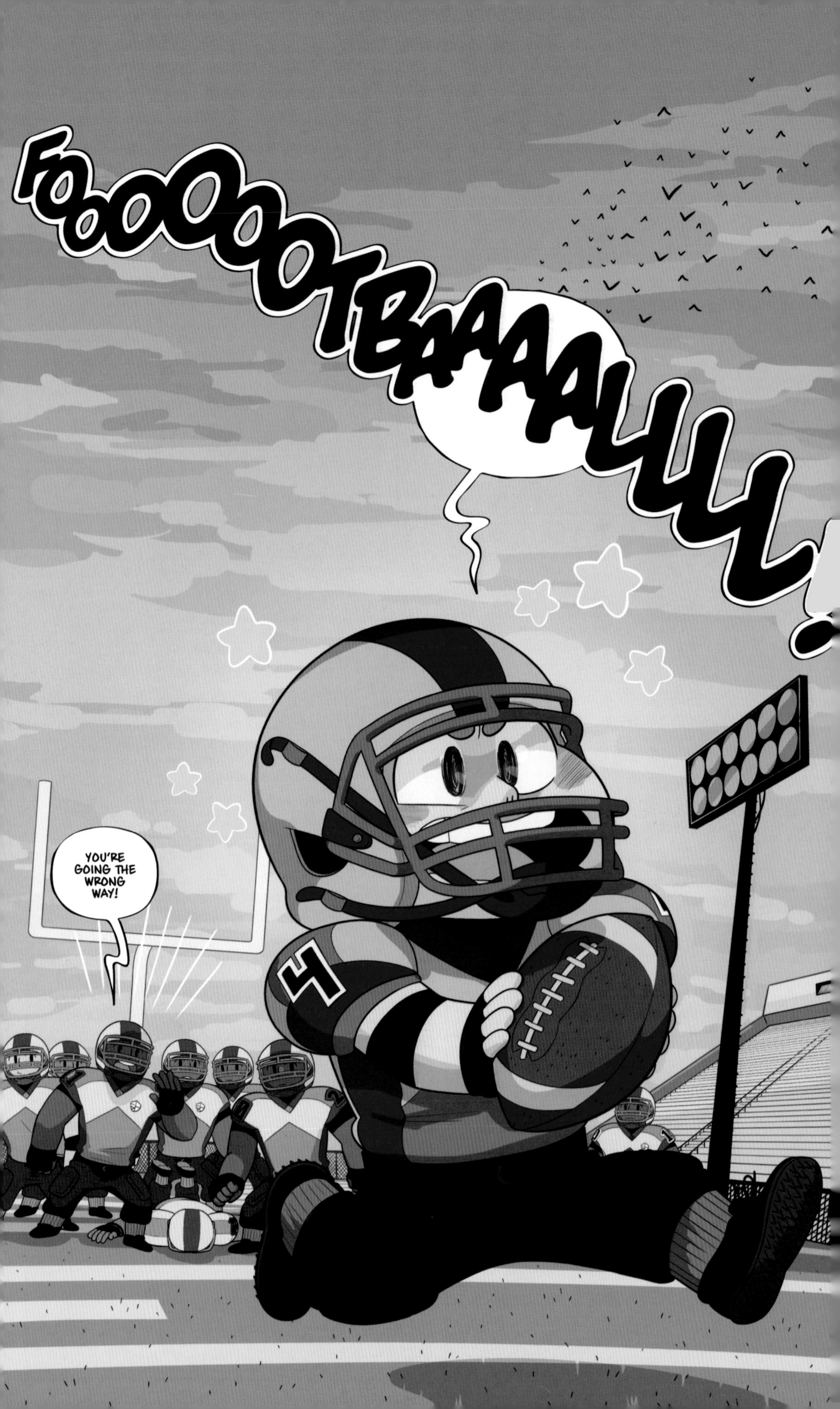

FOOOOOOTBAAAALLLL!
YOU'RE GOING THE WRONG WAY!

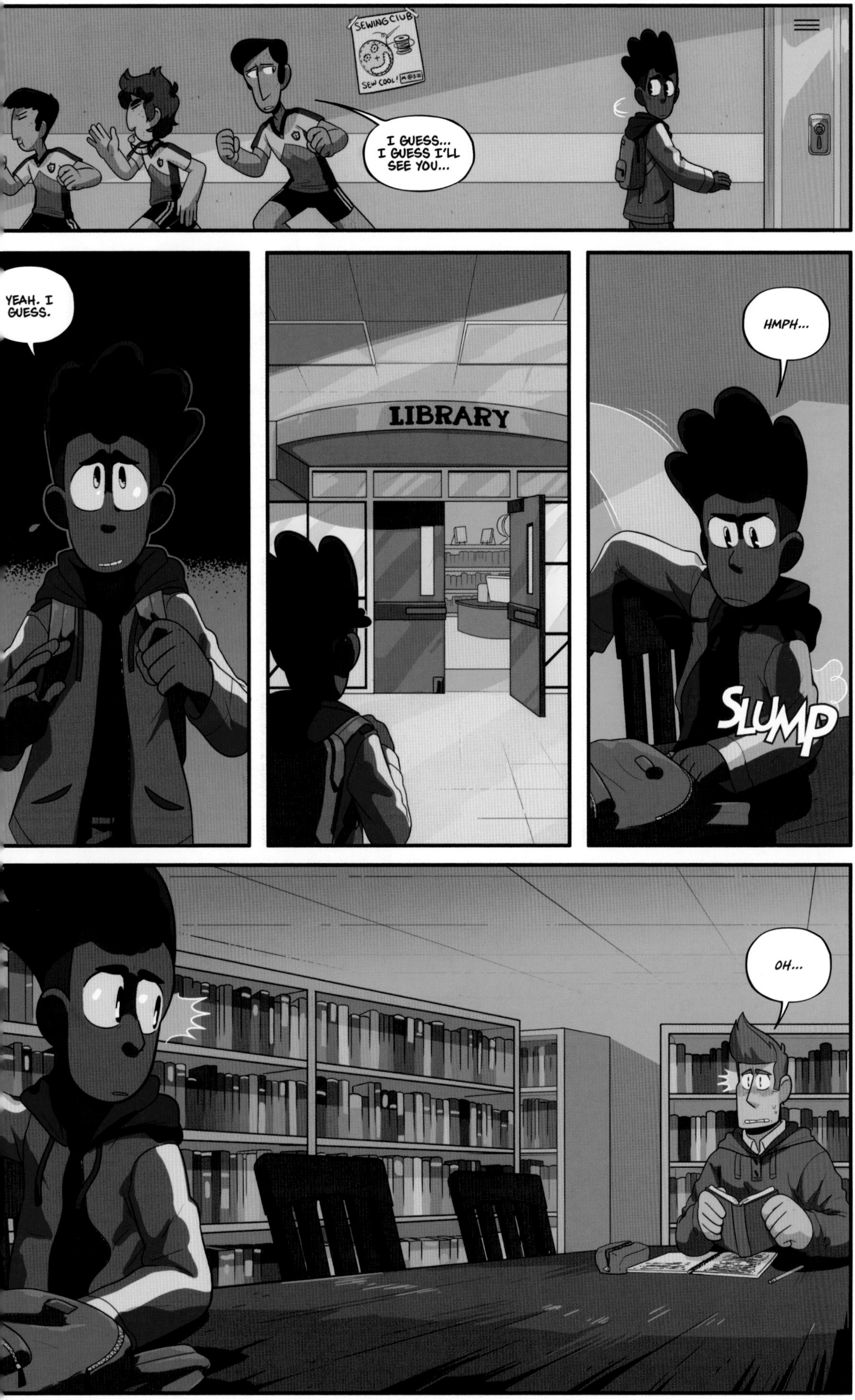
SEWING CLUB
SEW COOL!
I GUESS... I GUESS I'LL SEE YOU...
YEAH. I GUESS.
LIBRARY
HMPH...
SLUMP
OH...

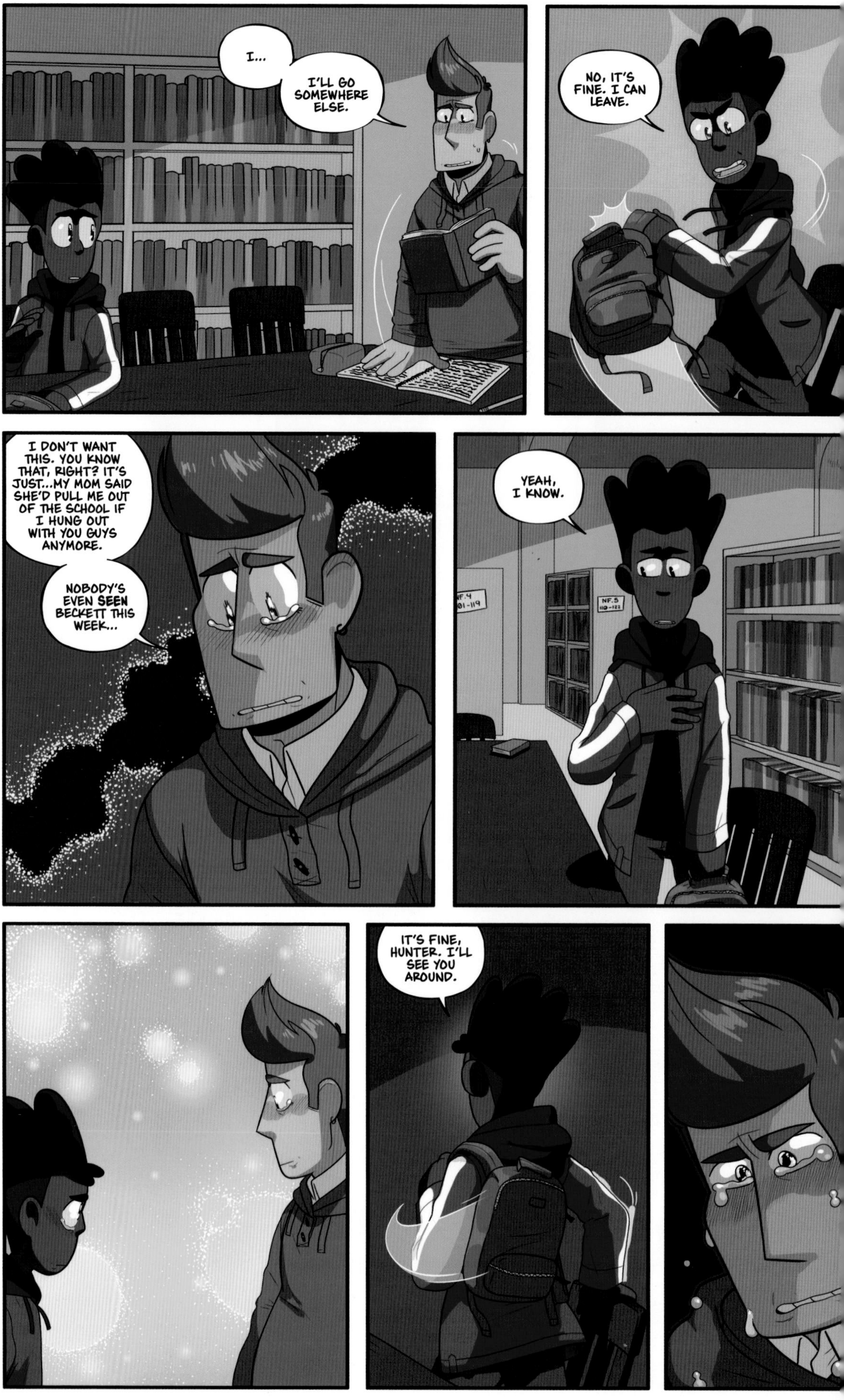
I...
I'LL GO SOMEWHERE ELSE.
NO, IT'S FINE. I CAN LEAVE.
I DON'T WANT THIS. YOU KNOW THAT, RIGHT? IT'S JUST...MY MOM SAID SHE'D PULL ME OUT OF THE SCHOOL IF I HUNG OUT WITH YOU GUYS ANYMORE.
NOBODY'S EVEN SEEN BECKETT THIS WEEK...
YEAH, I KNOW.
IT'S FINE, HUNTER. I'LL SEE YOU AROUND.

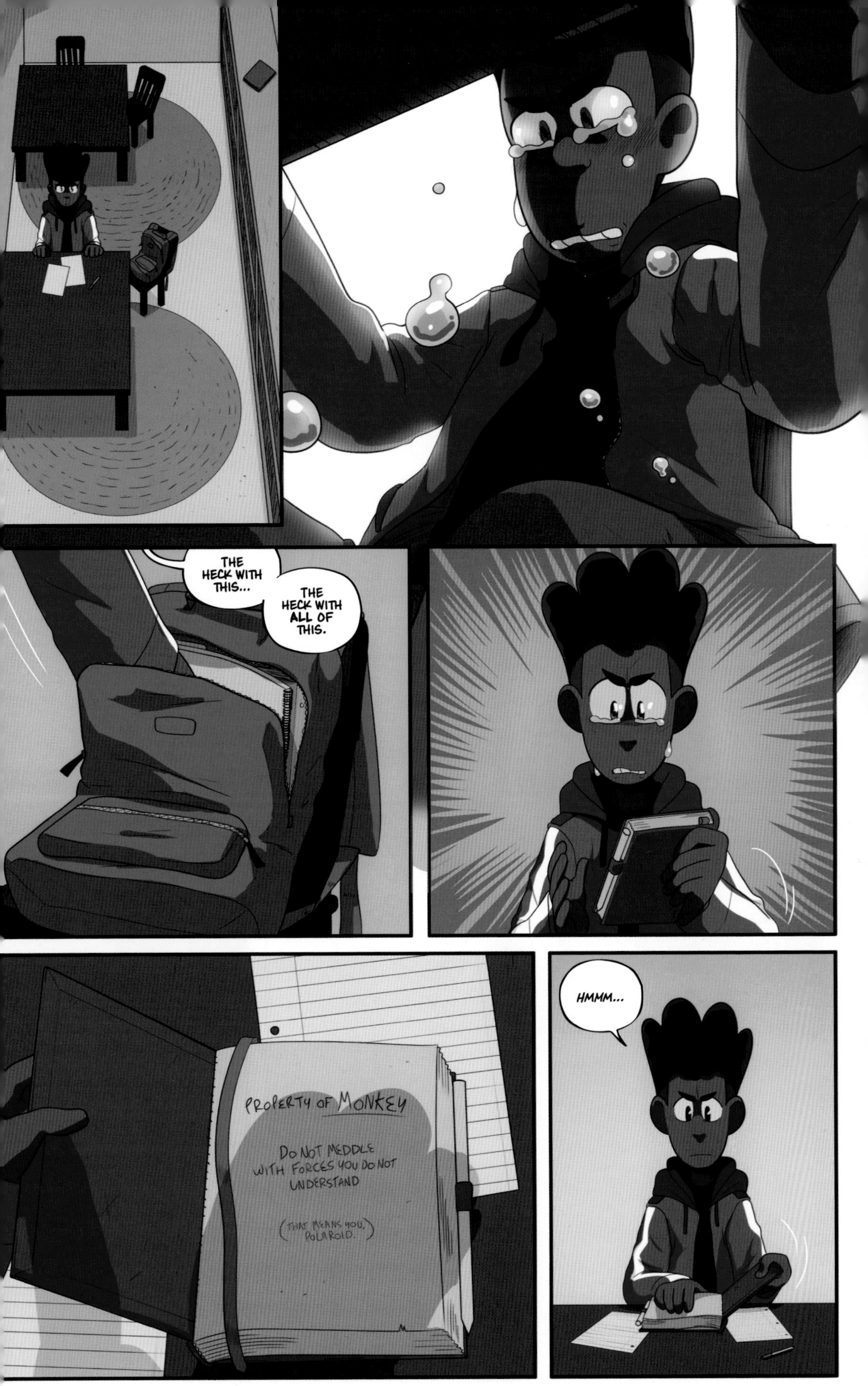

THE HECK WITH THIS...
THE HECK WITH ALL OF THIS.
PROPERTY OF MONKEY
DO NOT MEDDLE WITH FORCES YOU DO NOT UNDERSTAND
(THAT MEANS YOU, POLAROID.)
HMMM...

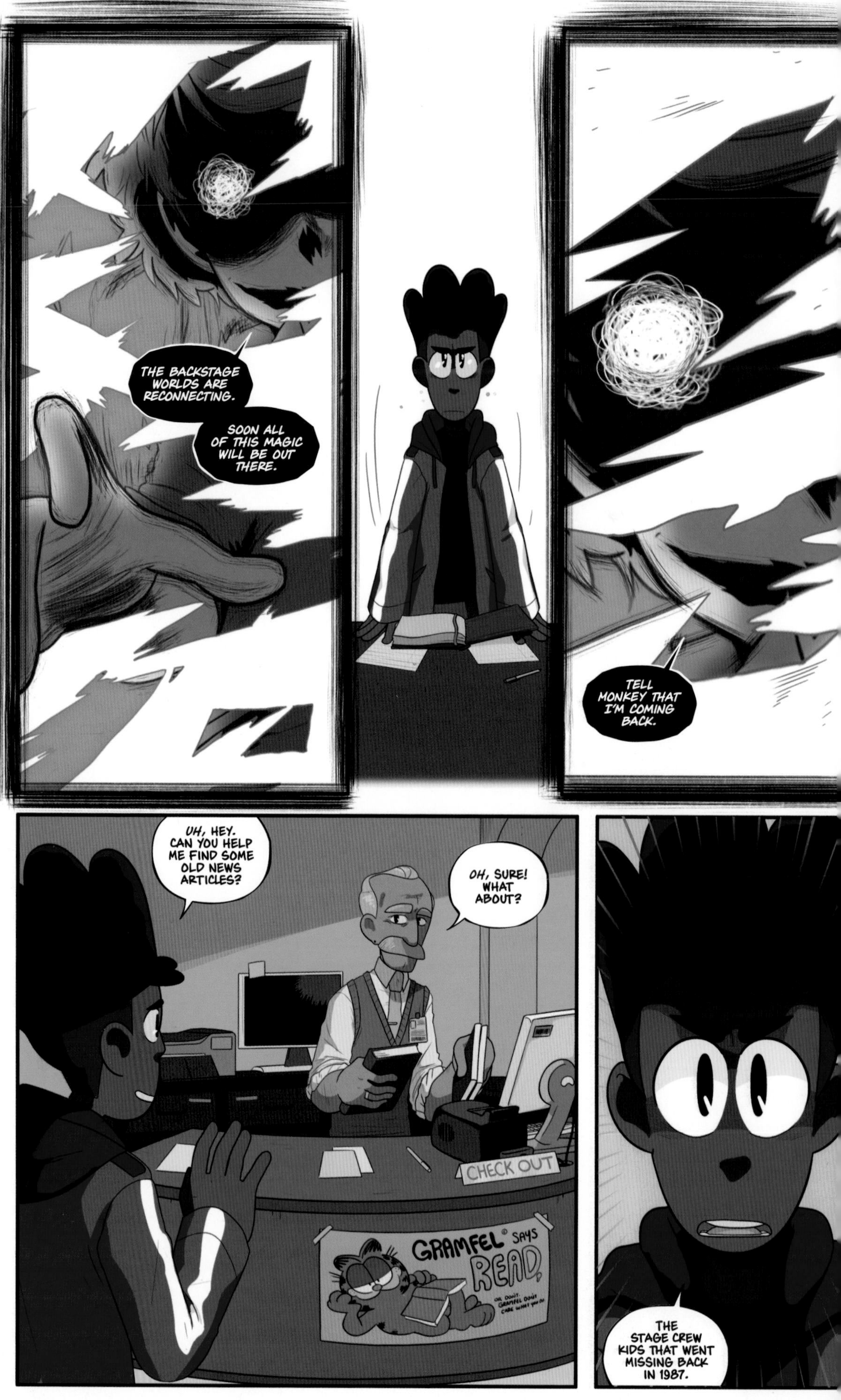

THE BACKSTAGE WORLDS ARE RECONNECTING.
SOON ALL OF THIS MAGIC WILL BE OUT THERE.
TELL MONKEY THAT I'M COMING BACK.
UH, HEY. CAN YOU HELP ME FIND SOME OLD NEWS ARTICLES?
OH, SURE! WHAT ABOUT?
CHECK OUT
GRAMFEL® SAYS READ
OR DON'T. GRAMFEL DON'T CARE WHAT YOU DO
THE STAGE CREW KIDS THAT WENT MISSING BACK IN 1987.

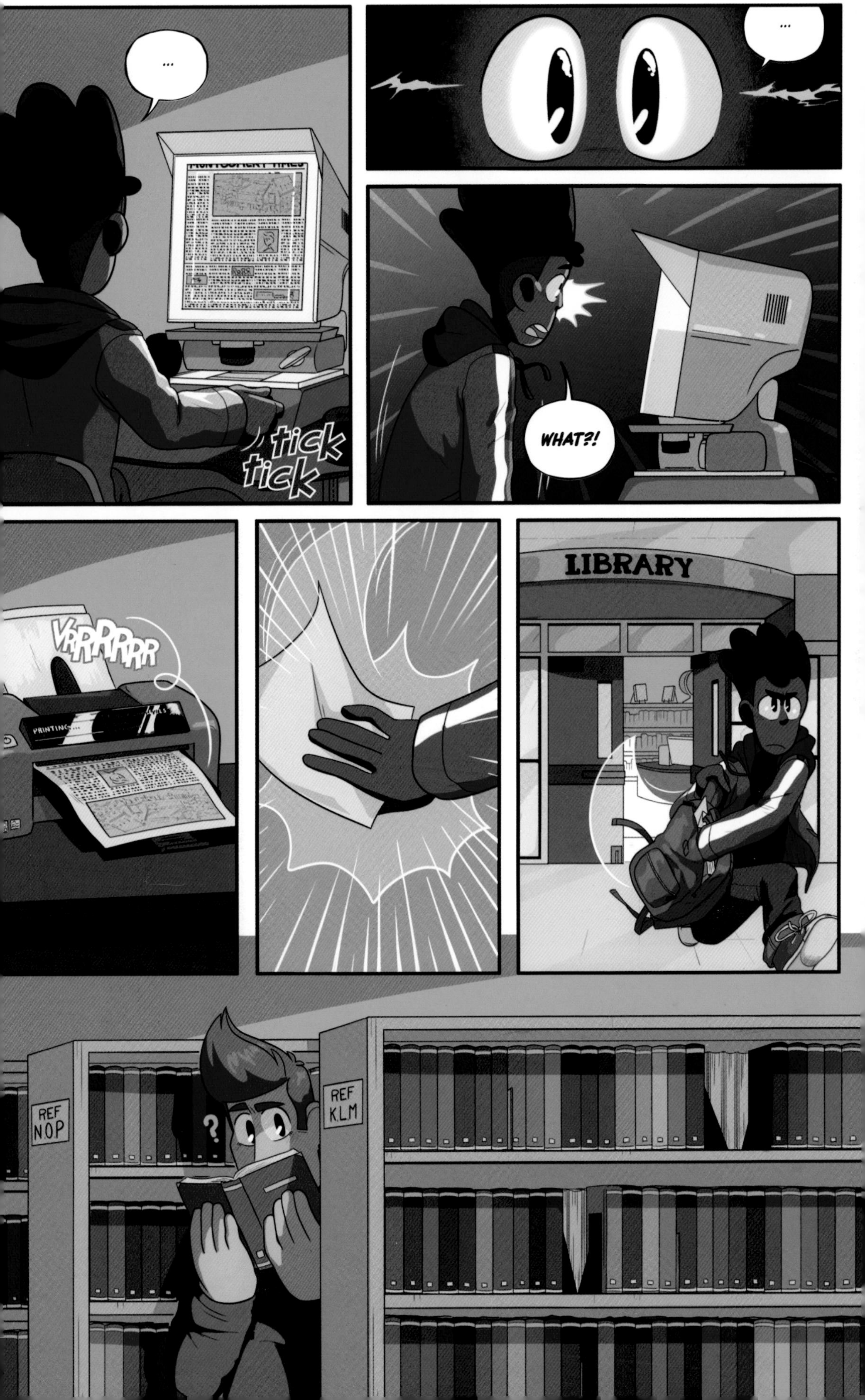
...
tick
tick
...
WHAT?!
VRRRRRR
PRINTING....
LIBRARY
?
REF
N.O.P
REF
K.L.M

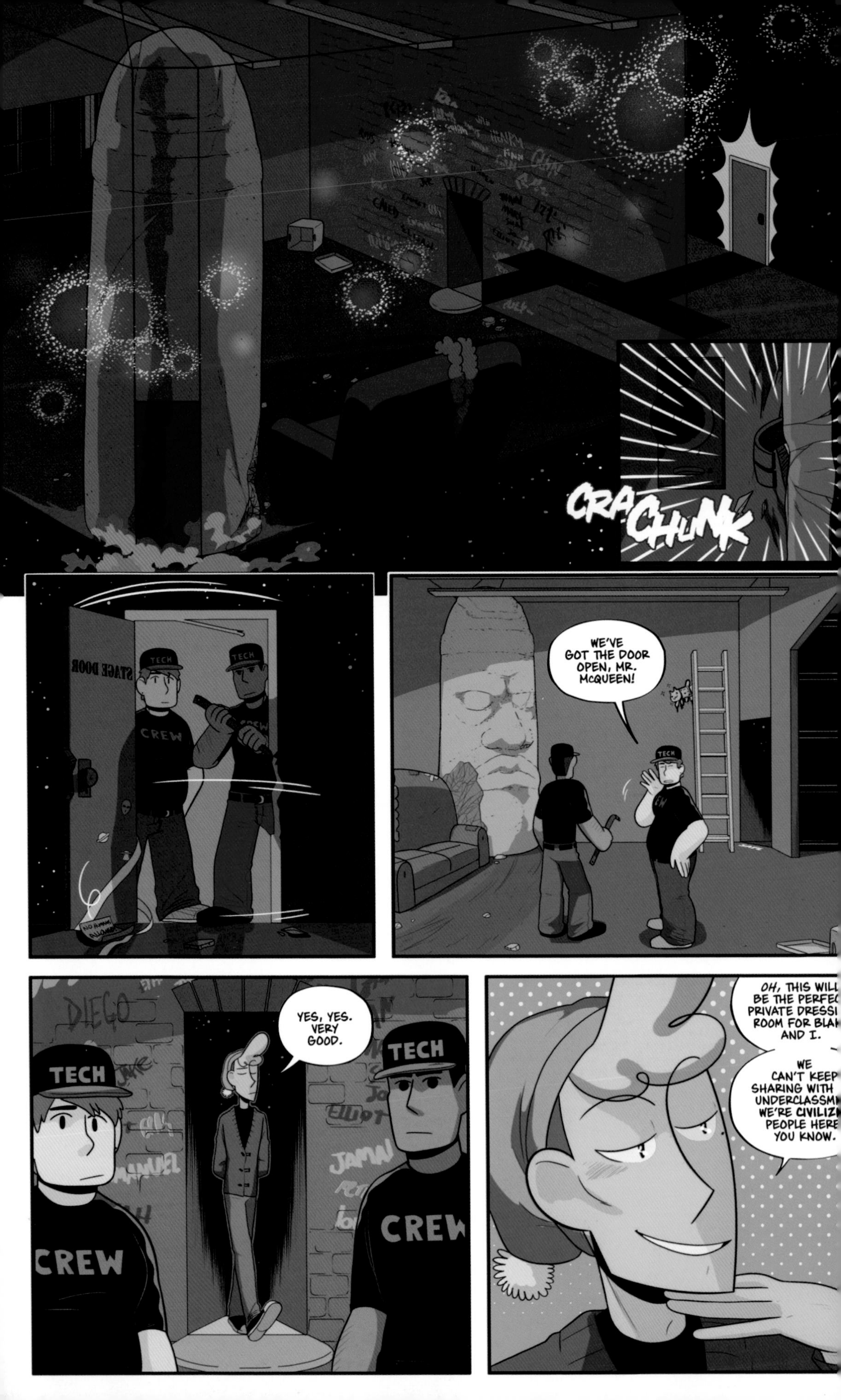
CRA CHUNK
STAGE DOOR
TECH CREW
WE'VE GOT THE DOOR OPEN, MR. McQUEEN!
YES, YES. VERY GOOD.
OH, THIS WILL BE THE PERFEC PRIVATE DRESSI ROOM FOR BLAI AND I.
WE CAN'T KEEP SHARING WITH UNDERCLASSM WE'RE CIVILIZ PEOPLE HERE YOU KNOW.

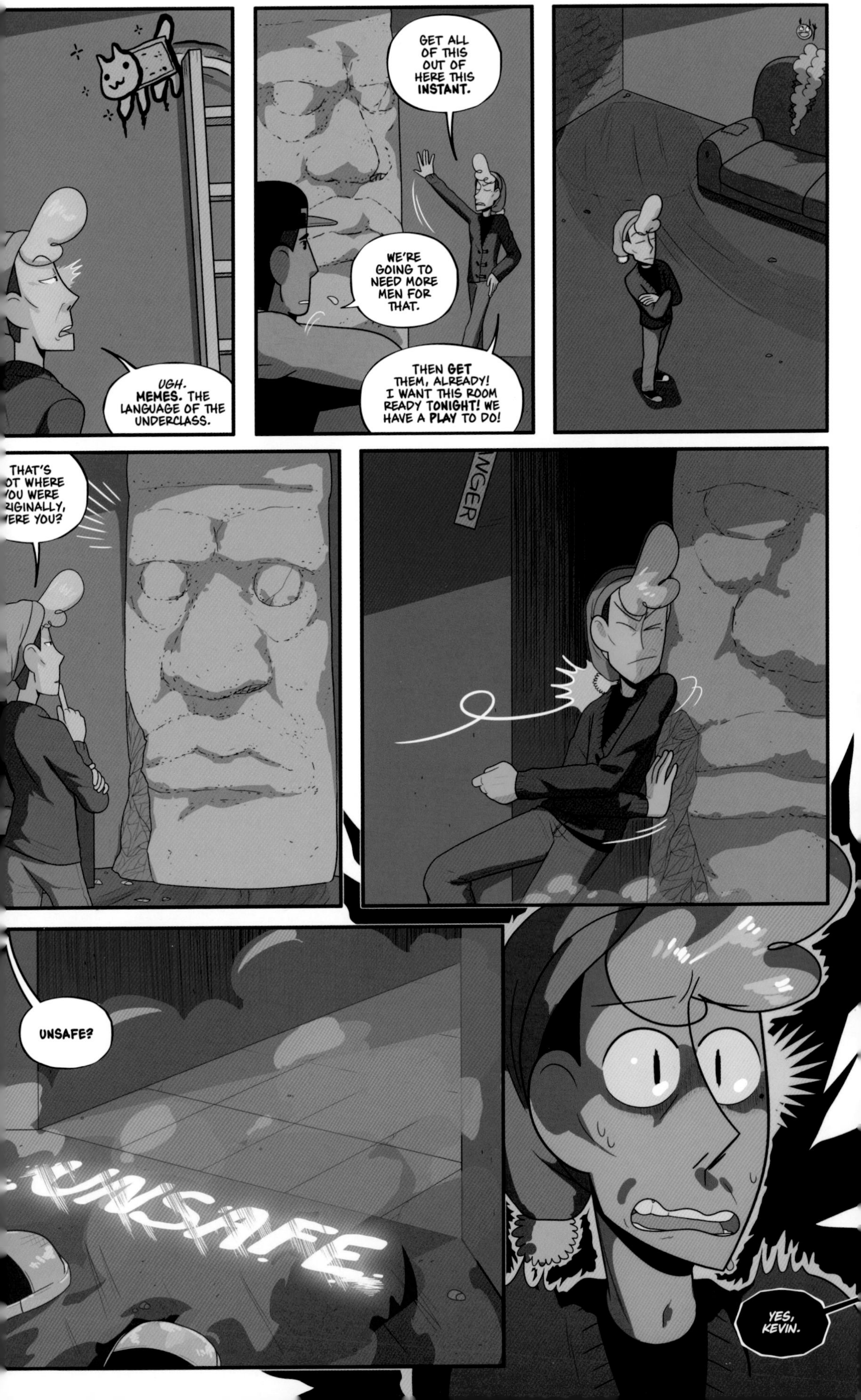
UGH. MEMES. THE LANGUAGE OF THE UNDERCLASS.
GET ALL OF THIS OUT OF HERE THIS INSTANT.
WE'RE GOING TO NEED MORE MEN FOR THAT.
THEN GET THEM, ALREADY! I WANT THIS ROOM READY TONIGHT! WE HAVE A PLAY TO DO!
THAT'S OT WHERE OU WERE RIGINALLY, ERE YOU?
UNSAFE?
UNSAFE.
YES, KEVIN.

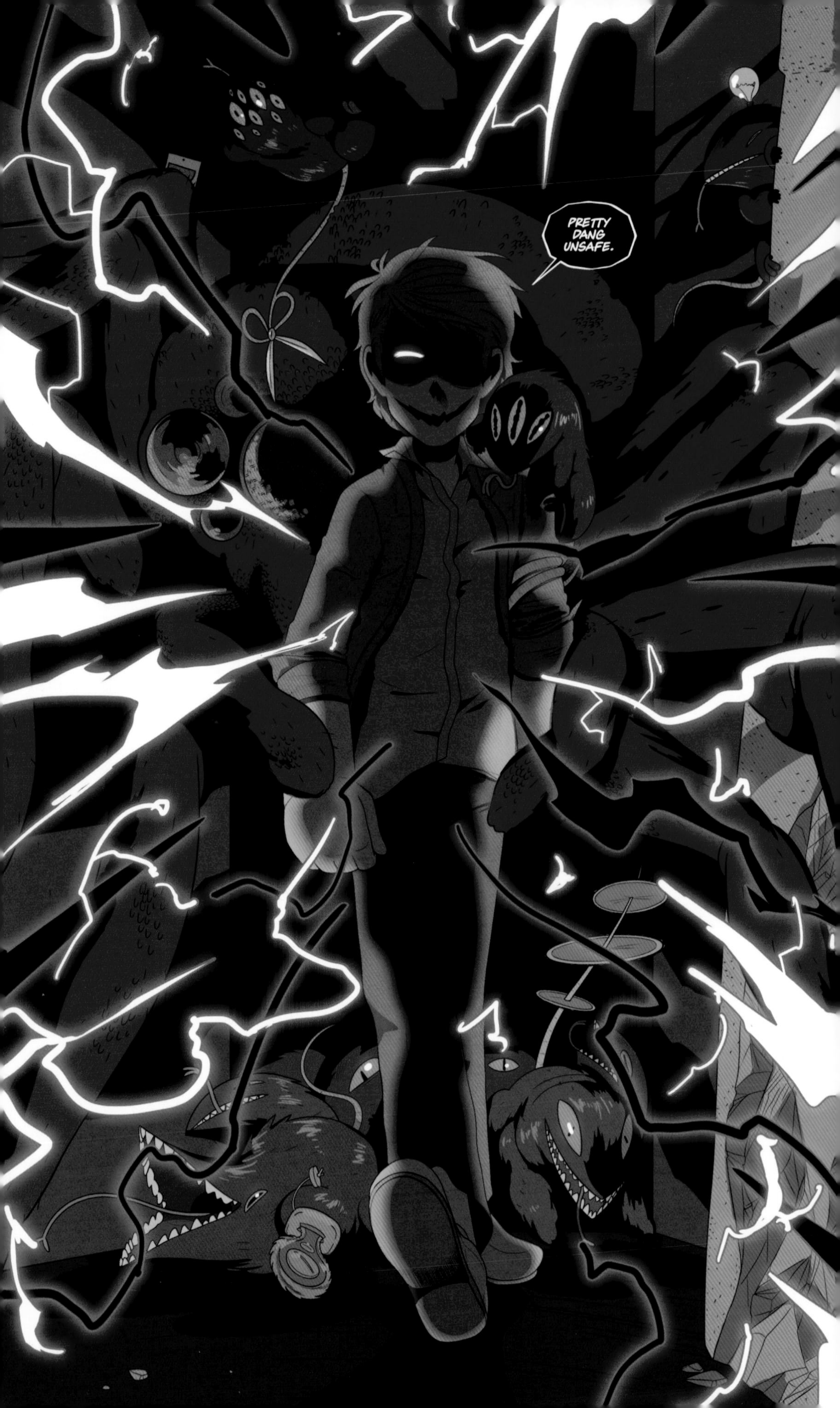
PRETTY DANG UNSAFE.

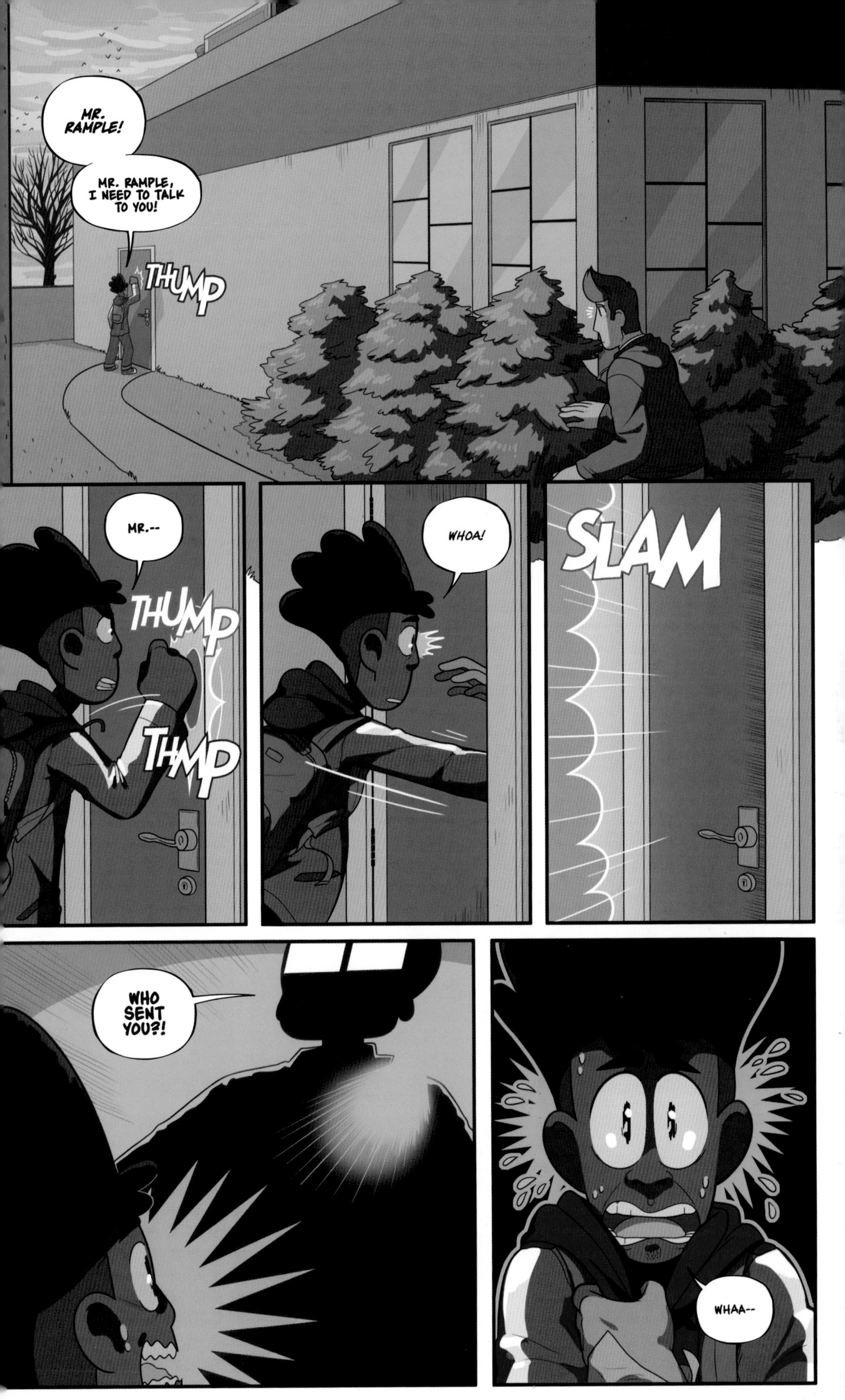

MR. RAMPLE!
MR. RAMPLE, I NEED TO TALK TO YOU!
THUMP
MR.--
THUMP
THMP
WHOA!
SLAM
WHO SENT YOU?!
WHAA--

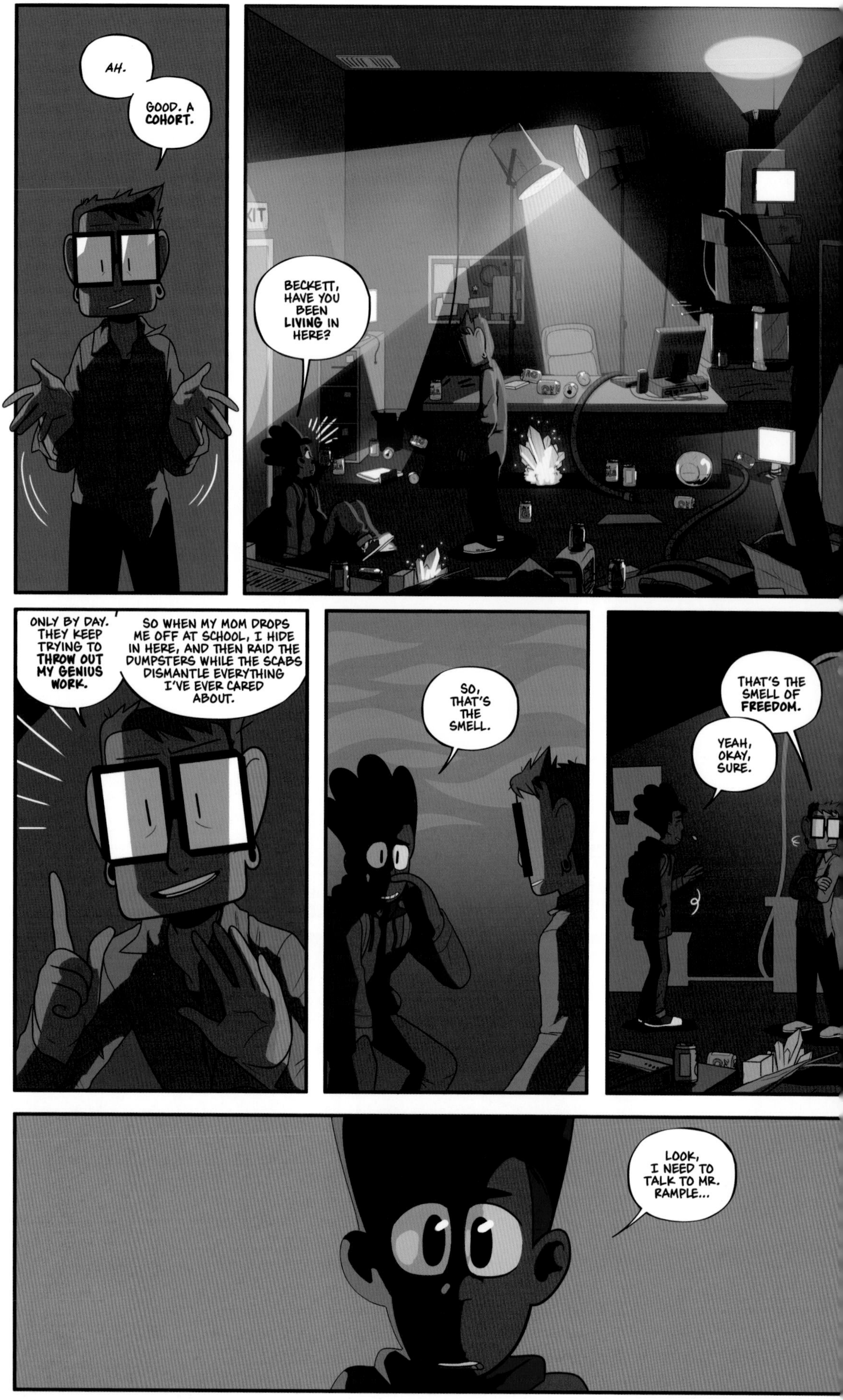
AH.
GOOD. A COHORT.
BECKETT, HAVE YOU BEEN LIVING IN HERE?
ONLY BY DAY. THEY KEEP TRYING TO THROW OUT MY GENIUS WORK.
SO WHEN MY MOM DROPS ME OFF AT SCHOOL, I HIDE IN HERE, AND THEN RAID THE DUMPSTERS WHILE THE SCABS DISMANTLE EVERYTHING I'VE EVER CARED ABOUT.
SO, THAT'S THE SMELL.
THAT'S THE SMELL OF FREEDOM.
YEAH, OKAY, SURE.
LOOK, I NEED TO TALK TO MR. RAMPLE...

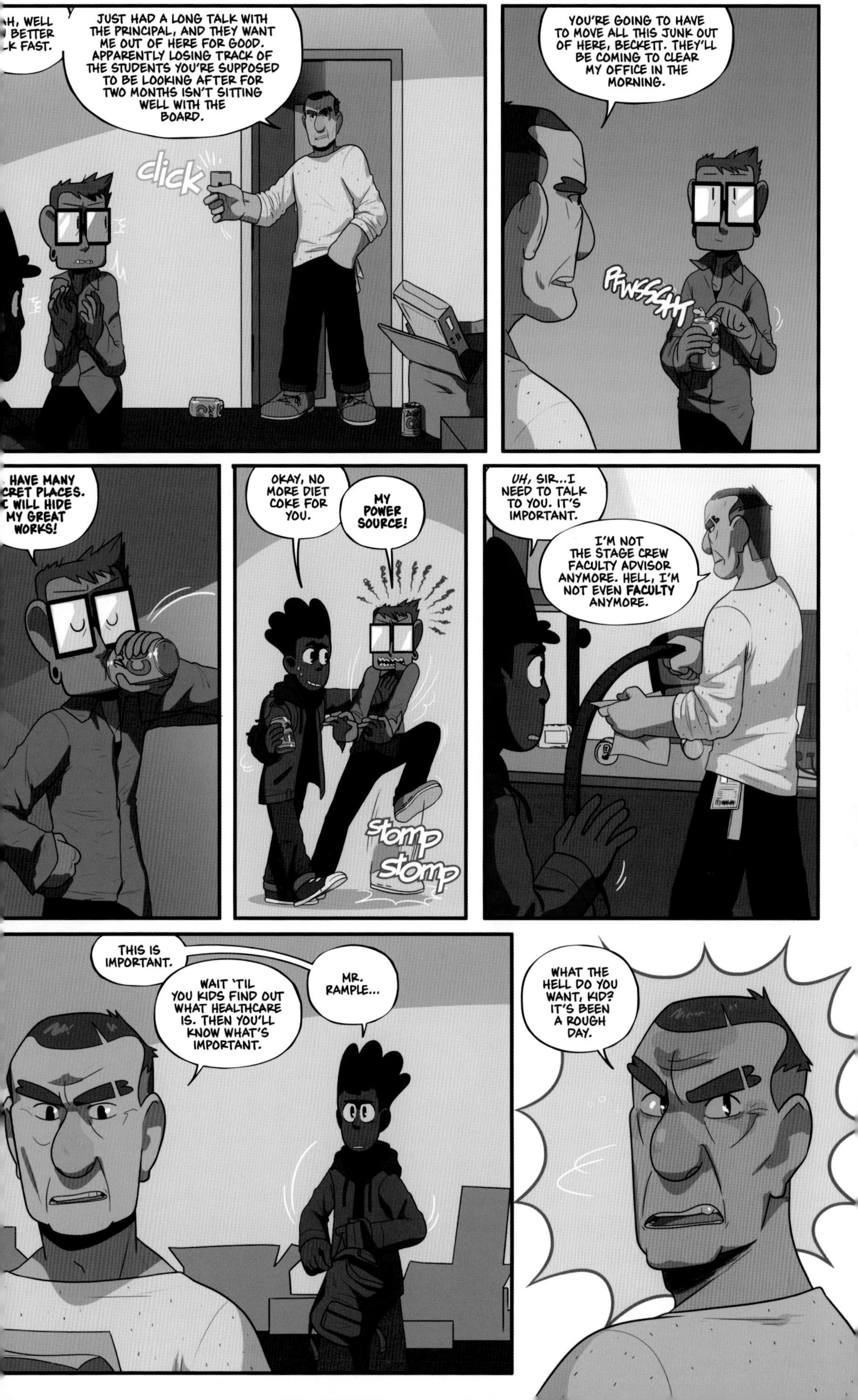

...H, WELL ...BETTER ...K FAST.
JUST HAD A LONG TALK WITH THE PRINCIPAL, AND THEY WANT ME OUT OF HERE FOR GOOD. APPARENTLY LOSING TRACK OF THE STUDENTS YOU'RE SUPPOSED TO BE LOOKING AFTER FOR TWO MONTHS ISN'T SITTING WELL WITH THE BOARD.
click
YOU'RE GOING TO HAVE TO MOVE ALL THIS JUNK OUT OF HERE, BECKETT. THEY'LL BE COMING TO CLEAR MY OFFICE IN THE MORNING.
PFWSSSHT
...HAVE MANY ...CRET PLACES. ...C WILL HIDE MY GREAT WORKS!
OKAY, NO MORE DIET COKE FOR YOU.
MY POWER SOURCE!
stomp stomp
UH, SIR...I NEED TO TALK TO YOU. IT'S IMPORTANT.
I'M NOT THE STAGE CREW FACULTY ADVISOR ANYMORE. HELL, I'M NOT EVEN FACULTY ANYMORE.
MR. RAMPLE...
THIS IS IMPORTANT.
WAIT 'TIL YOU KIDS FIND OUT WHAT HEALTHCARE IS. THEN YOU'LL KNOW WHAT'S IMPORTANT.
WHAT THE HELL DO YOU WANT, KID? IT'S BEEN A ROUGH DAY.

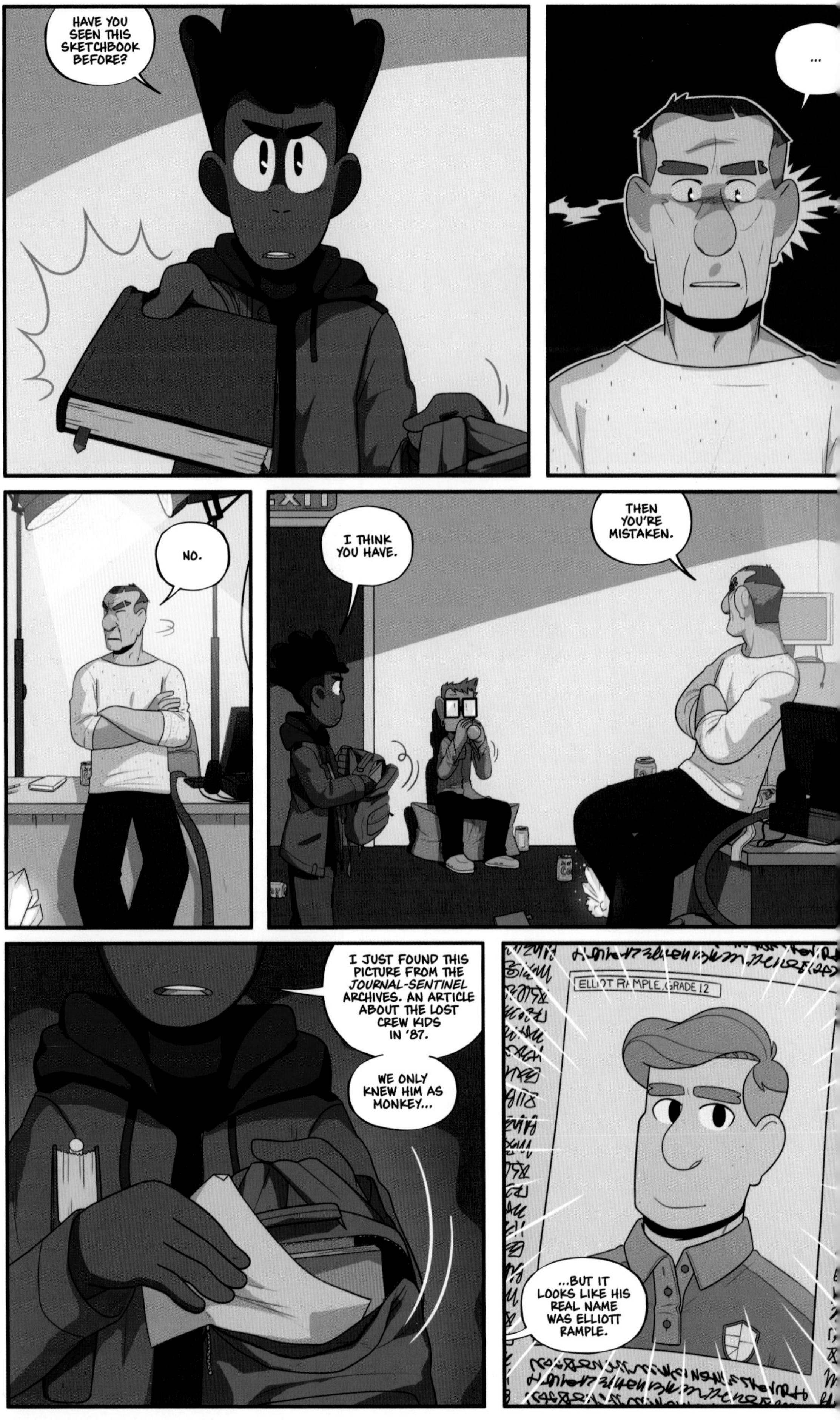
HAVE YOU SEEN THIS SKETCHBOOK BEFORE?
...
NO.
I THINK YOU HAVE.
THEN YOU'RE MISTAKEN.
I JUST FOUND THIS PICTURE FROM THE *JOURNAL-SENTINEL* ARCHIVES. AN ARTICLE ABOUT THE LOST CREW KIDS IN '87.
WE ONLY KNEW HIM AS MONKEY...
ELLIOT RAMPLE, GRADE 12
...BUT IT LOOKS LIKE HIS REAL NAME WAS ELLIOTT RAMPLE.

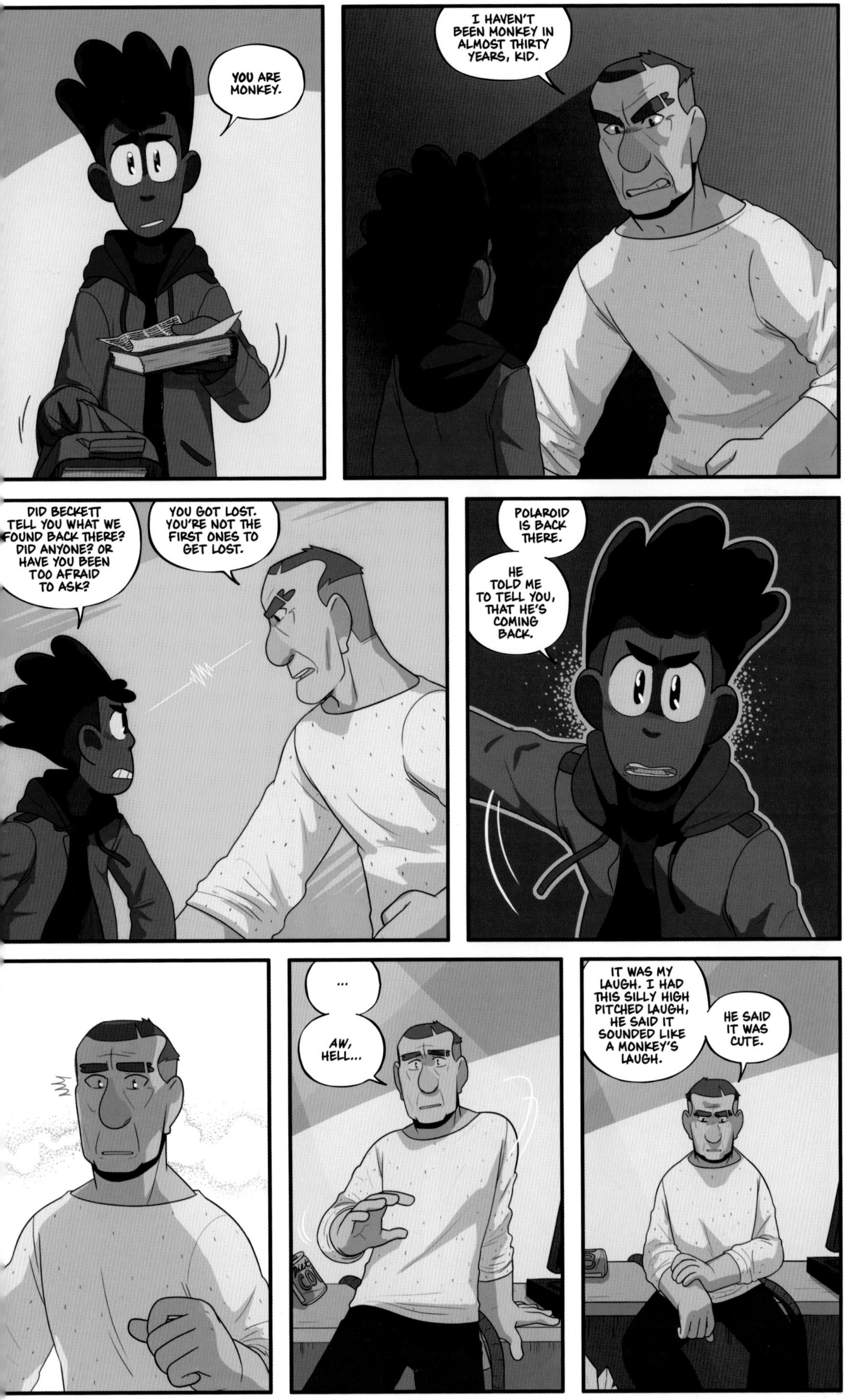
YOU ARE MONKEY.
I HAVEN'T BEEN MONKEY IN ALMOST THIRTY YEARS, KID.
DID BECKETT TELL YOU WHAT WE FOUND BACK THERE? DID ANYONE? OR HAVE YOU BEEN TOO AFRAID TO ASK?
YOU GOT LOST. YOU'RE NOT THE FIRST ONES TO GET LOST.
POLAROID IS BACK THERE.
HE TOLD ME TO TELL YOU, THAT HE'S COMING BACK.
...
AW, HELL...
IT WAS MY LAUGH. I HAD THIS SILLY HIGH PITCHED LAUGH, HE SAID IT SOUNDED LIKE A MONKEY'S LAUGH.
HE SAID IT WAS CUTE.

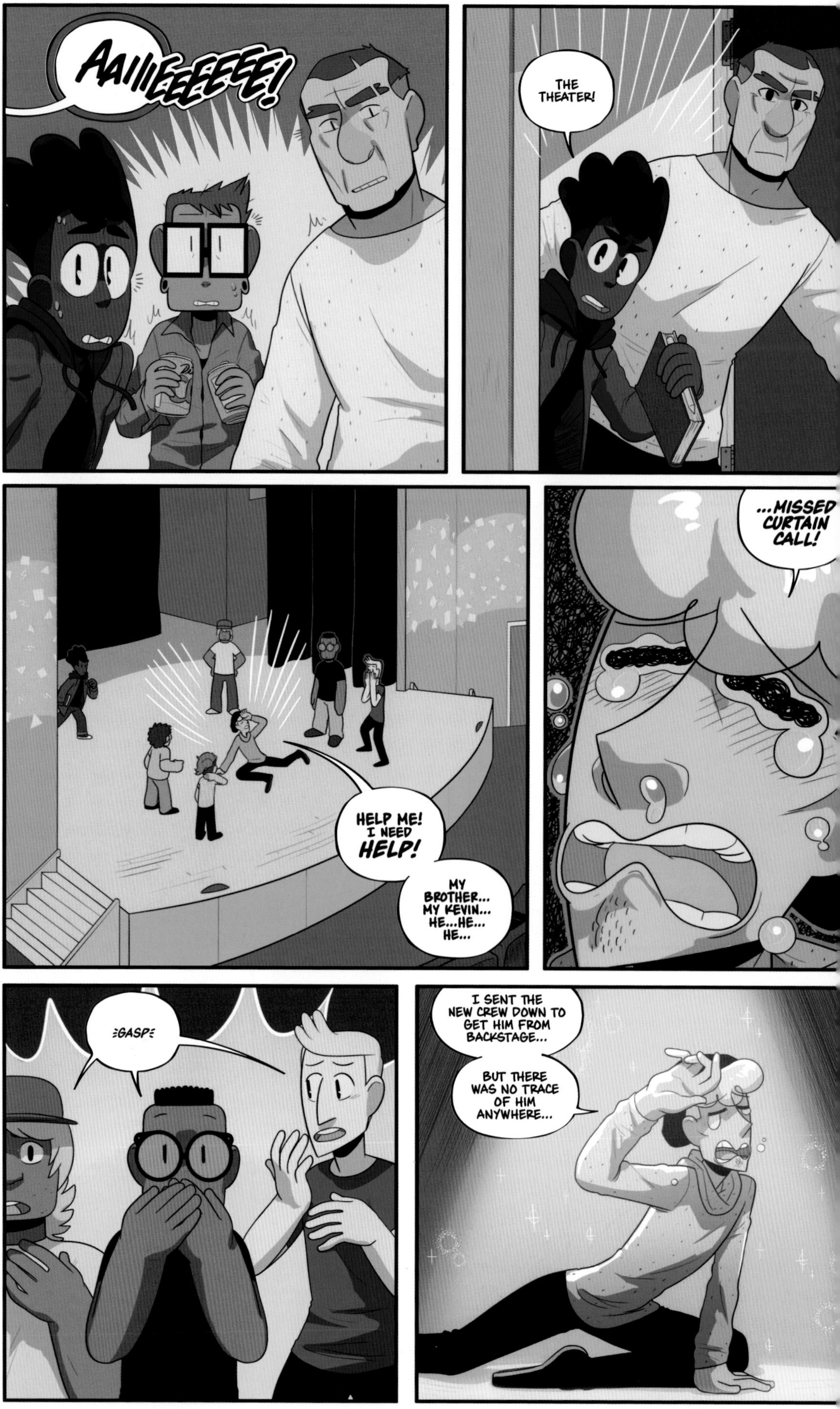
AAIIIEEEEEE!
THE THEATER!
HELP ME! I NEED HELP!
MY BROTHER... MY KEVIN... HE...HE... HE...
...MISSED CURTAIN CALL!
GASP
I SENT THE NEW CREW DOWN TO GET HIM FROM BACKSTAGE...
BUT THERE WAS NO TRACE OF HIM ANYWHERE...

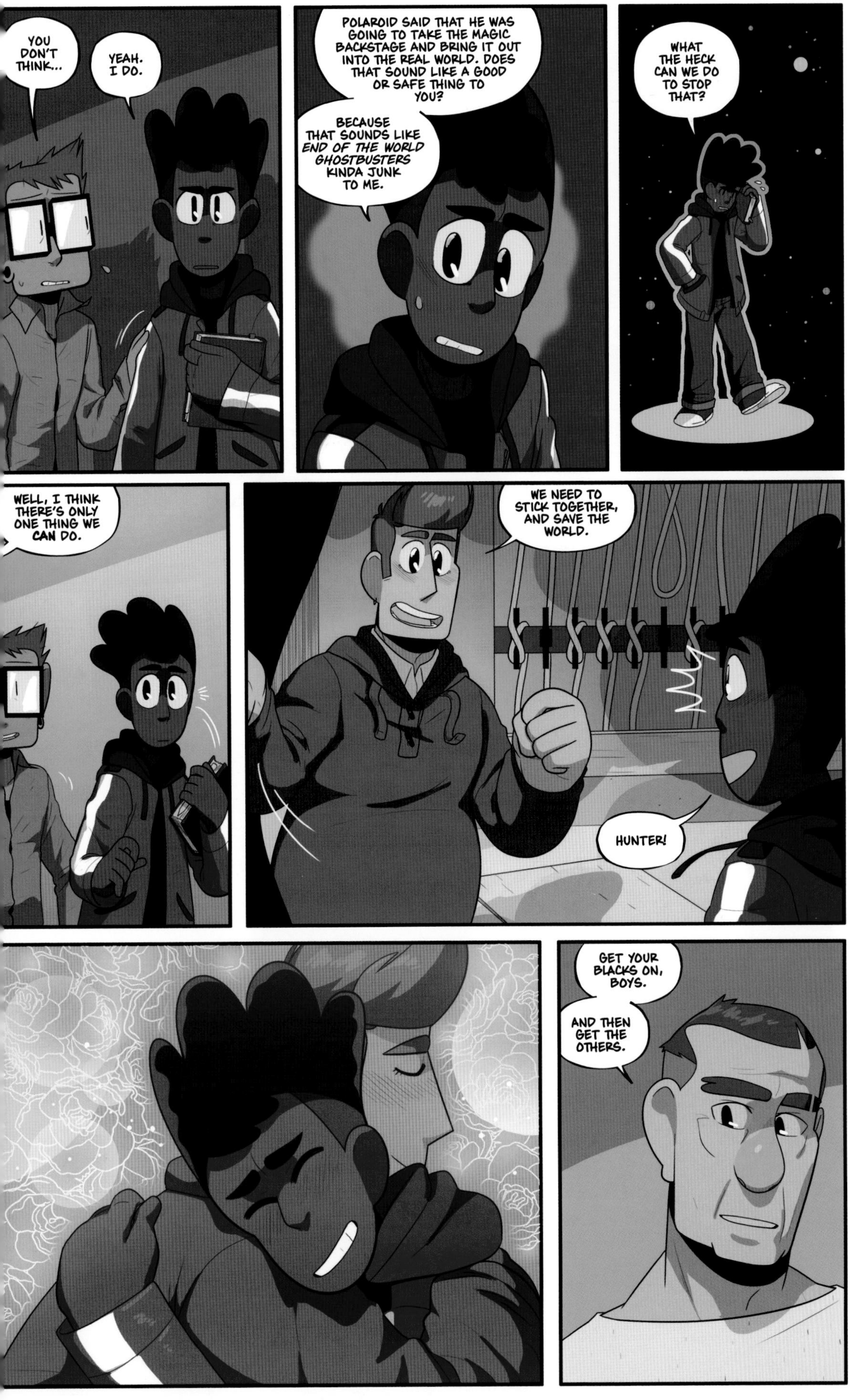
YOU DON'T THINK...
YEAH. I DO.
POLAROID SAID THAT HE WAS GOING TO TAKE THE MAGIC BACKSTAGE AND BRING IT OUT INTO THE REAL WORLD. DOES THAT SOUND LIKE A GOOD OR SAFE THING TO YOU?
BECAUSE THAT SOUNDS LIKE END OF THE WORLD GHOSTBUSTERS KINDA JUNK TO ME.
WHAT THE HECK CAN WE DO TO STOP THAT?
WELL, I THINK THERE'S ONLY ONE THING WE CAN DO.
WE NEED TO STICK TOGETHER, AND SAVE THE WORLD.
HUNTER!
GET YOUR BLACKS ON, BOYS.
AND THEN GET THE OTHERS.

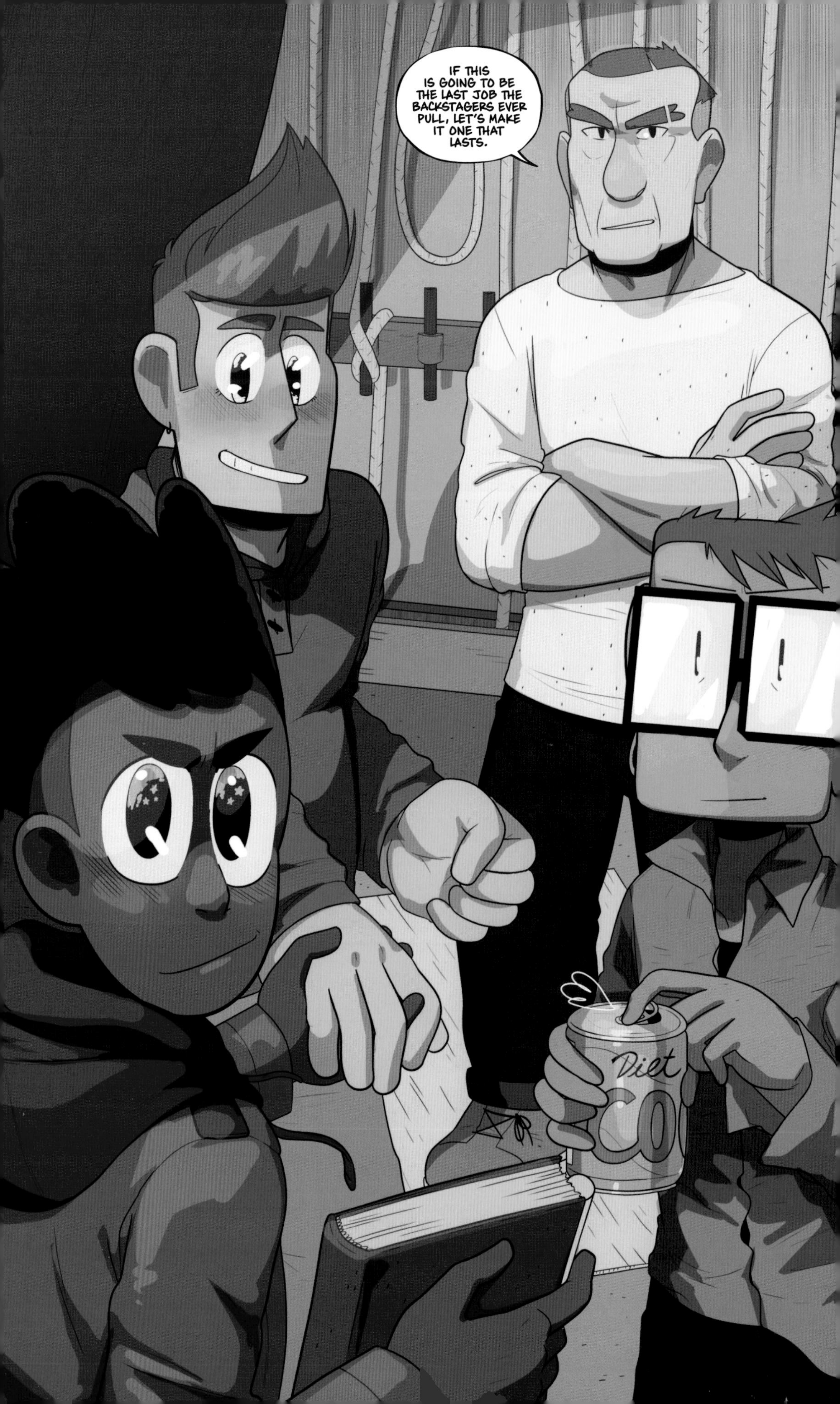
IF THIS IS GOING TO BE THE LAST JOB THE BACKSTAGERS EVER PULL, LET'S MAKE IT ONE THAT LASTS.
Diet

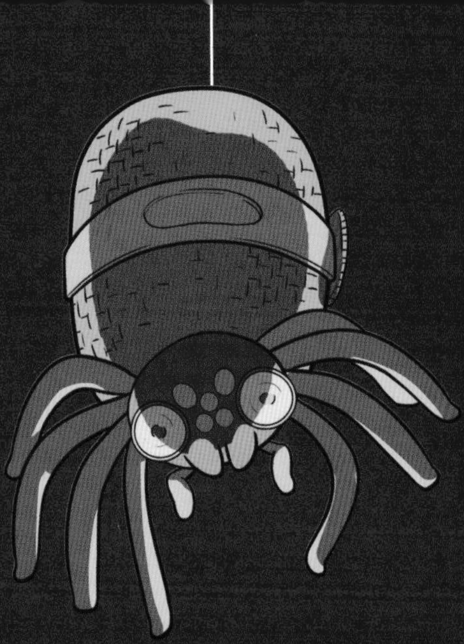

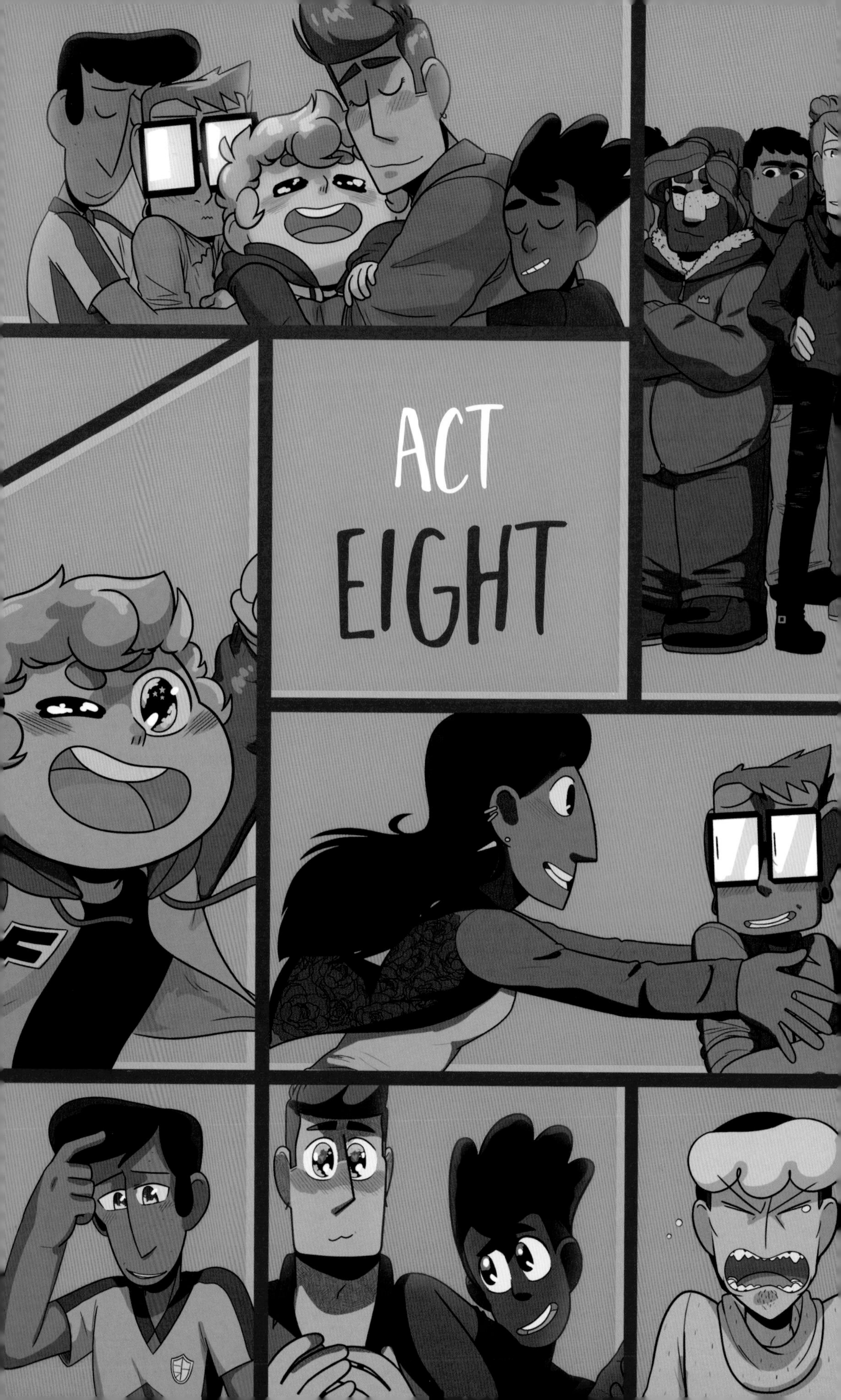
ACT
EIGHT

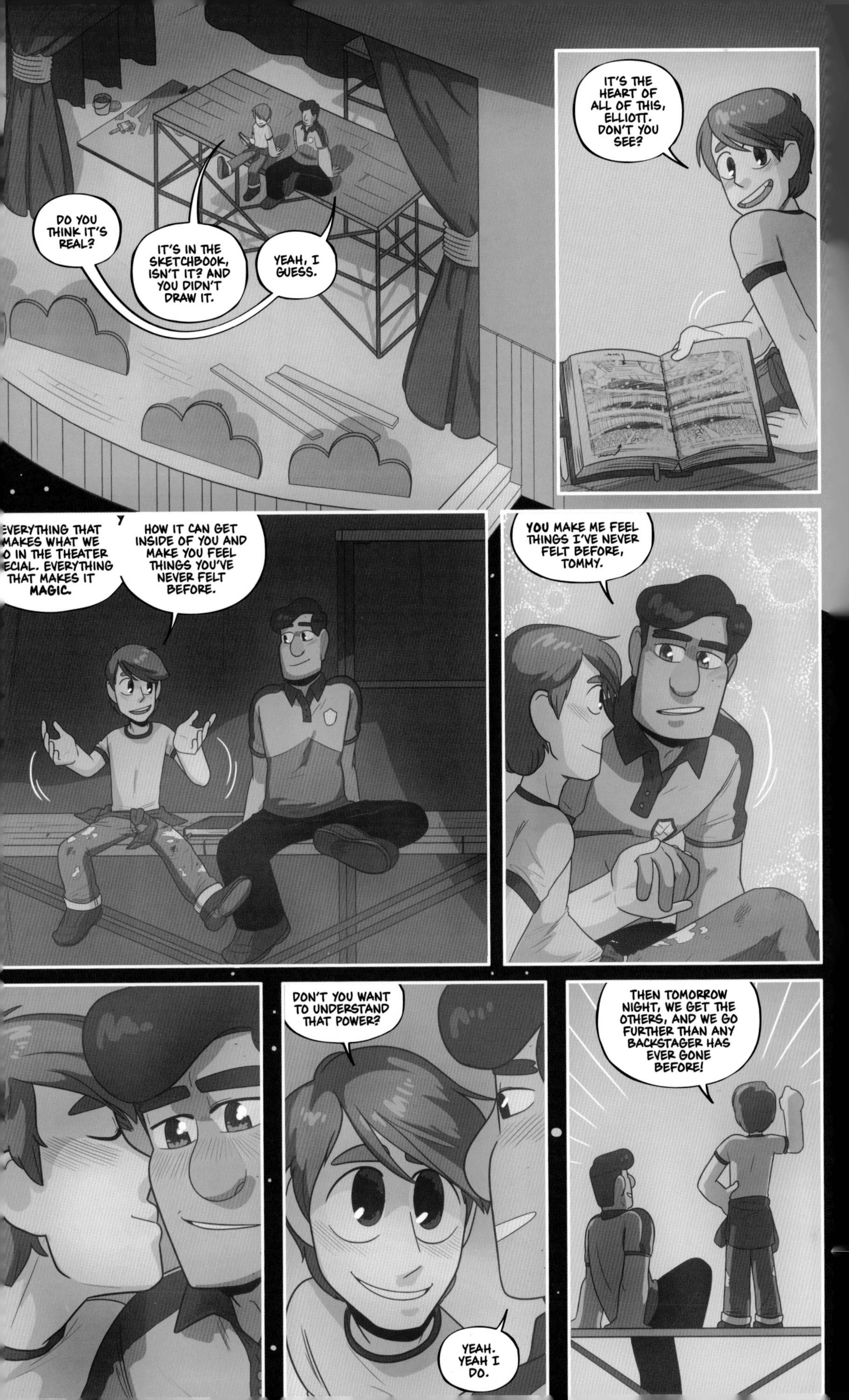
DO YOU THINK IT'S REAL?
IT'S IN THE SKETCHBOOK, ISN'T IT? AND YOU DIDN'T DRAW IT.
YEAH, I GUESS.
IT'S THE HEART OF ALL OF THIS, ELLIOTT. DON'T YOU SEE?
EVERYTHING THAT MAKES WHAT WE DO IN THE THEATER SPECIAL. EVERYTHING THAT MAKES IT MAGIC.
HOW IT CAN GET INSIDE OF YOU AND MAKE YOU FEEL THINGS YOU'VE NEVER FELT BEFORE.
YOU MAKE ME FEEL THINGS I'VE NEVER FELT BEFORE, TOMMY.
DON'T YOU WANT TO UNDERSTAND THAT POWER?
YEAH. YEAH I DO.
THEN TOMORROW NIGHT, WE GET THE OTHERS, AND WE GO FURTHER THAN ANY BACKSTAGER HAS EVER GONE BEFORE!

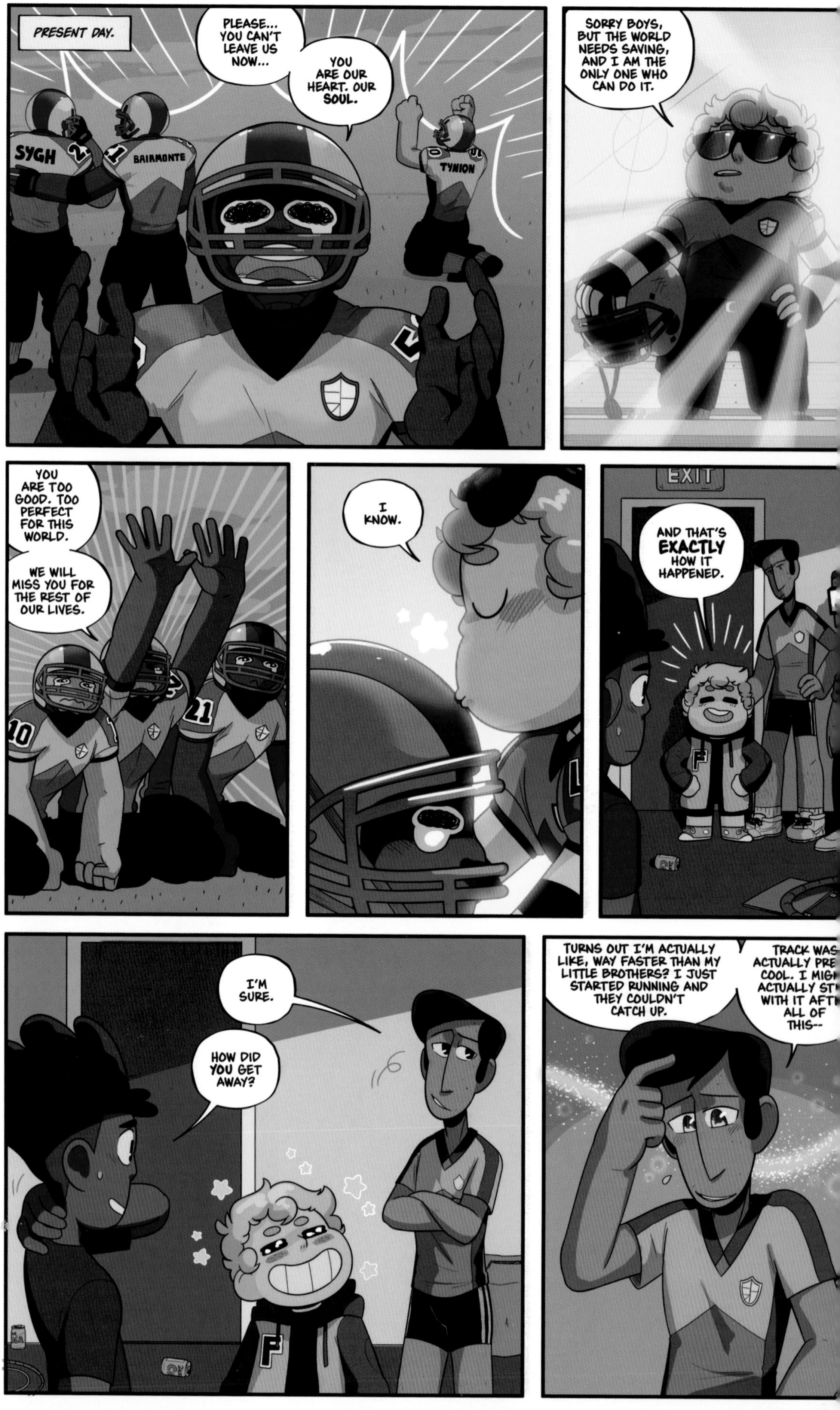
PRESENT DAY.
PLEASE... YOU CAN'T LEAVE US NOW...
YOU ARE OUR HEART. OUR SOUL.
SYGH
BAIRMONTE
TYNION
SORRY BOYS, BUT THE WORLD NEEDS SAVING, AND I AM THE ONLY ONE WHO CAN DO IT.
YOU ARE TOO GOOD. TOO PERFECT FOR THIS WORLD.
WE WILL MISS YOU FOR THE REST OF OUR LIVES.
I KNOW.
EXIT
AND THAT'S EXACTLY HOW IT HAPPENED.
I'M SURE.
HOW DID YOU GET AWAY?
TURNS OUT I'M ACTUALLY LIKE, WAY FASTER THAN MY LITTLE BROTHERS? I JUST STARTED RUNNING AND THEY COULDN'T CATCH UP.
TRACK WAS ACTUALLY PRE COOL. I MIG ACTUALLY ST WITH IT AFT ALL OF THIS--

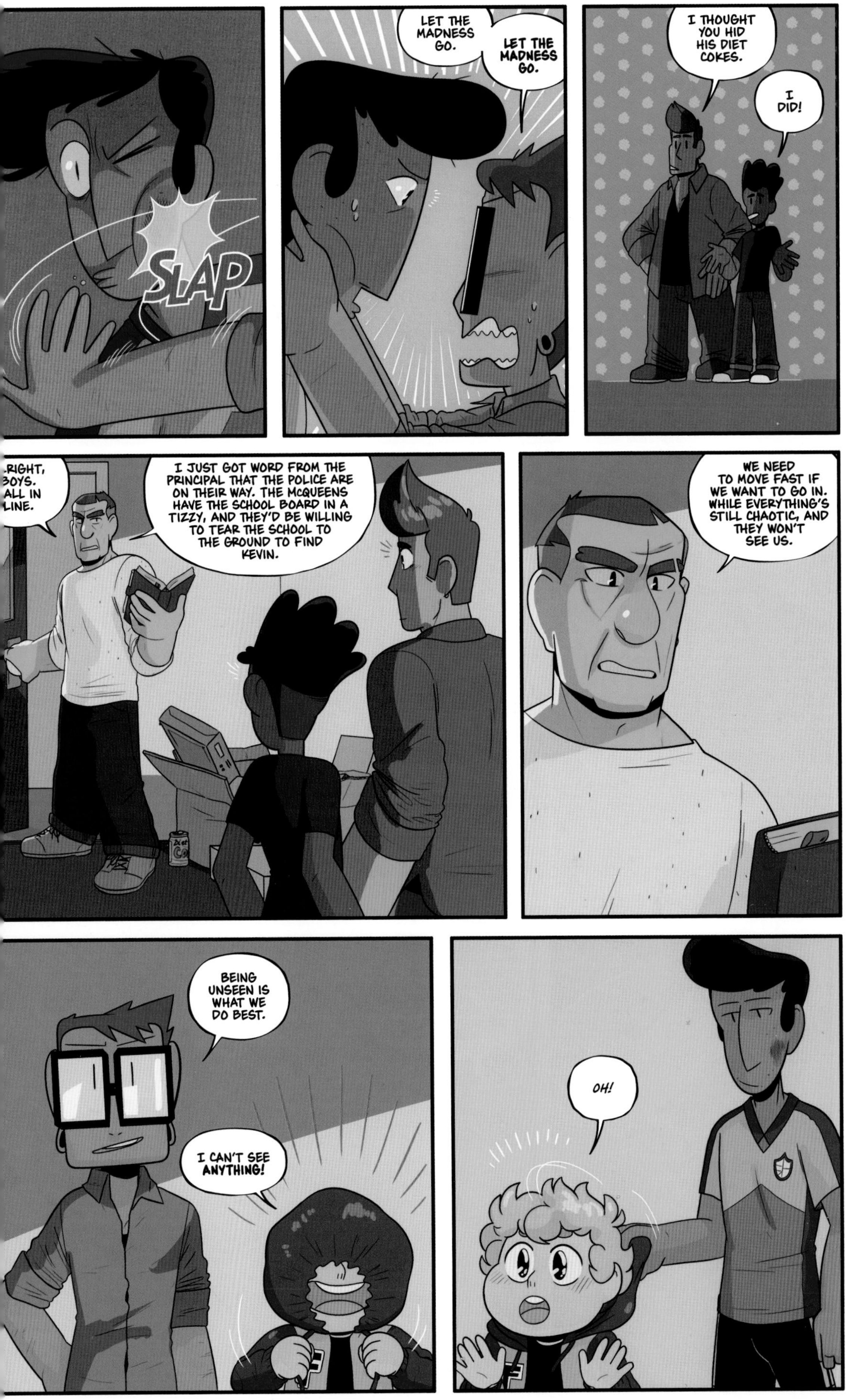
LET THE MADNESS GO.
LET THE MADNESS GO.
I THOUGHT YOU HID HIS DIET COKES.
I DID!
RIGHT, BOYS. ALL IN LINE.
I JUST GOT WORD FROM THE PRINCIPAL THAT THE POLICE ARE ON THEIR WAY. THE McQUEENS HAVE THE SCHOOL BOARD IN A TIZZY, AND THEY'D BE WILLING TO TEAR THE SCHOOL TO THE GROUND TO FIND KEVIN.
WE NEED TO MOVE FAST IF WE WANT TO GO IN. WHILE EVERYTHING'S STILL CHAOTIC, AND THEY WON'T SEE US.
BEING UNSEEN IS WHAT WE DO BEST.
I CAN'T SEE ANYTHING!
OH!

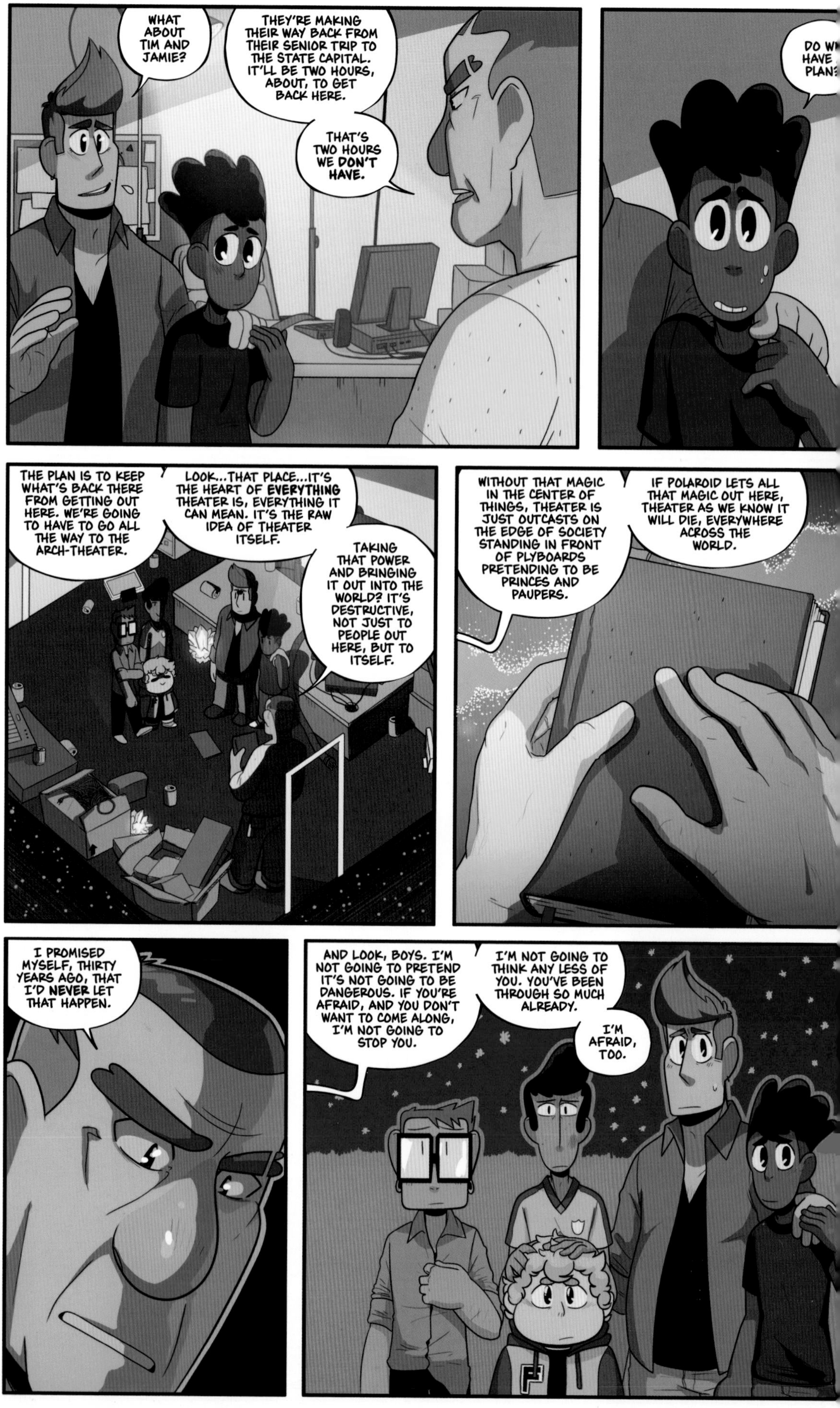
WHAT ABOUT TIM AND JAMIE?
THEY'RE MAKING THEIR WAY BACK FROM THEIR SENIOR TRIP TO THE STATE CAPITAL. IT'LL BE TWO HOURS, ABOUT, TO GET BACK HERE.
THAT'S TWO HOURS WE DON'T HAVE.
THE PLAN IS TO KEEP WHAT'S BACK THERE FROM GETTING OUT HERE. WE'RE GOING TO HAVE TO GO ALL THE WAY TO THE ARCH-THEATER.
LOOK...THAT PLACE...IT'S THE HEART OF EVERYTHING THEATER IS, EVERYTHING IT CAN MEAN. IT'S THE RAW IDEA OF THEATER ITSELF.
TAKING THAT POWER AND BRINGING IT OUT INTO THE WORLD? IT'S DESTRUCTIVE, NOT JUST TO PEOPLE OUT HERE, BUT TO ITSELF.
WITHOUT THAT MAGIC IN THE CENTER OF THINGS, THEATER IS JUST OUTCASTS ON THE EDGE OF SOCIETY STANDING IN FRONT OF PLYBOARDS PRETENDING TO BE PRINCES AND PAUPERS.
IF POLAROID LETS ALL THAT MAGIC OUT HERE, THEATER AS WE KNOW IT WILL DIE, EVERYWHERE ACROSS THE WORLD.
I PROMISED MYSELF, THIRTY YEARS AGO, THAT I'D NEVER LET THAT HAPPEN.
AND LOOK, BOYS. I'M NOT GOING TO PRETEND IT'S NOT GOING TO BE DANGEROUS. IF YOU'RE AFRAID, AND YOU DON'T WANT TO COME ALONG, I'M NOT GOING TO STOP YOU.
I'M NOT GOING TO THINK ANY LESS OF YOU. YOU'VE BEEN THROUGH SO MUCH ALREADY.
I'M AFRAID, TOO.

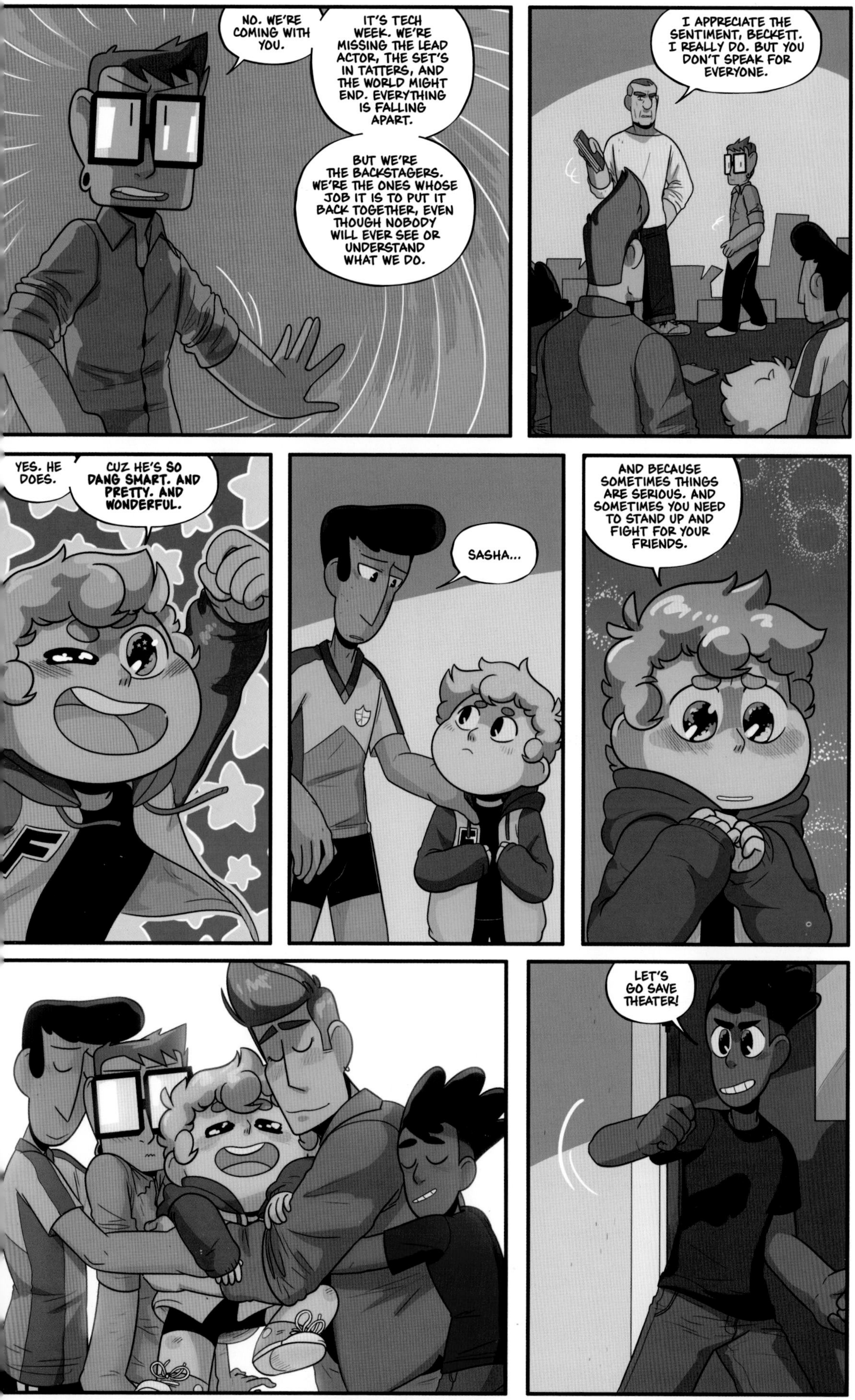

NO. WE'RE COMING WITH YOU.
IT'S TECH WEEK. WE'RE MISSING THE LEAD ACTOR, THE SET'S IN TATTERS, AND THE WORLD MIGHT END. EVERYTHING IS FALLING APART.
BUT WE'RE THE BACKSTAGERS. WE'RE THE ONES WHOSE JOB IT IS TO PUT IT BACK TOGETHER, EVEN THOUGH NOBODY WILL EVER SEE OR UNDERSTAND WHAT WE DO.
I APPRECIATE THE SENTIMENT, BECKETT. I REALLY DO. BUT YOU DON'T SPEAK FOR EVERYONE.
YES. HE DOES.
CUZ HE'S SO DANG SMART. AND PRETTY. AND WONDERFUL.
SASHA...
AND BECAUSE SOMETIMES THINGS ARE SERIOUS. AND SOMETIMES YOU NEED TO STAND UP AND FIGHT FOR YOUR FRIENDS.
LET'S GO SAVE THEATER!

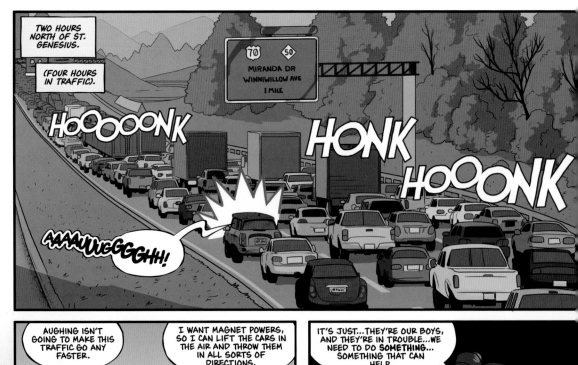

TWO HOURS NORTH OF ST. GENESIUS.

(FOUR HOURS IN TRAFFIC).

70   50
MIRANDA DR
WINNIWILLOW AVE
1 MILE

HOOOOONK

HONK

HOOONK

AAAAUUGGGGHH!

AUGHING ISN'T GOING TO MAKE THIS TRAFFIC GO ANY FASTER.

I WANT MAGNET POWERS, SO I CAN LIFT THE CARS IN THE AIR AND THROW THEM IN ALL SORTS OF DIRECTIONS.

IT'S JUST...THEY'RE OUR BOYS, AND THEY'RE IN TROUBLE...WE NEED TO DO **SOMETHING**... SOMETHING THAT CAN HELP.

WAIT...

...I HAVE A TOTALLY BONKERS, CRAZY, IMPOSSIBLE IDEA... PULL OFF AT THIS NEXT EXIT.

WINNIWILLOW AVE

MIRANDA DRAMA HIGHSCHOOL PRESENTS: "THE PYJAMA SANCTION"

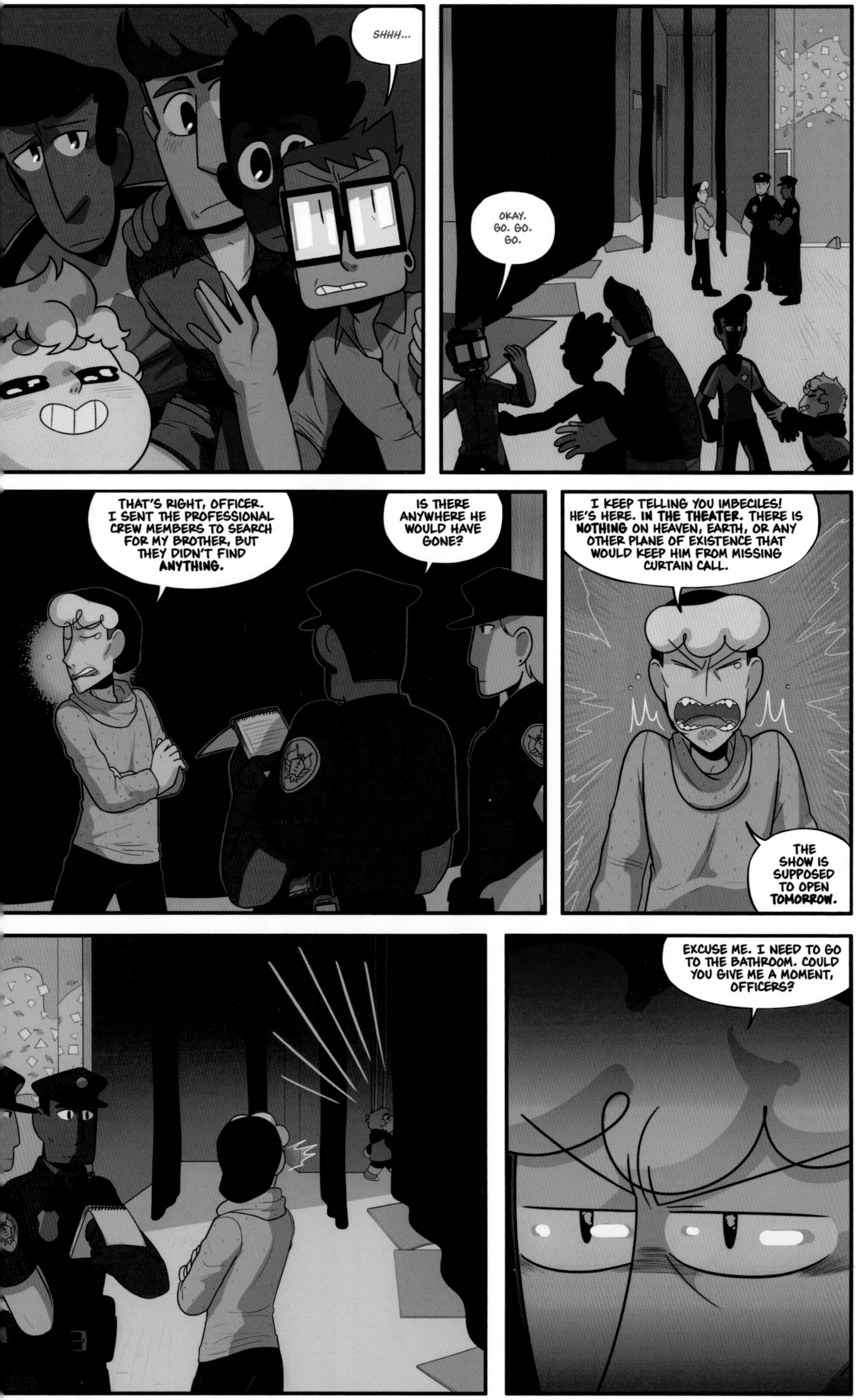
SHHH...
OKAY. GO. GO. GO.
THAT'S RIGHT, OFFICER. I SENT THE PROFESSIONAL CREW MEMBERS TO SEARCH FOR MY BROTHER, BUT THEY DIDN'T FIND ANYTHING.
IS THERE ANYWHERE HE WOULD HAVE GONE?
I KEEP TELLING YOU IMBECILES! HE'S HERE. IN THE THEATER. THERE IS NOTHING ON HEAVEN, EARTH, OR ANY OTHER PLANE OF EXISTENCE THAT WOULD KEEP HIM FROM MISSING CURTAIN CALL.
THE SHOW IS SUPPOSED TO OPEN TOMORROW.
EXCUSE ME. I NEED TO GO TO THE BATHROOM. COULD YOU GIVE ME A MOMENT, OFFICERS?

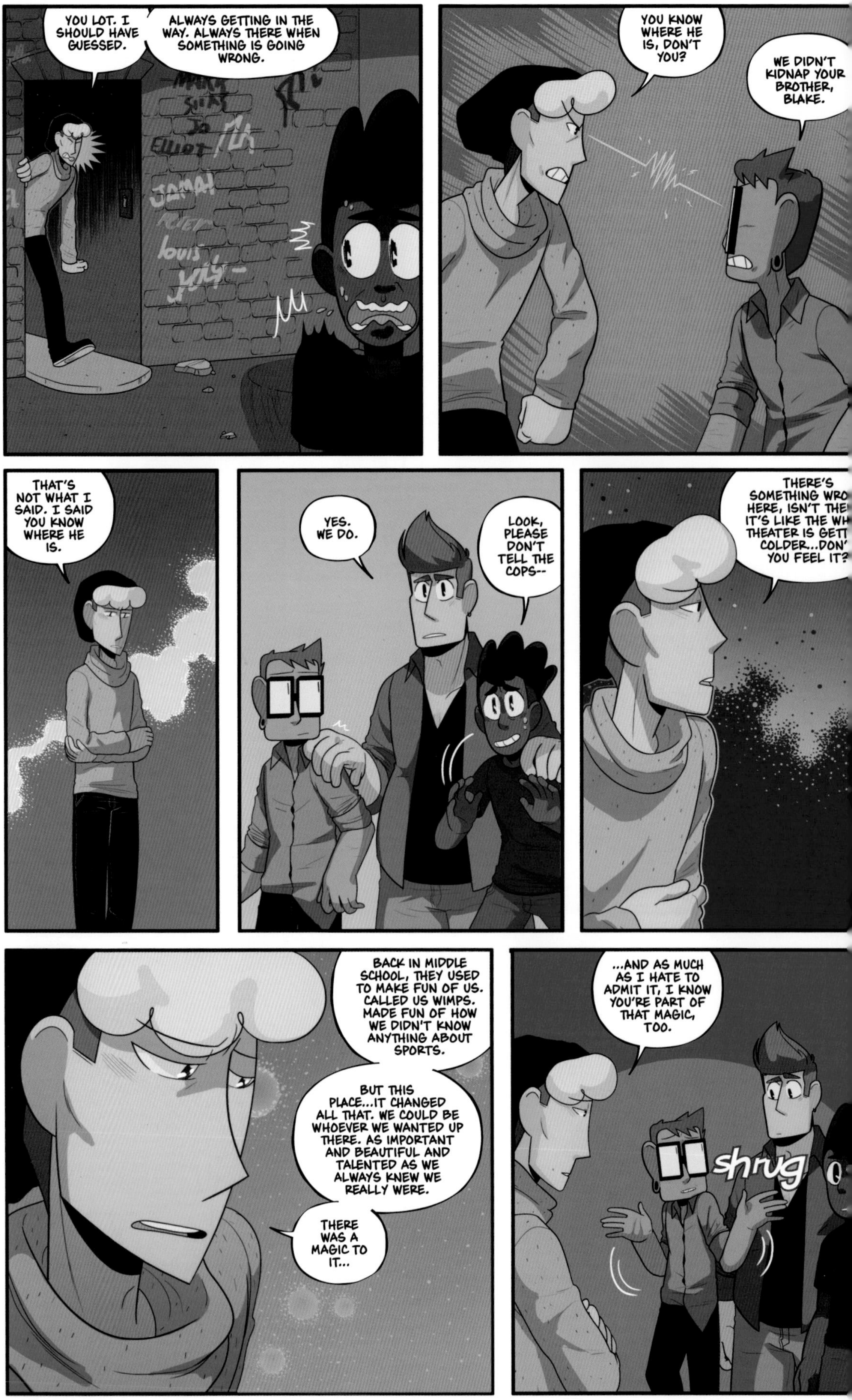
YOU LOT. I SHOULD HAVE GUESSED.
ALWAYS GETTING IN THE WAY. ALWAYS THERE WHEN SOMETHING IS GOING WRONG.
YOU KNOW WHERE HE IS, DON'T YOU?
WE DIDN'T KIDNAP YOUR BROTHER, BLAKE.
THAT'S NOT WHAT I SAID. I SAID YOU KNOW WHERE HE IS.
YES. WE DO.
LOOK, PLEASE DON'T TELL THE COPS--
THERE'S SOMETHING WRO HERE, ISN'T THE IT'S LIKE THE WH THEATER IS GETT COLDER...DON' YOU FEEL IT?
BACK IN MIDDLE SCHOOL, THEY USED TO MAKE FUN OF US. CALLED US WIMPS. MADE FUN OF HOW WE DIDN'T KNOW ANYTHING ABOUT SPORTS.
BUT THIS PLACE...IT CHANGED ALL THAT. WE COULD BE WHOEVER WE WANTED UP THERE. AS IMPORTANT AND BEAUTIFUL AND TALENTED AS WE ALWAYS KNEW WE REALLY WERE.
THERE WAS A MAGIC TO IT...
...AND AS MUCH AS I HATE TO ADMIT IT, I KNOW YOU'RE PART OF THAT MAGIC, TOO.
shrug

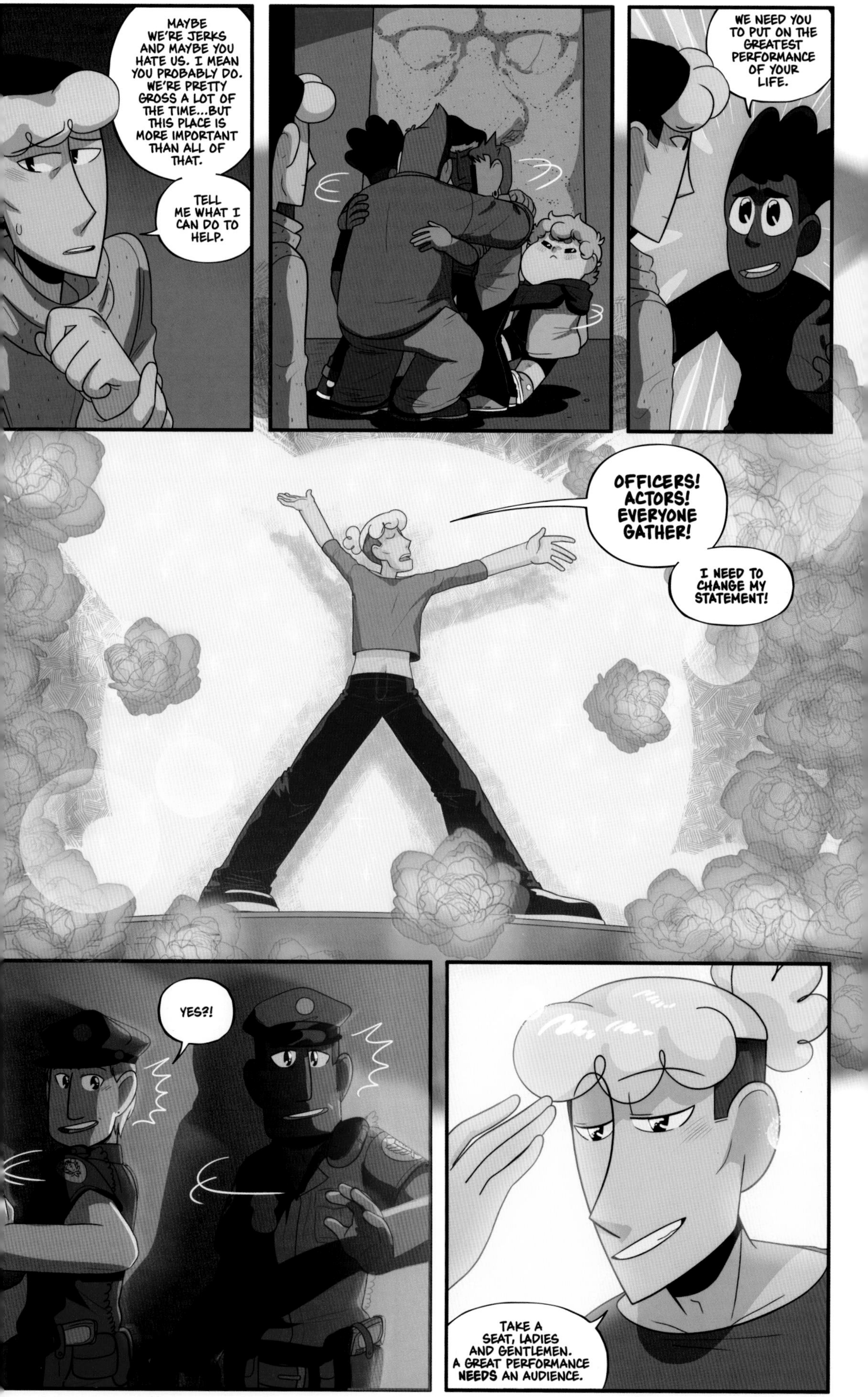
MAYBE WE'RE JERKS AND MAYBE YOU HATE US. I MEAN YOU PROBABLY DO. WE'RE PRETTY GROSS A LOT OF THE TIME...BUT THIS PLACE IS MORE IMPORTANT THAN ALL OF THAT.
TELL ME WHAT I CAN DO TO HELP.
WE NEED YOU TO PUT ON THE GREATEST PERFORMANCE OF YOUR LIFE.
OFFICERS! ACTORS! EVERYONE GATHER!
I NEED TO CHANGE MY STATEMENT!
YES?!
TAKE A SEAT, LADIES AND GENTLEMEN. A GREAT PERFORMANCE NEEDS AN AUDIENCE.

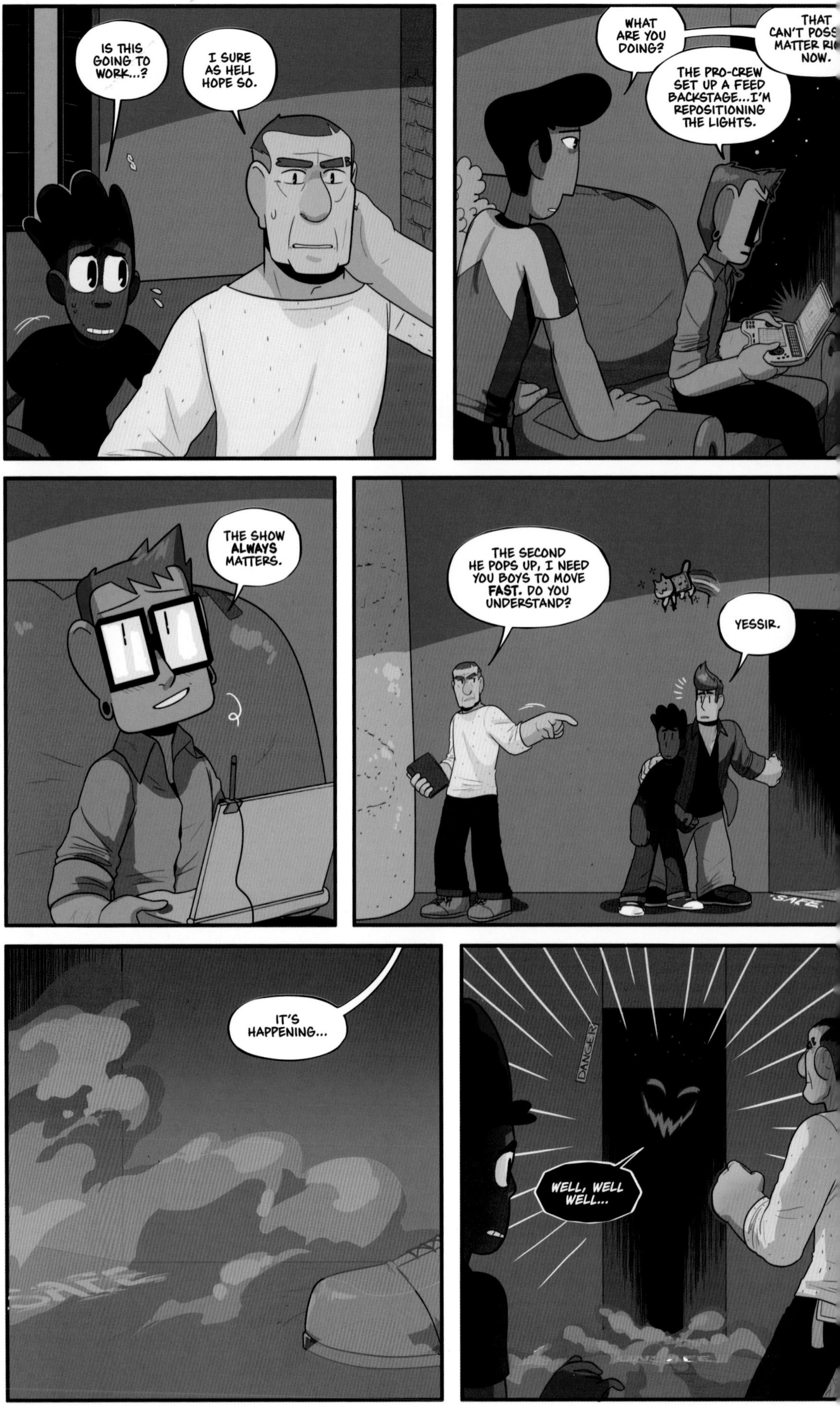
IS THIS GOING TO WORK...?
I SURE AS HELL HOPE SO.
WHAT ARE YOU DOING?
THAT CAN'T POSS MATTER RI NOW.
THE PRO-CREW SET UP A FEED BACKSTAGE...I'M REPOSITIONING THE LIGHTS.
THE SHOW **ALWAYS** MATTERS.
THE SECOND HE POPS UP, I NEED YOU BOYS TO MOVE **FAST.** DO YOU UNDERSTAND?
YESSIR.
SAFE
IT'S HAPPENING...
SAFE
DANGER
WELL, WELL WELL...

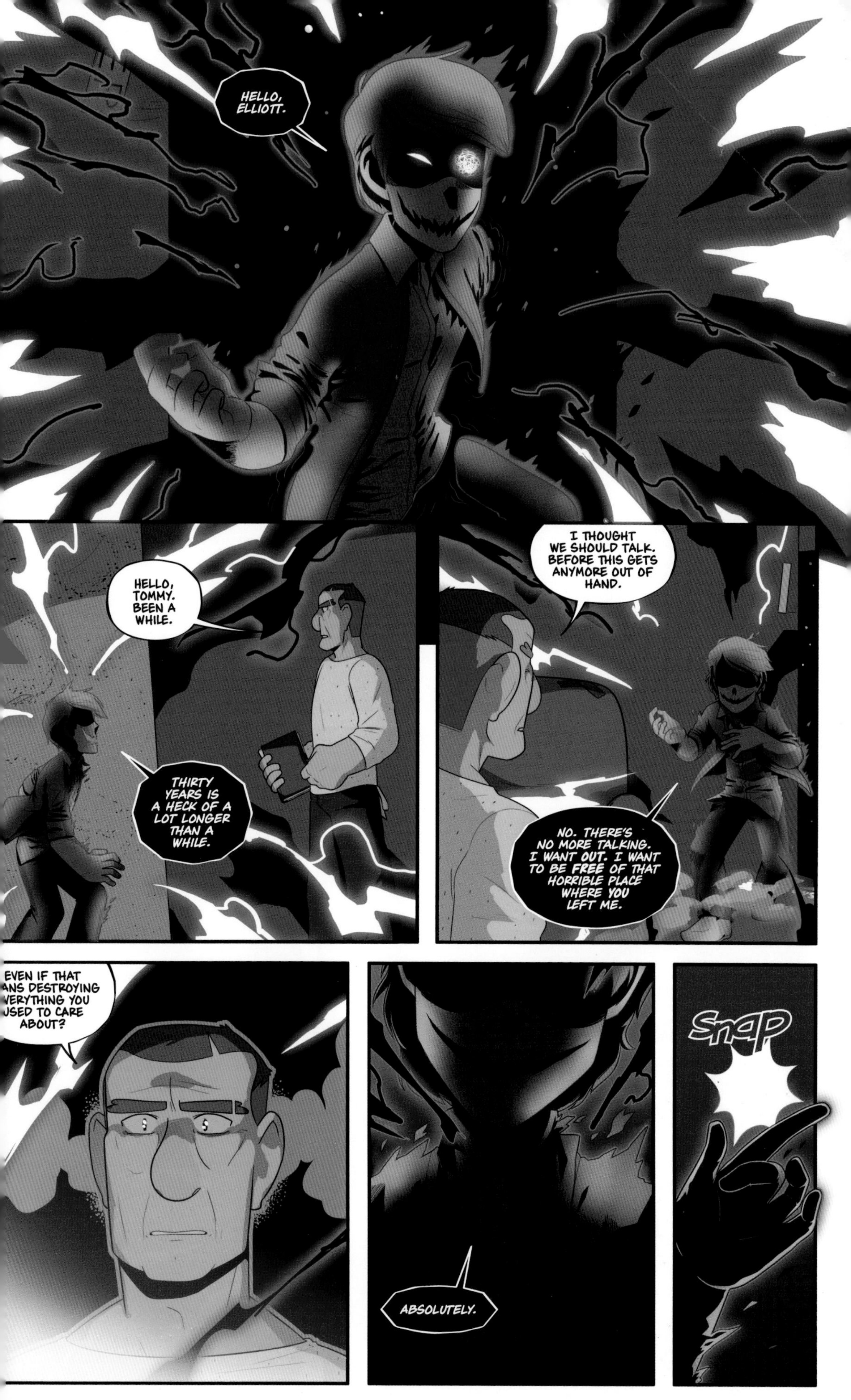
HELLO, ELLIOTT.
HELLO, TOMMY. BEEN A WHILE.
THIRTY YEARS IS A HECK OF A LOT LONGER THAN A WHILE.
I THOUGHT WE SHOULD TALK. BEFORE THIS GETS ANYMORE OUT OF HAND.
NO. THERE'S NO MORE TALKING. I WANT OUT. I WANT TO BE FREE OF THAT HORRIBLE PLACE WHERE YOU LEFT ME.
EVEN IF THAT ANS DESTROYING VERYTHING YOU USED TO CARE ABOUT?
ABSOLUTELY.
SNAP

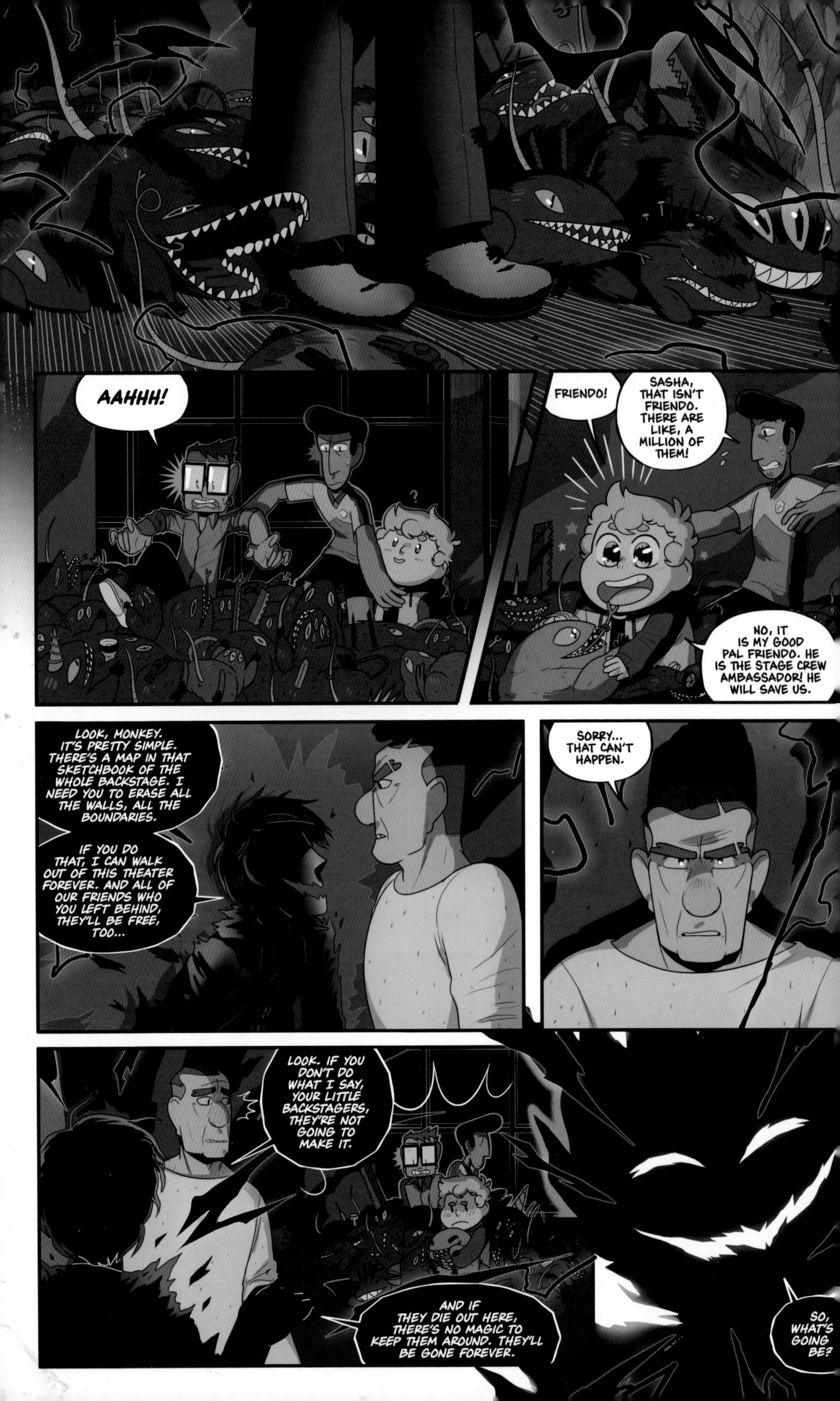
AAHHH!
FRIENDO!
SASHA, THAT ISN'T FRIENDO. THERE ARE LIKE, A MILLION OF THEM!
NO, IT IS MY GOOD PAL FRIENDO. HE IS THE STAGE CREW AMBASSADOR! HE WILL SAVE US.
LOOK, MONKEY. IT'S PRETTY SIMPLE. THERE'S A MAP IN THAT SKETCHBOOK OF THE WHOLE BACKSTAGE. I NEED YOU TO ERASE ALL THE WALLS, ALL THE BOUNDARIES.
IF YOU DO THAT, I CAN WALK OUT OF THIS THEATER FOREVER. AND ALL OF OUR FRIENDS WHO YOU LEFT BEHIND, THEY'LL BE FREE, TOO...
SORRY... THAT CAN'T HAPPEN.
LOOK. IF YOU DON'T DO WHAT I SAY, YOUR LITTLE BACKSTAGERS, THEY'RE NOT GOING TO MAKE IT.
AND IF THEY DIE OUT HERE, THERE'S NO MAGIC TO KEEP THEM AROUND. THEY'LL BE GONE FOREVER.
SO, WHAT'S GOING BE?

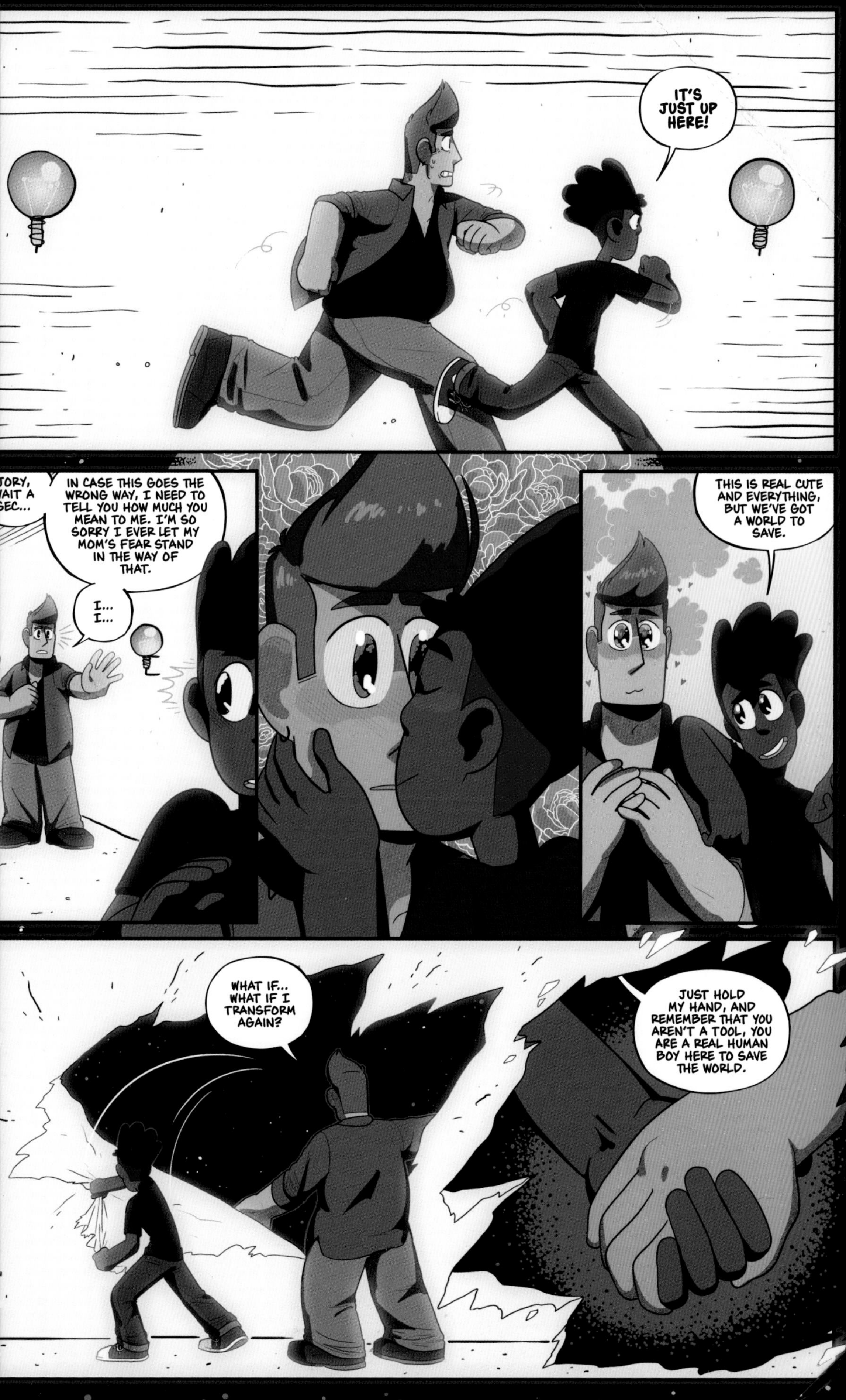

IT'S JUST UP HERE!
JORY, WAIT A SEC...
IN CASE THIS GOES THE WRONG WAY, I NEED TO TELL YOU HOW MUCH YOU MEAN TO ME. I'M SO SORRY I EVER LET MY MOM'S FEAR STAND IN THE WAY OF THAT.
I... I...
THIS IS REAL CUTE AND EVERYTHING, BUT WE'VE GOT A WORLD TO SAVE.
WHAT IF... WHAT IF I TRANSFORM AGAIN?
JUST HOLD MY HAND, AND REMEMBER THAT YOU AREN'T A TOOL, YOU ARE A REAL HUMAN BOY HERE TO SAVE THE WORLD.

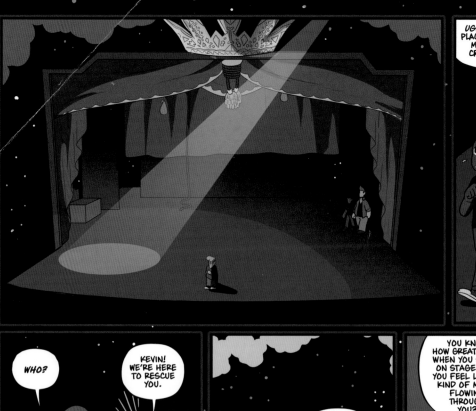

UGH, THIS PLACE GIVES ME THE CREEPS.

TELL ME ABOUT I

WHO?

KEVIN! WE'RE HERE TO RESCUE YOU.

I DON'T UNDERSTAND WHERE I AM.

YOU KNOW HOW GREAT IT IS, WHEN YOU STAND ON STAGE, AND YOU FEEL LIKE, A KIND OF MAGIC FLOWING THROUGH YOU?

THIS IS WHERE THA MAGIC COMES FR AND IF WE'RE N FAST, IT'S GOI TO BE DESTROY

THAT'S STUPID. THAT'S MADE UP AND IT'S STUPID.

THIS IS A DREAM.

THIS IS A DREAM.

THIS IS A DREAM.

LOOK UP, KEVIN. LOOK AT THE STAGE...

BLAKE?

BLAKE, IS THAT YOU?

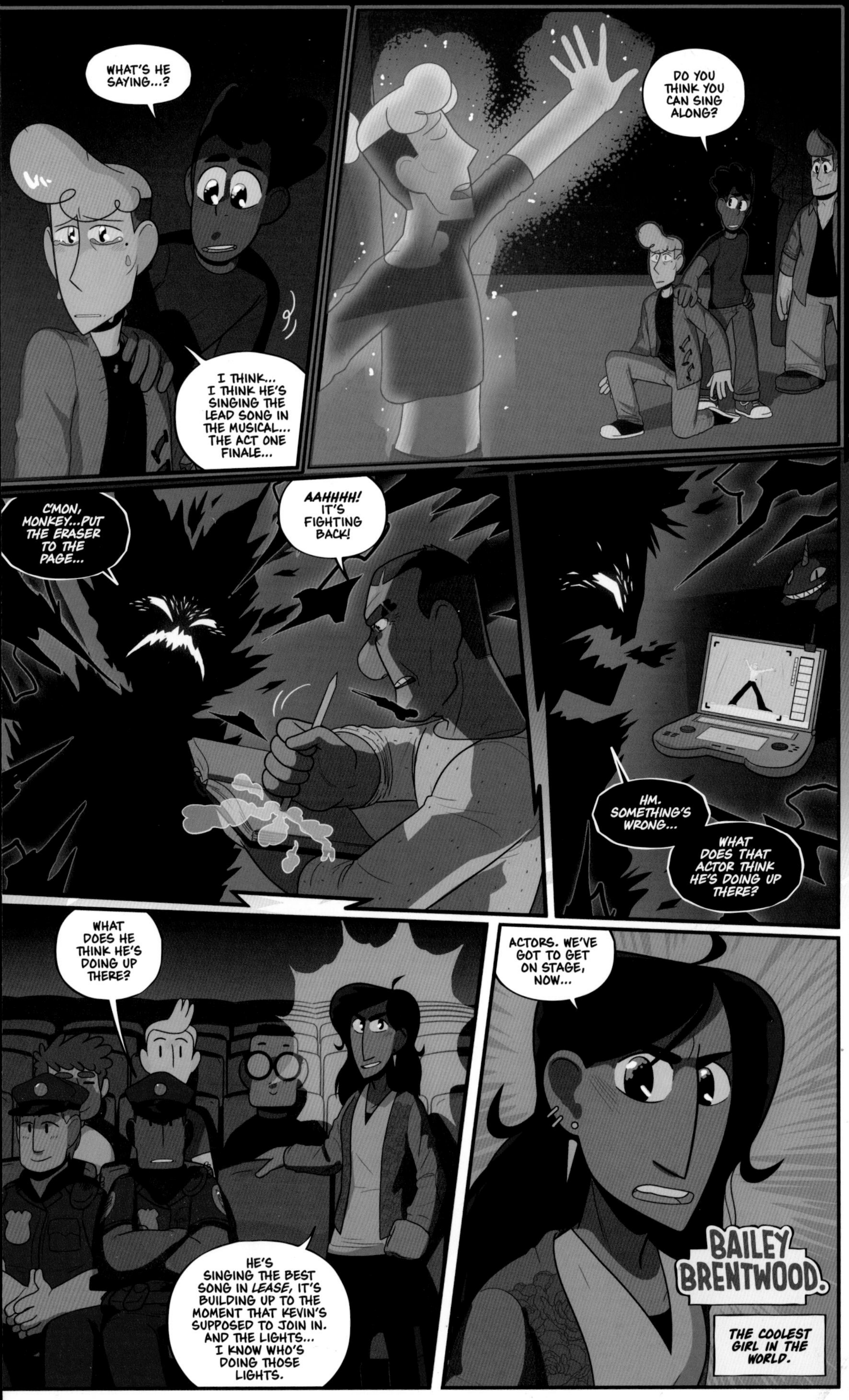

WHAT'S HE SAYING...?
I THINK... I THINK HE'S SINGING THE LEAD SONG IN THE MUSICAL... THE ACT ONE FINALE...
DO YOU THINK YOU CAN SING ALONG?
C'MON, MONKEY...PUT THE ERASER TO THE PAGE...
AAHHHH! IT'S FIGHTING BACK!
HM. SOMETHING'S WRONG...
WHAT DOES THAT ACTOR THINK HE'S DOING UP THERE?
WHAT DOES HE THINK HE'S DOING UP THERE?
HE'S SINGING THE BEST SONG IN LEASE, IT'S BUILDING UP TO THE MOMENT THAT KEVIN'S SUPPOSED TO JOIN IN. AND THE LIGHTS... I KNOW WHO'S DOING THOSE LIGHTS.
ACTORS. WE'VE GOT TO GET ON STAGE, NOW...
BAILEY BRENTWOOD.
THE COOLEST GIRL IN THE WORLD.

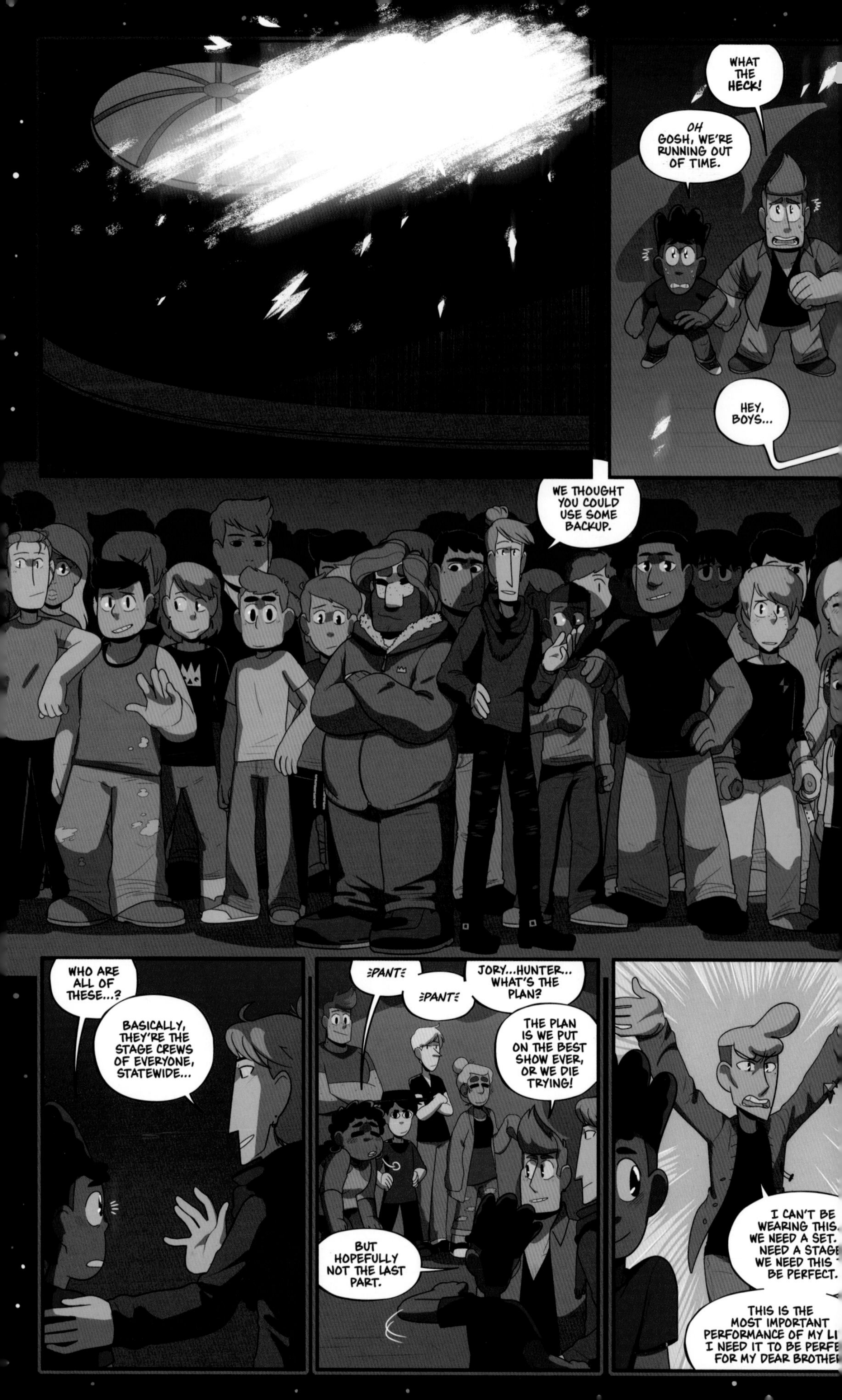
WHAT THE HECK!
OH GOSH, WE'RE RUNNING OUT OF TIME.
HEY, BOYS...
WE THOUGHT YOU COULD USE SOME BACKUP.
WHO ARE ALL OF THESE...?
BASICALLY, THEY'RE THE STAGE CREWS OF EVERYONE, STATEWIDE...
PANT
PANT
JORY...HUNTER... WHAT'S THE PLAN?
THE PLAN IS WE PUT ON THE BEST SHOW EVER, OR WE DIE TRYING!
BUT HOPEFULLY NOT THE LAST PART.
I CAN'T BE WEARING THIS. WE NEED A SET. NEED A STAGE WE NEED THIS BE PERFECT.
THIS IS THE MOST IMPORTANT PERFORMANCE OF MY LI I NEED IT TO BE PERFE FOR MY DEAR BROTHE

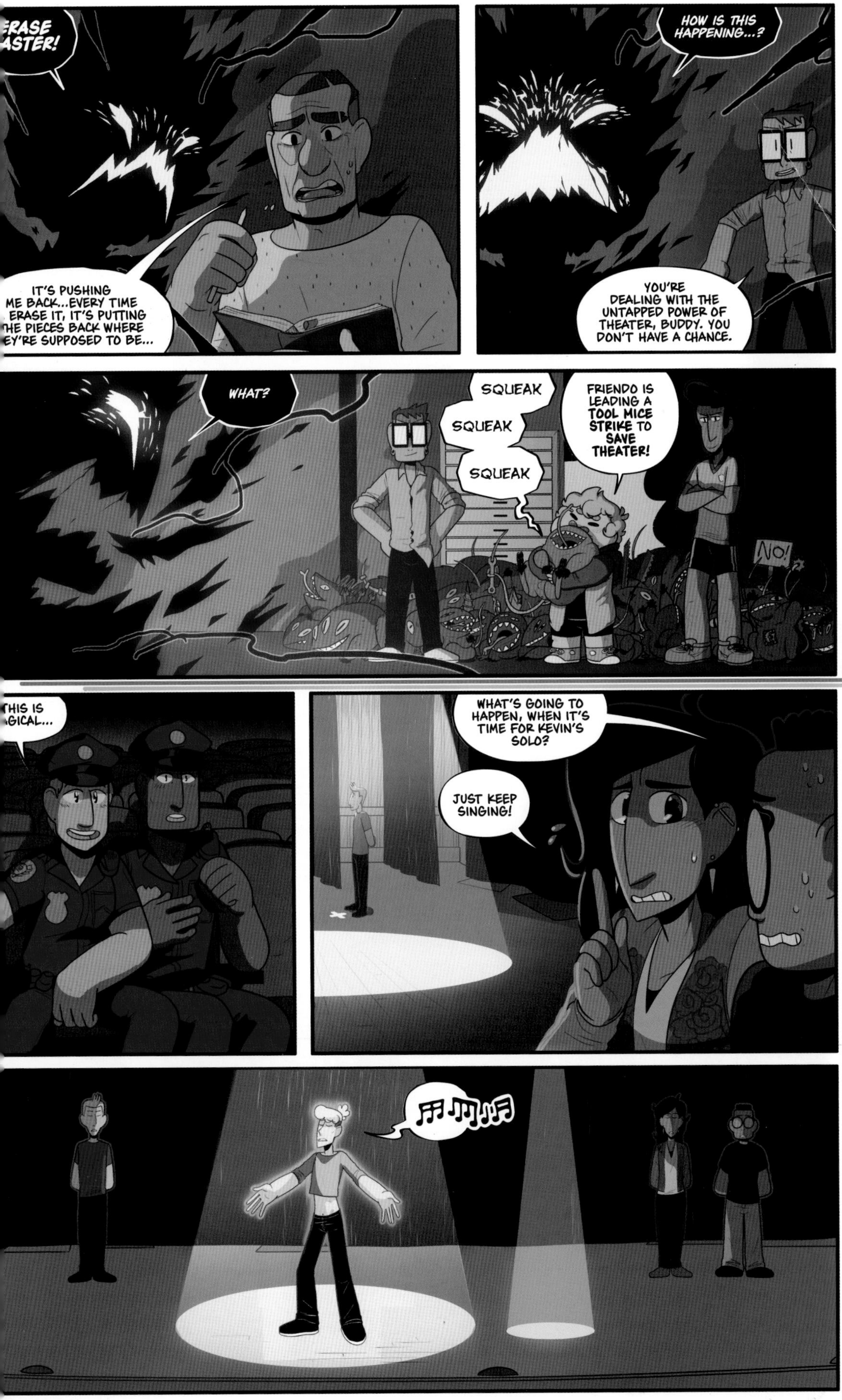

ERASE
ASTER!
IT'S PUSHING
ME BACK...EVERY TIME
ERASE IT, IT'S PUTTING
THE PIECES BACK WHERE
EY'RE SUPPOSED TO BE...
HOW IS THIS HAPPENING...?
YOU'RE DEALING WITH THE UNTAPPED POWER OF THEATER, BUDDY. YOU DON'T HAVE A CHANCE.
WHAT?
SQUEAK
SQUEAK
SQUEAK
FRIENDO IS LEADING A TOOL MICE STRIKE TO SAVE THEATER!
NO!
THIS IS
AGICAL...
WHAT'S GOING TO HAPPEN, WHEN IT'S TIME FOR KEVIN'S SOLO?
JUST KEEP SINGING!

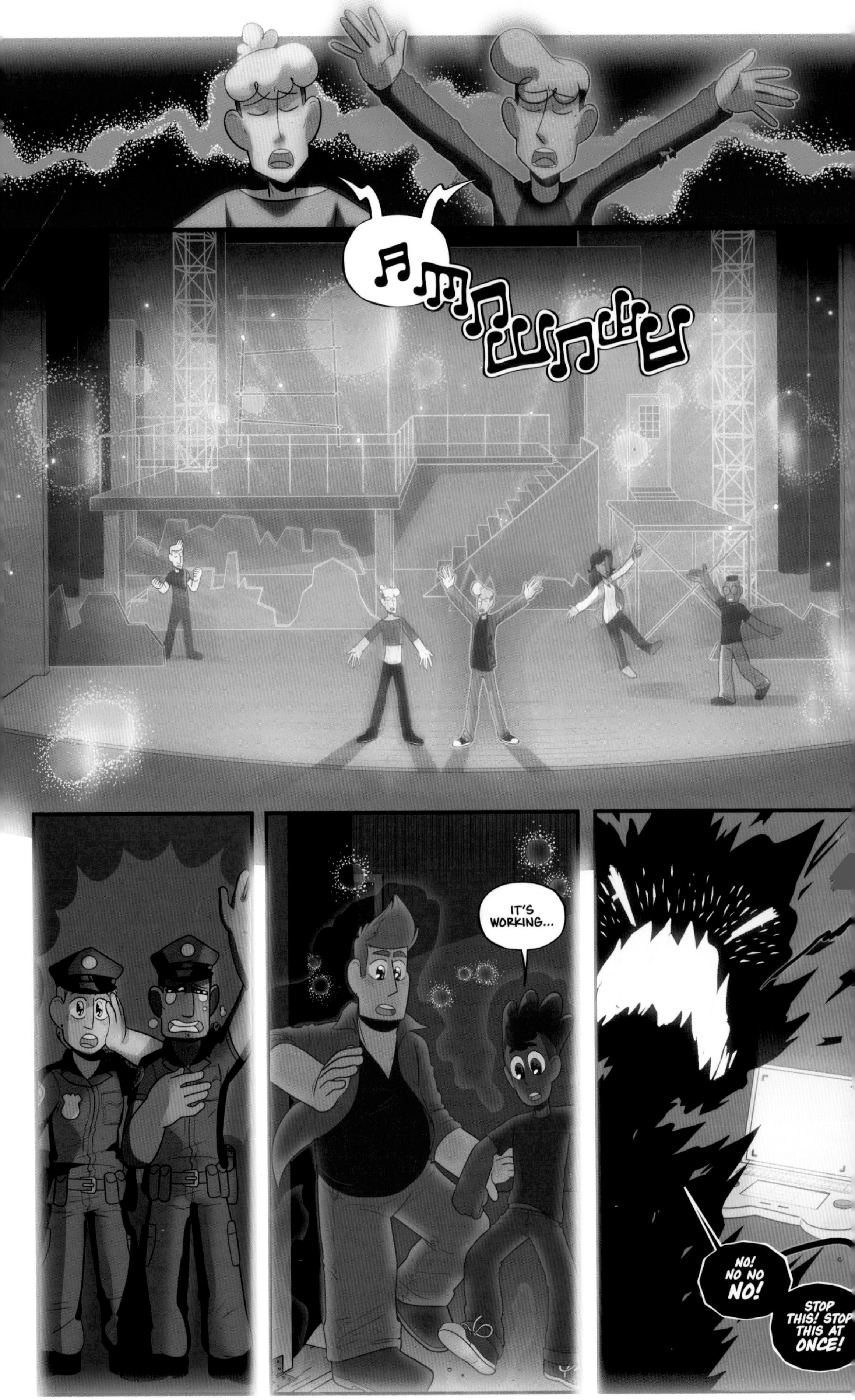
IT'S WORKING...
NO! NO NO NO!
STOP THIS! STOP THIS AT ONCE!

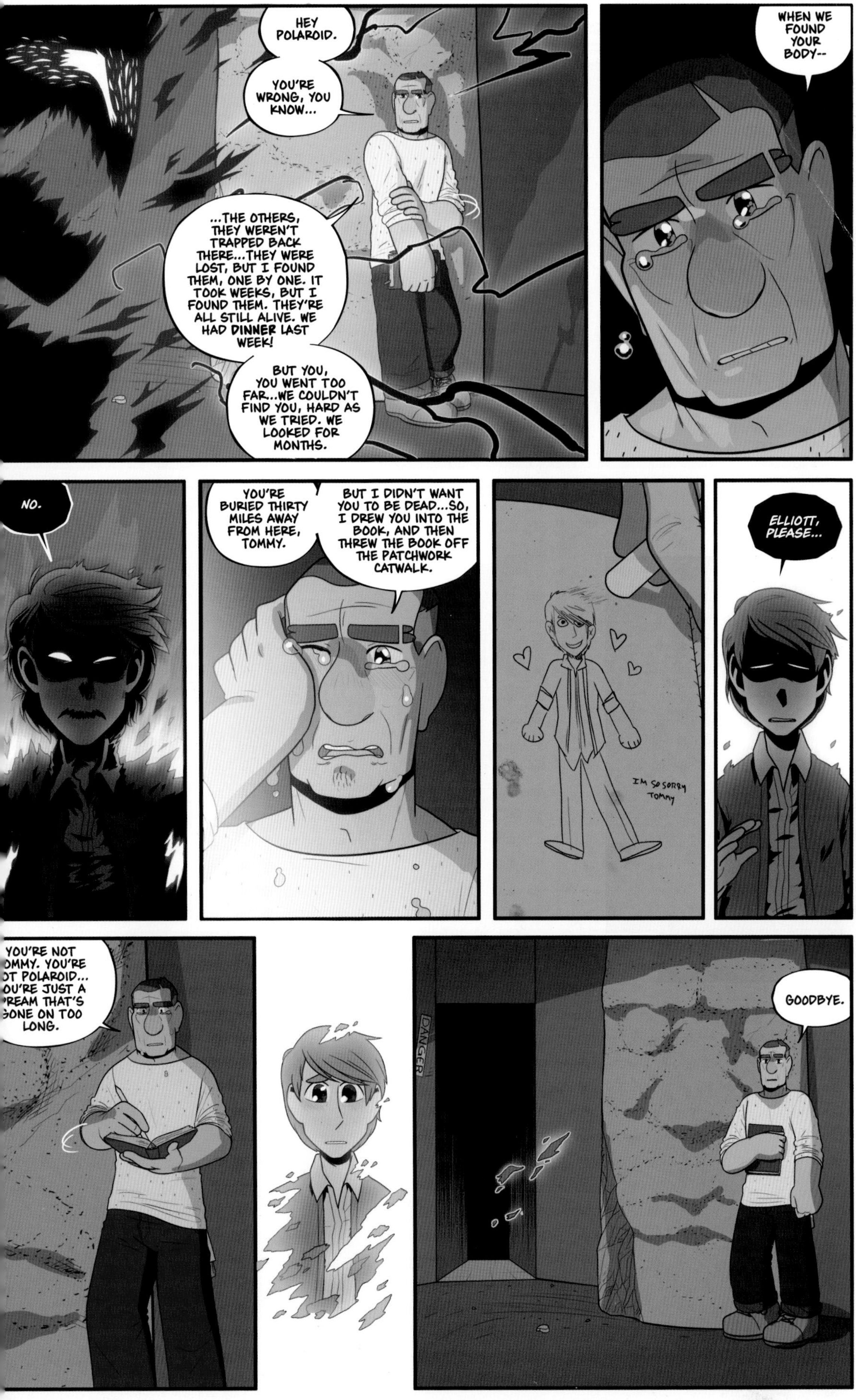
HEY POLAROID.
YOU'RE WRONG, YOU KNOW...
...THE OTHERS, THEY WEREN'T TRAPPED BACK THERE...THEY WERE LOST, BUT I FOUND THEM, ONE BY ONE. IT TOOK WEEKS, BUT I FOUND THEM. THEY'RE ALL STILL ALIVE. WE HAD DINNER LAST WEEK!
BUT YOU, YOU WENT TOO FAR...WE COULDN'T FIND YOU, HARD AS WE TRIED. WE LOOKED FOR MONTHS.
WHEN WE FOUND YOUR BODY--
NO.
YOU'RE BURIED THIRTY MILES AWAY FROM HERE, TOMMY.
BUT I DIDN'T WANT YOU TO BE DEAD...SO, I DREW YOU INTO THE BOOK, AND THEN THREW THE BOOK OFF THE PATCHWORK CATWALK.
IM SO SORRY TOMMY
ELLIOTT, PLEASE...
YOU'RE NOT OMMY. YOU'RE OT POLAROID... OU'RE JUST A REAM THAT'S GONE ON TOO LONG.
DANGER
GOODBYE.

THAT WAS T MOST BEAUT PRODUCTION EVER SEEN MY LIFE.

WHERE THE HECK ARE WE?!

MY MOM'S GOING TO KILL ME.

WE ARE NOT GETTING PAID ENOUGH FOR THIS CRAZY BS.

PRO CREW! ROLL OUT!

BROTHER!

BROTH

MR. RAMPLE, ARE YOU OKAY?

I'M SORRY I CAUSED SO MUCH TROUBLE, BOYS. HE WAS JUST...I LOVED HIM VERY MUCH ONCE UPON A TIME.

I DIDN'T REALIZE WHAT HOLDING ONTO THAT WOULD COST IN THE END.

IT'S OKAY.

WE UNDERSTAN

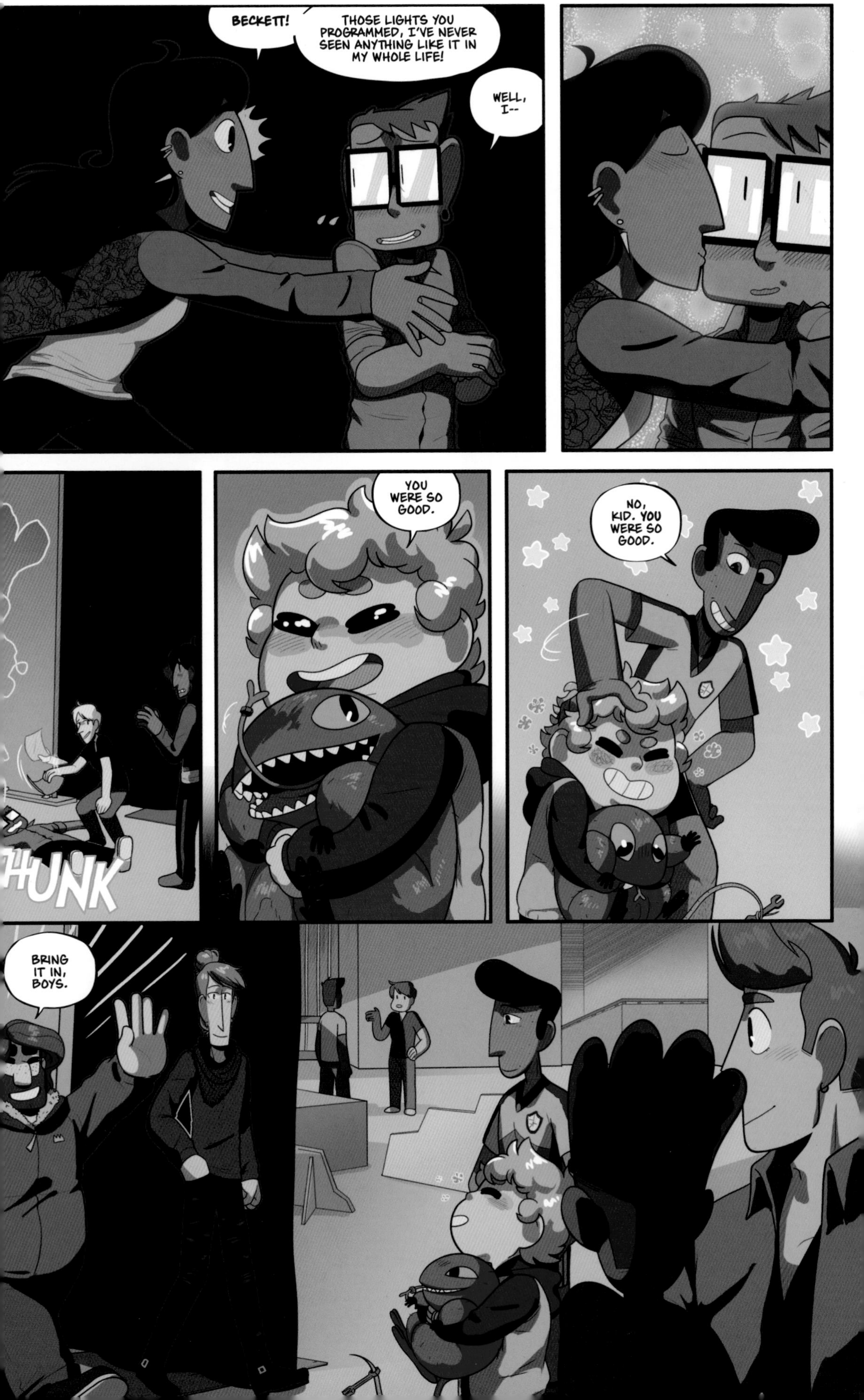
BECKETT!
THOSE LIGHTS YOU PROGRAMMED, I'VE NEVER SEEN ANYTHING LIKE IT IN MY WHOLE LIFE!
WELL, I--
HUNK
YOU WERE SO GOOD.
NO, KID. YOU WERE SO GOOD.
BRING IT IN, BOYS.

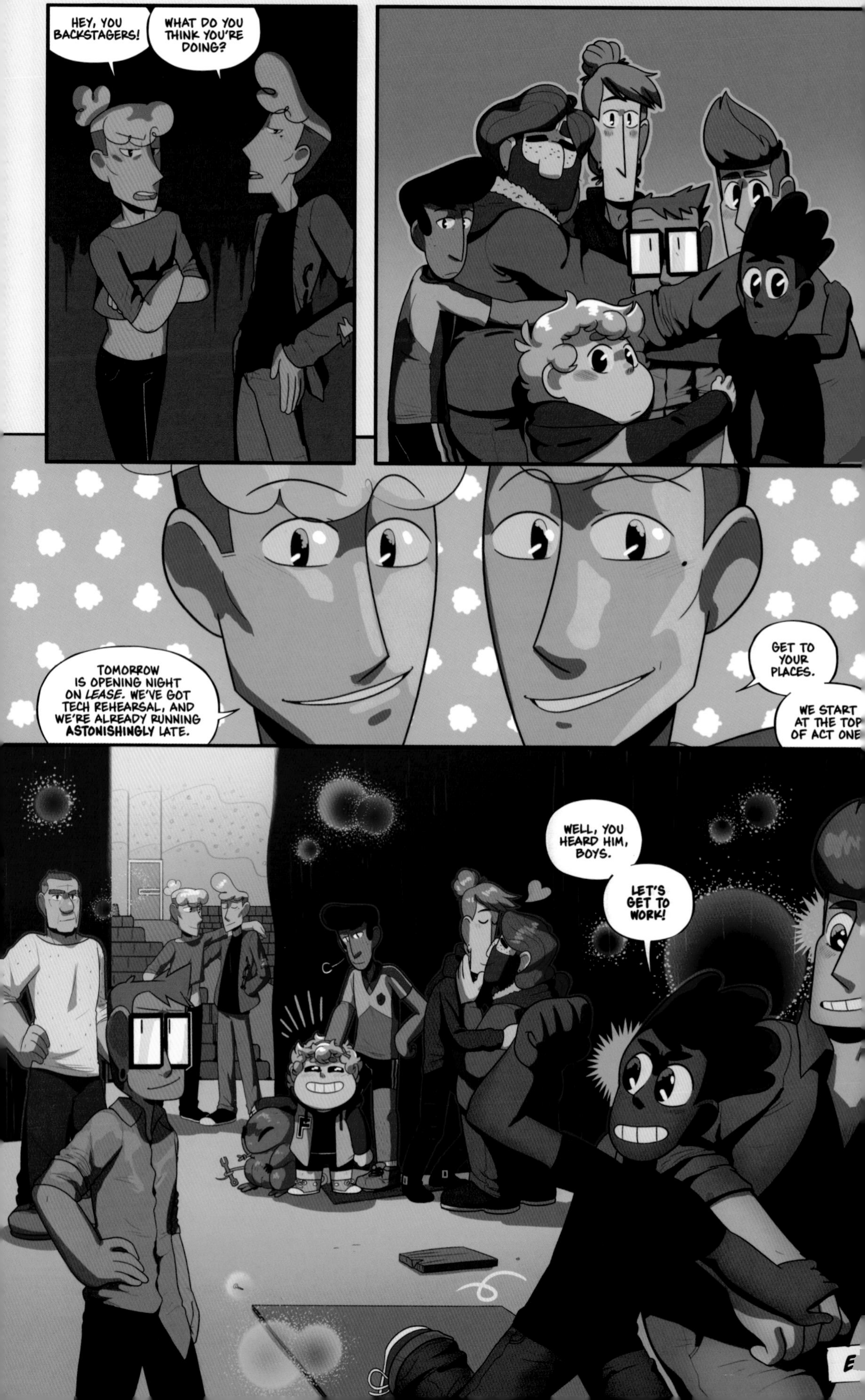
HEY, YOU BACKSTAGERS!
WHAT DO YOU THINK YOU'RE DOING?
TOMORROW IS OPENING NIGHT ON *LEASE*. WE'VE GOT TECH REHEARSAL, AND WE'RE ALREADY RUNNING **ASTONISHINGLY** LATE.
GET TO YOUR PLACES.
WE START AT THE TOP OF ACT ONE
WELL, YOU HEARD HIM, BOYS.
LET'S GET TO WORK!
E

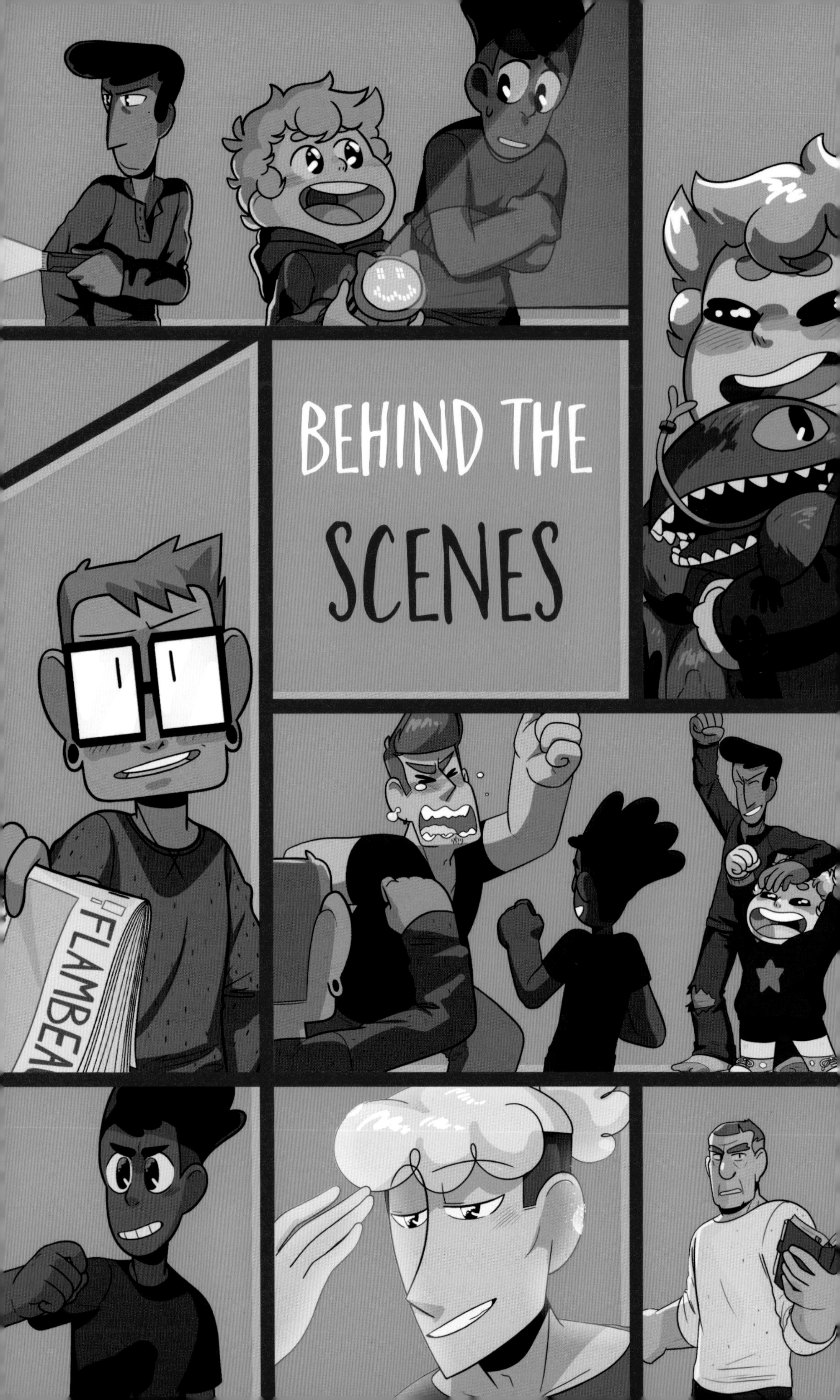

BEHIND THE SCENES
FLAMBEA

ISSUE #5 COVER BY
VERONICA FISH

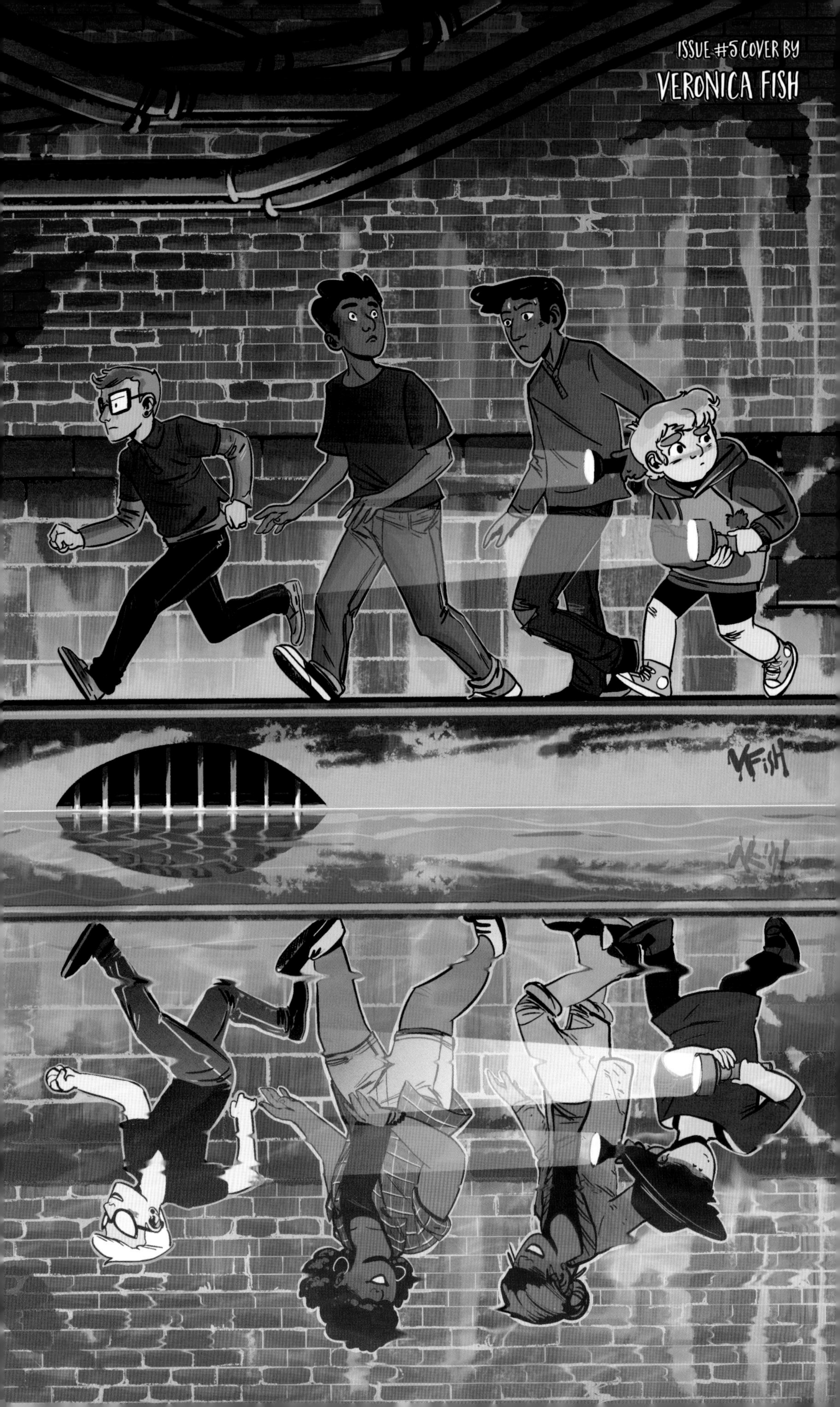
VFISH

ISSUE #6 COVER BY
VERONICA FISH

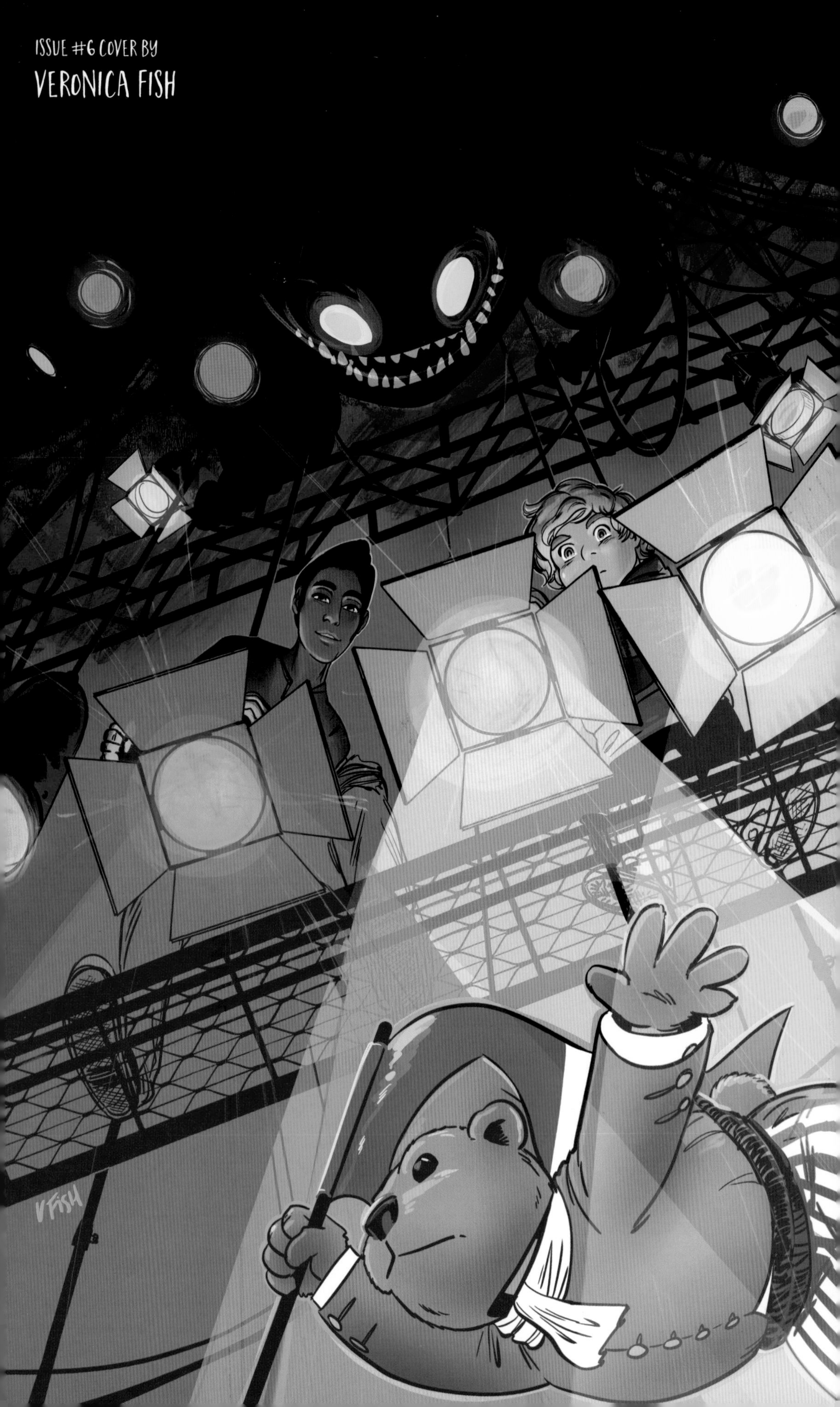
VFISH

ISSUE #7 COVER BY
VERONICA FISH

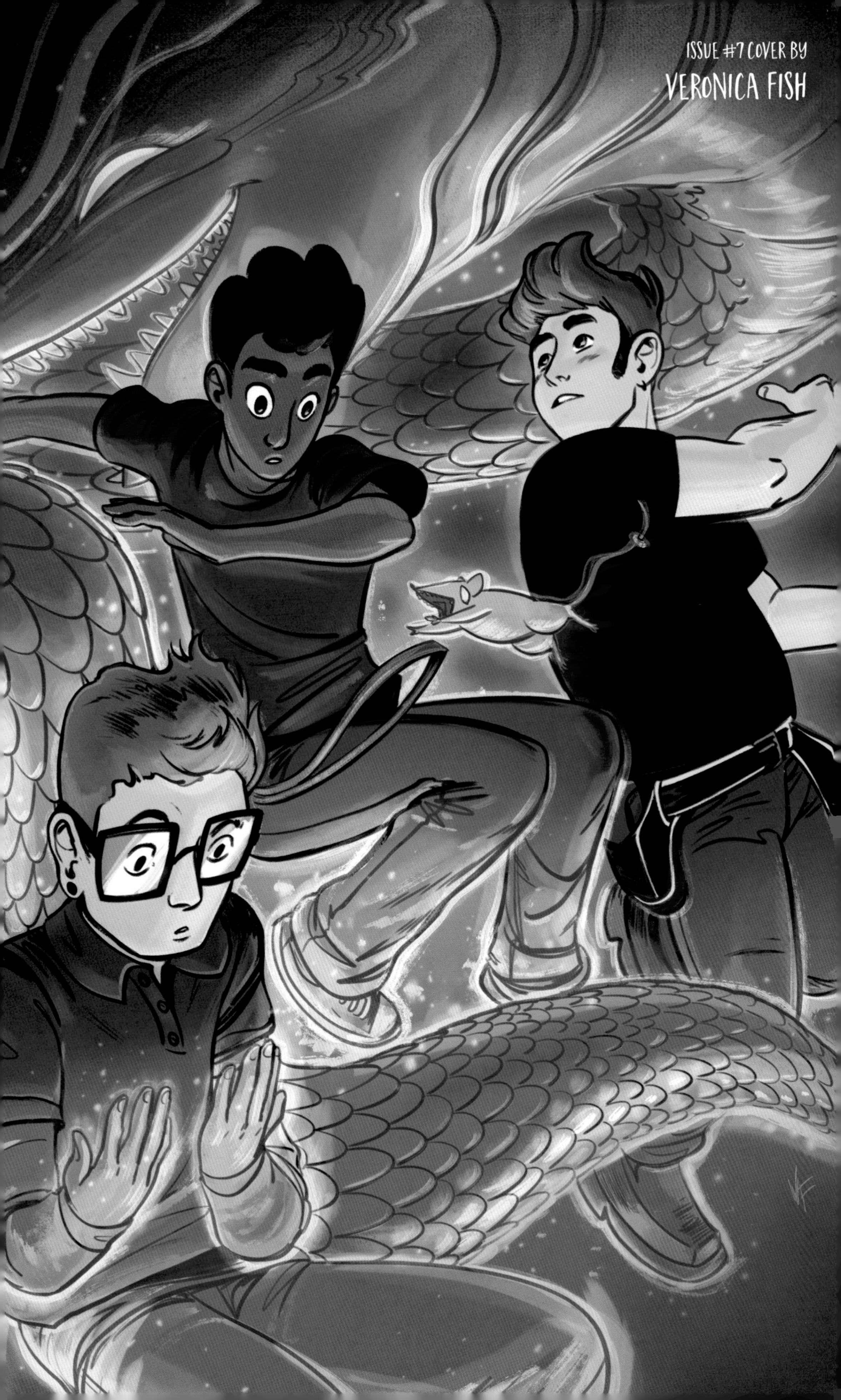
VF

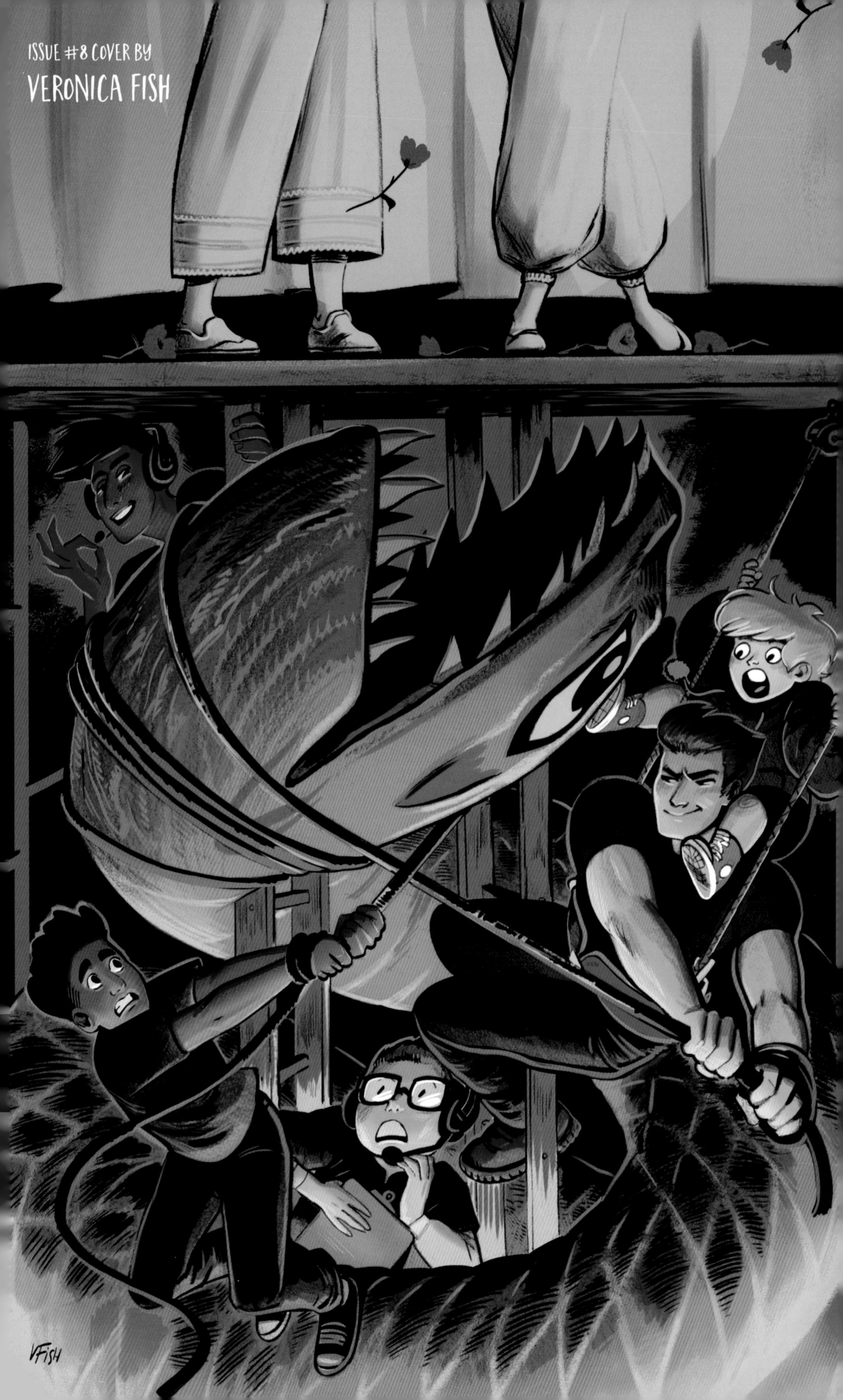
ISSUE #8 COVER BY
VERONICA FISH
VFISH

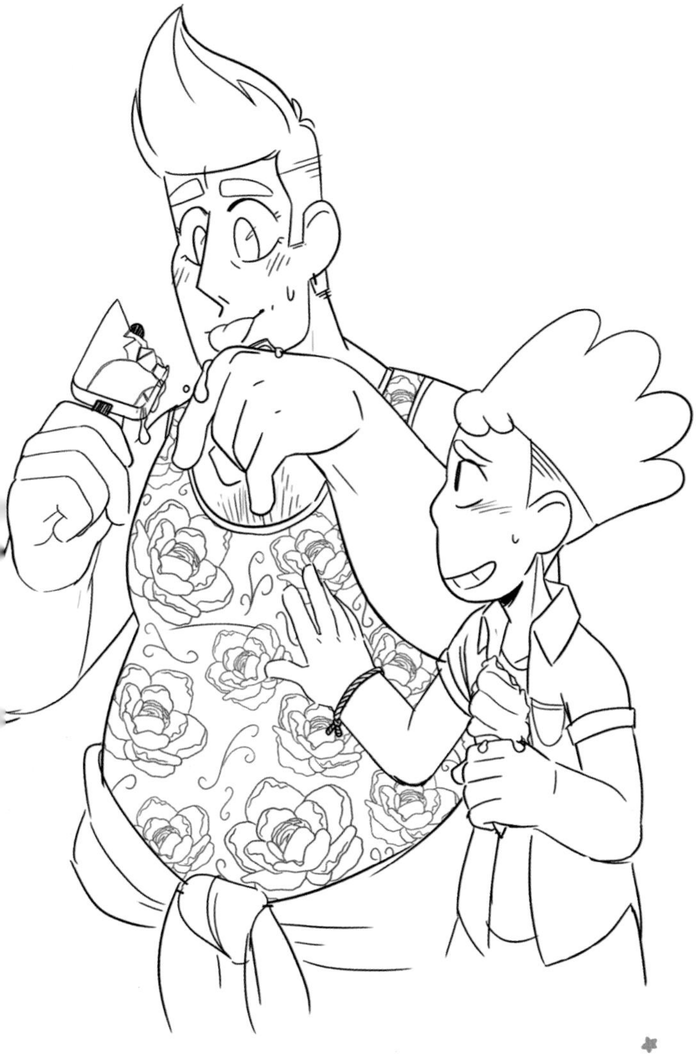

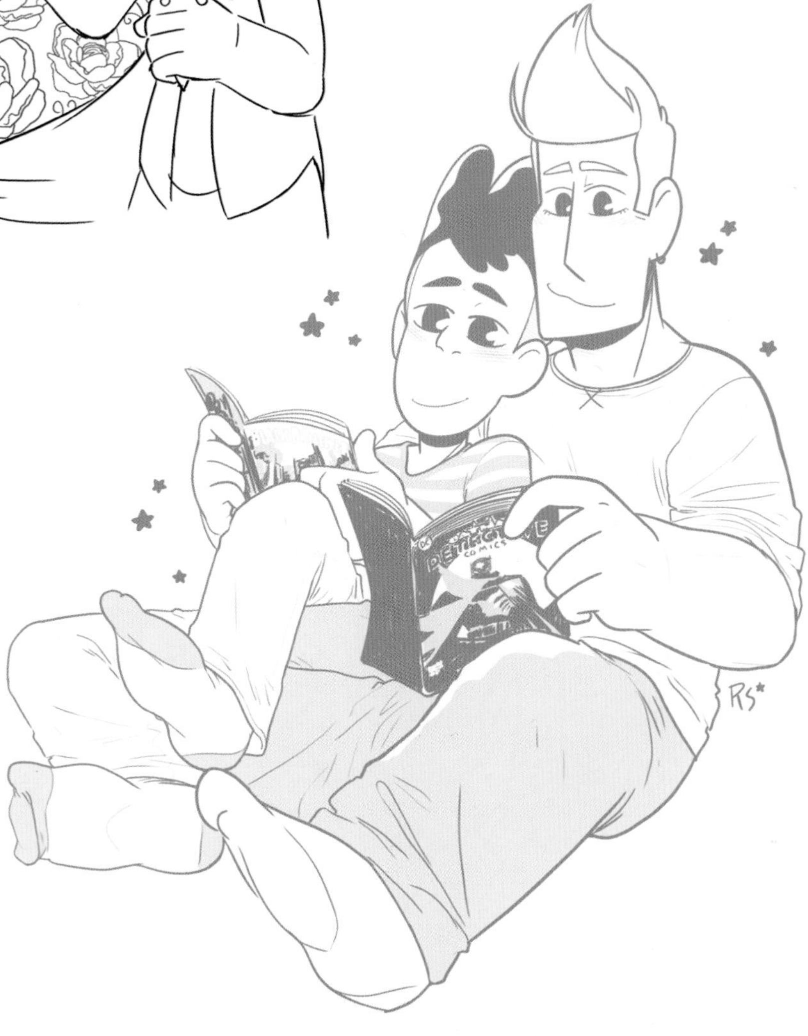
RS*

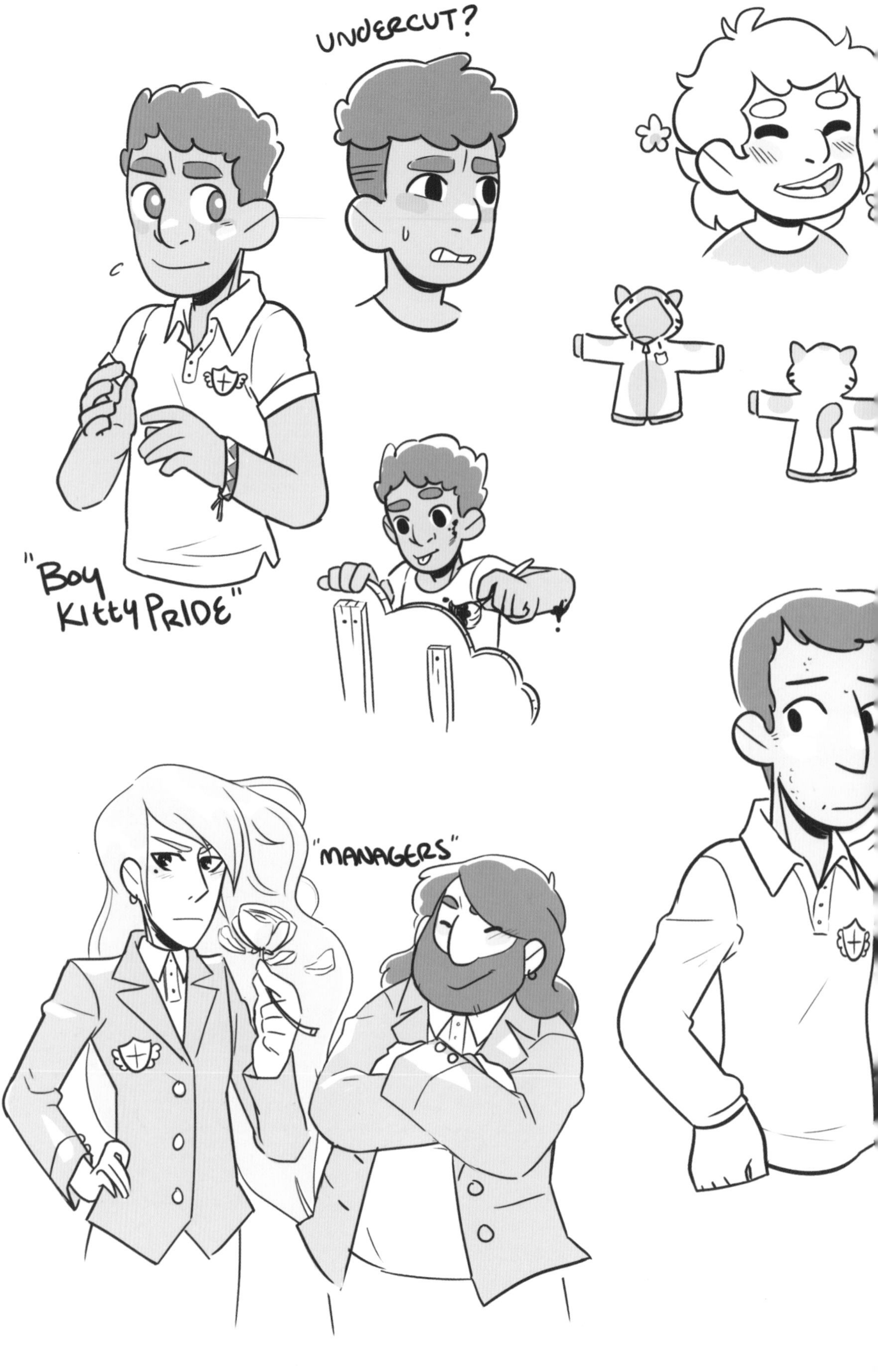
UNDERCUT?
"BOY KITTY PRIDE"
"MANAGERS"

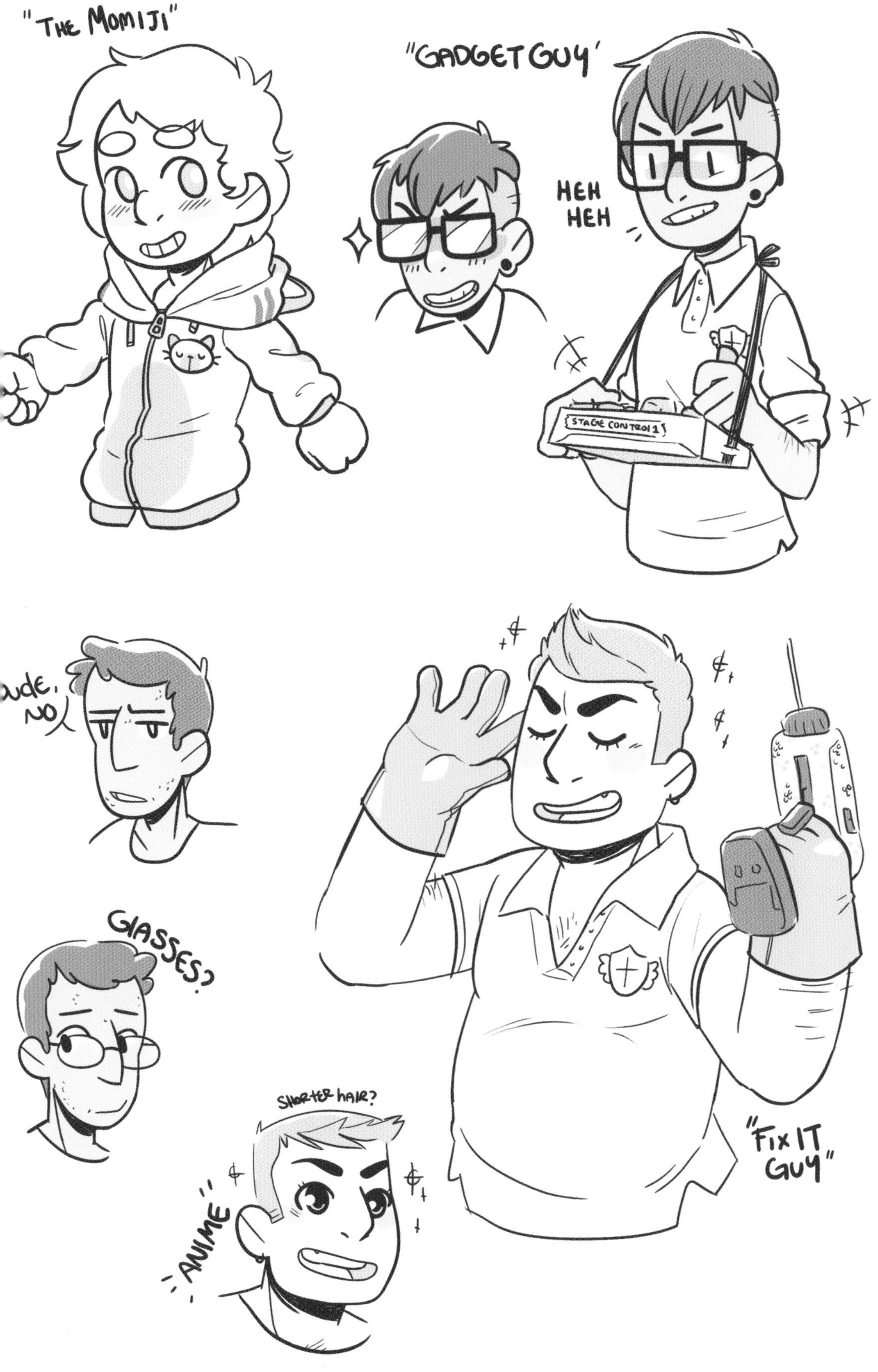
"THE MOMIJI"
"GADGET GUY"
HEH HEH
STAGE CONTROL 1
NO
GLASSES?
SHORTER HAIR?
"ANIME"
"FIX IT GUY"

CHARACTER DESIGNS BY RIAN SYGH

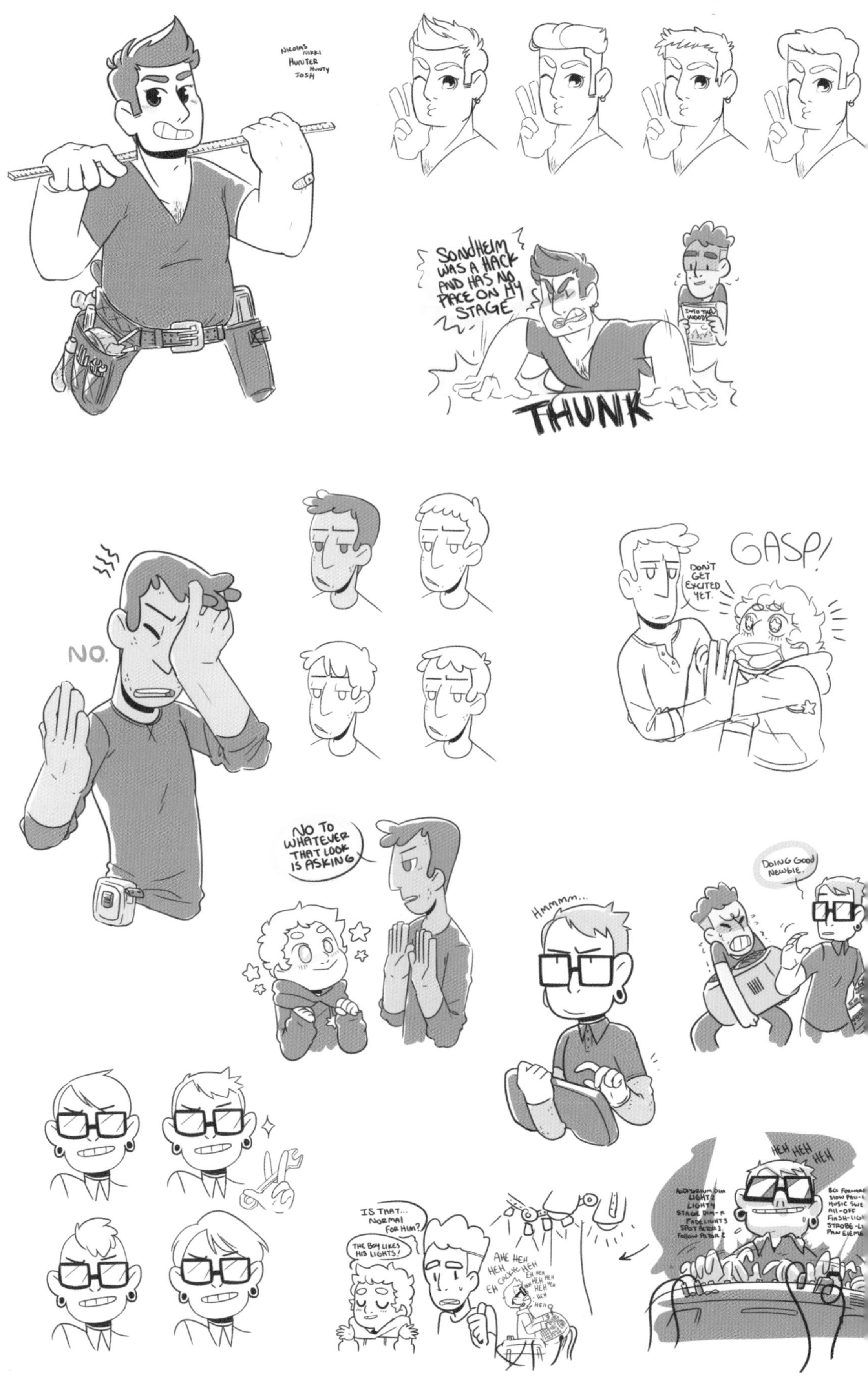
NICOLAS
NIKKI
HUNTER
HUNTY
JOSH
SONDHEIM WAS A HACK AND HAS NO PLACE ON MY STAGE
INTO THE WOODS
THUNK
NO.
GASP!
DON'T GET EXCITED YET.
NO TO WHATEVER THAT LOOK IS ASKING
HMMMM...
DOING GOOD NEWBIE.
IS THAT... NORMAL FOR HIM?
THE BOY LIKES HIS LIGHTS!
HEH HEH HEH

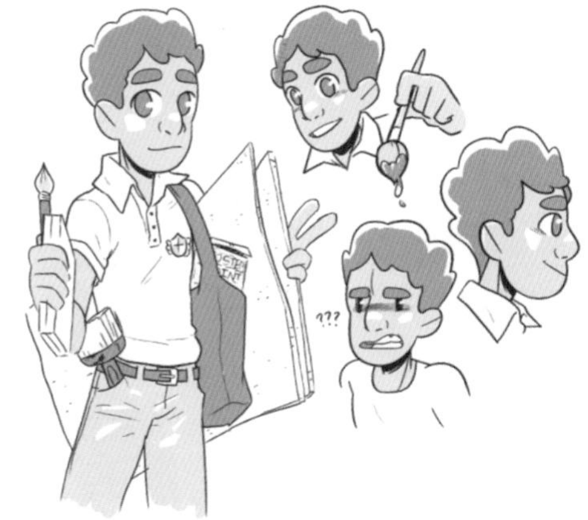
???

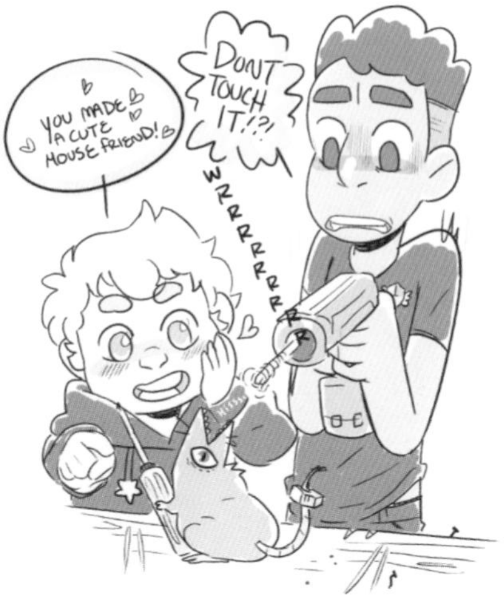
YOU MADE A CUTE HOUSE FRIEND!
DONT TOUCH IT!?!
WRRRRRRRR

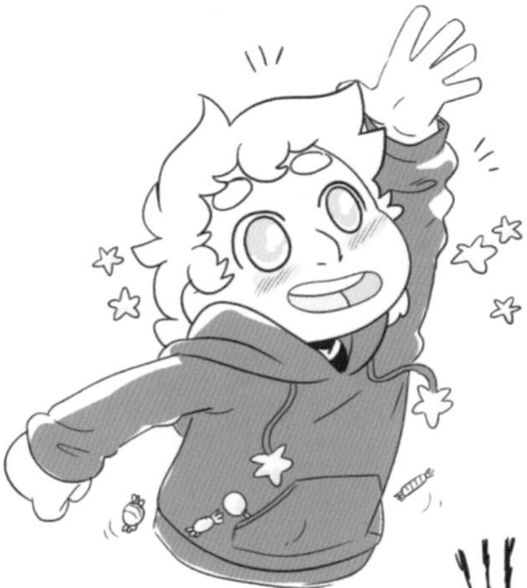

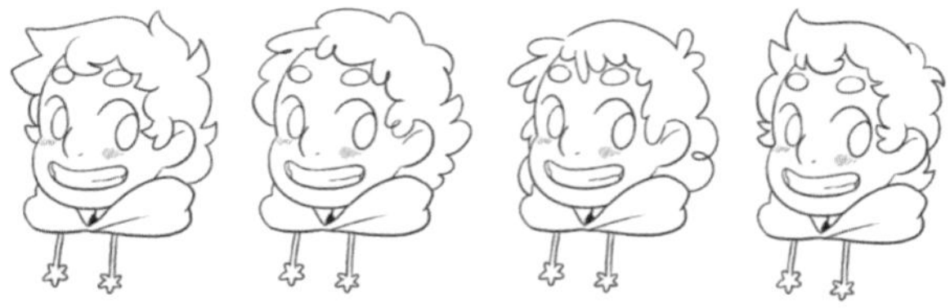

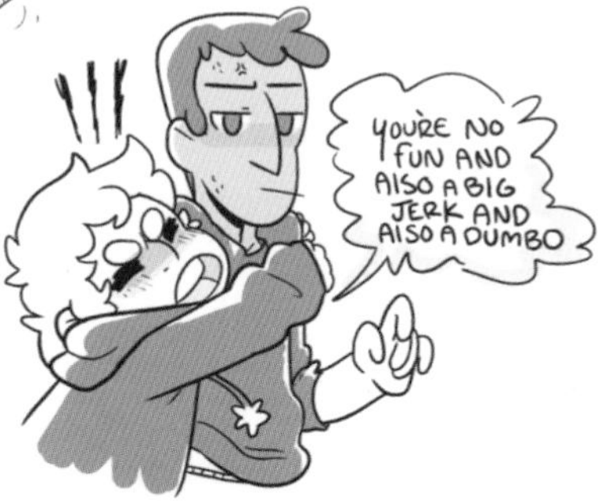
YOU'RE NO FUN AND ALSO A BIG JERK AND ALSO A DUMBO

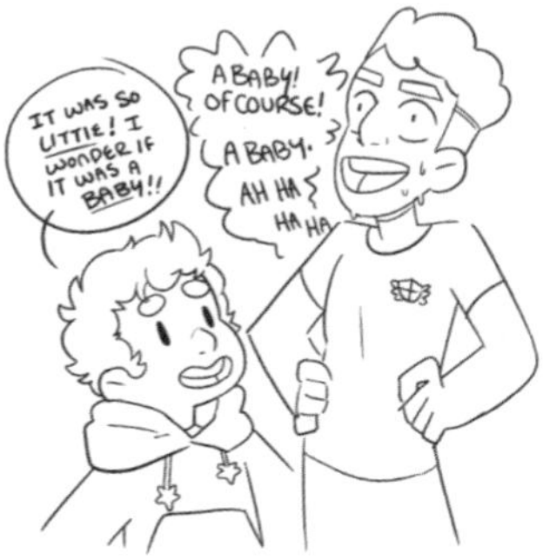
IT WAS SO LITTLE! I WONDER IF IT WAS A BABY!!
A BABY! OF COURSE!
A BABY. AH HA HA HA

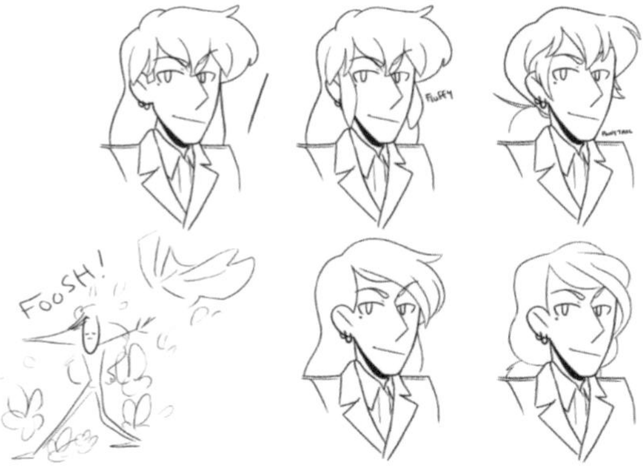
FOOSH!

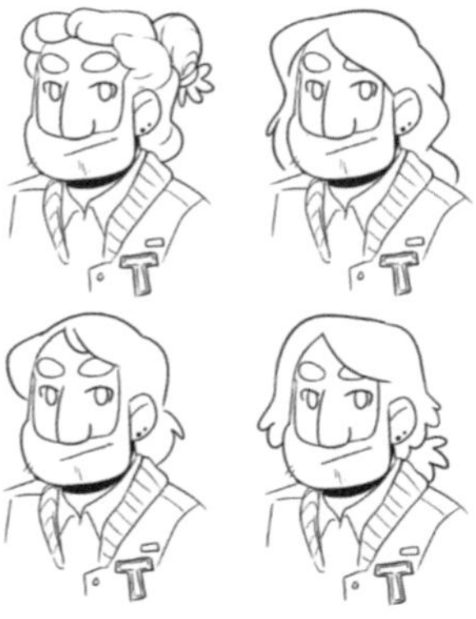

FINAL CHARACTER DESIGNS BY RIAN SYGH

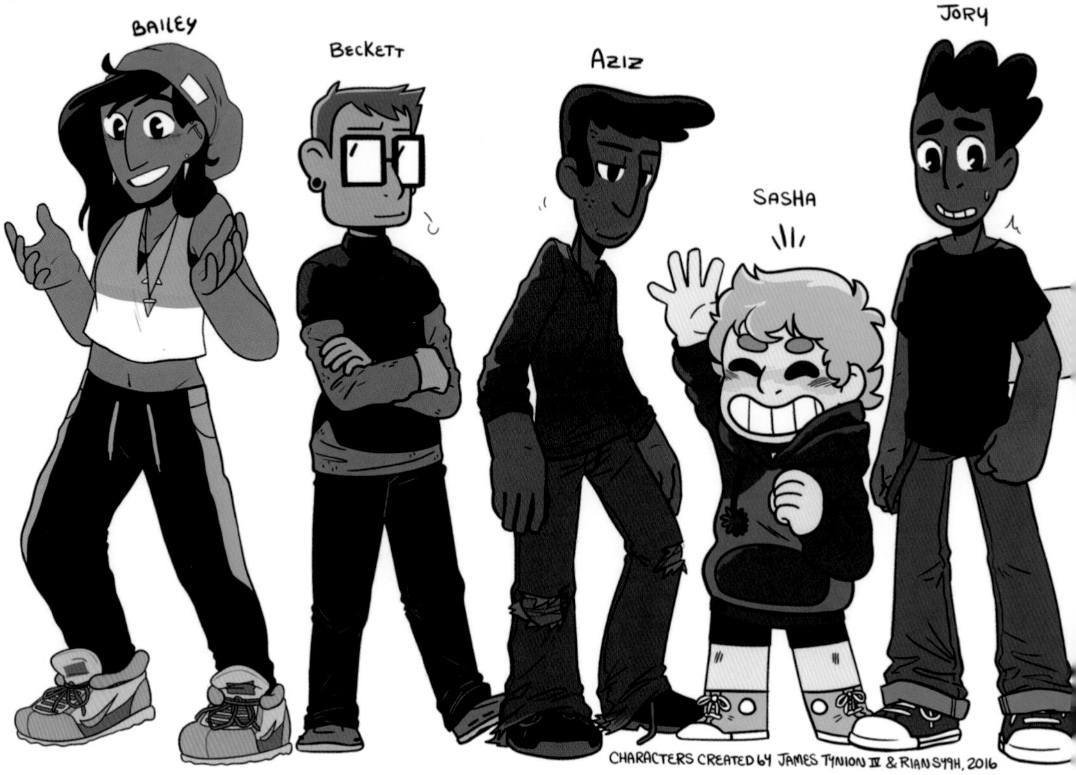

BAILEY
BECKETT
AZIZ
SASHA
JORY
CHARACTERS CREATED BY JAMES TYNION IV & RIAN SYGH, 2016

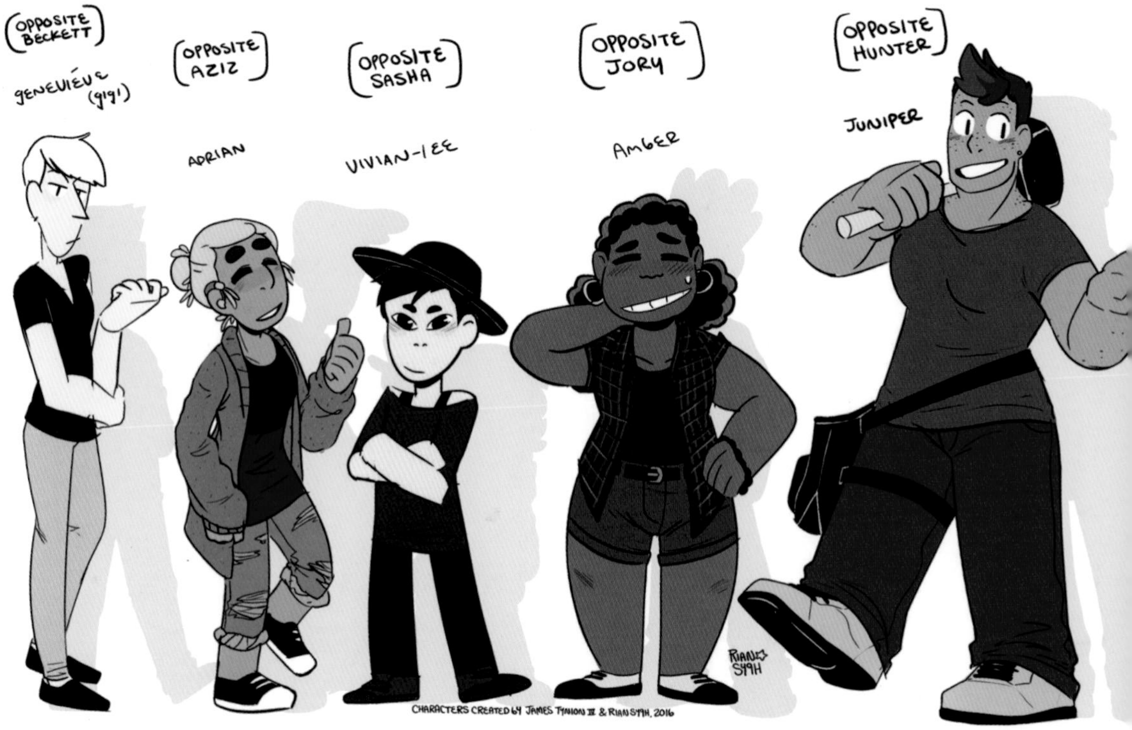

(OPPOSITE BECKETT)
GENEVIÉVE (GIGI)
(OPPOSITE AZIZ)
ADRIAN
(OPPOSITE SASHA)
VIVIAN-LEE
(OPPOSITE JORY)
AMBER
(OPPOSITE HUNTER)
JUNIPER
RIAN SYGH
CHARACTERS CREATED BY JAMES TYNION IV & RIAN SYGH, 2016